The Ancient Tree
The House &
Their Wizards

"AWAKENING"

The Meeting Tree The House & Their Wizards: Awakening
Copyright © 2018 by Stephen Francis Jordan. All rights reserved.

Published by Mindstir Media, LLC
45 Lafayette Rd | Suite 181| North Hampton, NH 03862 | USA
1.800.767.0531 | www.mindstirmedia.com

Printed in the United States of America
ISBN-13: 978-0-9998275-5-0
Library of Congress Control Number: 2018937616

STEPHEN FRANCIS JORDAN

The Meeting Tree
The House &
Their Wizards

"AWAKENING"

MINDSTIR MEDIA

To Jenna
Thank you
for reading.
Great Luck in
the future

Steve Jordan

Foreword

The house has sat empty for many of its years, now a family is going to make it their home after their last life was shredded into pieces. This mother and son have had a hard few last months, but they never in their lives thought that they would be learning so much in a short time.

The house has a past that you cannot find on a computer or even read in a book in a library. There are head stones in the cemetery nearby this house and in England, that are connected to this house but there is no one around to tell how that could be possible. Family members of the original builder and owner, are nowhere to be found, because time that has passed by, was the keeper of just who they were.

The house has not given up any of its secrets over the years and people would stay away from the old building, because of made up stories and rumors. Someone would clean the yard and the area every now and then, just to keep the neighborhood looking good but they would never go into the house. The house was sad, it had many great features that would make it an amazing home, but its owner has not returned and it has been decades since he left.

There is however, more to this house then meets the eye, but it is not giving its secrets out to just anyone. There are other people in the world, that want what this house has, but they cannot have it by owning the house, it will not let them! People tried to live in the house after agreeing to take over ownership from the town, but they left in fear, and the house now had a new image, it was haunted. A haunted house in a small New England town, that is nothing new, and there are many throughout this area of the country. However, for the house to be connected to something older then New England, that is different then what history has taught us in the many tales, is what makes this house special. Many things are not known about our world outside of what we see as our reality. There are dark secrets hidden within history and stories, one just needs to do the right research to find those answers. However, one just needs to be born into the right family, to find a life that can be different from the average person walking the streets of a town.

What if the many stories or folklores about history were somehow real and we were just unaware of it happening around us. What would life be like if you were even part of this world of mystic reality? Would it be as the movies and shows of the entertainment industries show us. Or, the great books that we read from, from the many written since the start of written language, or would it differ somehow in a way that we cannot conceive? Can a world of things that we dream, exist beyond what we know and see?

Dedicated to my four Granddaughters
April, Elizabeth, Kristle and Sarah Jordan

1

A New Land and New Life

THE CROCKER FAMILY CAME TO THE NEW WORLD, just after it was discovered by the early settlers. Many stayed in the New England area as it was called, but as the family grew, people expanded out to the lands beyond that area. In 1791, some went to the south, some to the west and one came to the area north of Boston Massachusetts. He decided to leave the expanding city area and went to the far north, into a country setting not far from the ocean. Horton Crocker was a young man of eighteen, full of energy, faith, and dreams to start a family. He found a nice little claim of land near a river, up on a little rise with a field just behind it, then filed to own the land to start a farm. It was in New Hampshire but it boarded Massachusetts by just less than a hundred feet on one of the proposed state lines. They were still deciding between the two states, where the state line would be in the southeastern part of the New Hampshire boarder, and the boarders of the towns in that area. He worked his land claim over the next ten years while living in a shack, until he cleared the land and built a house, then a large barn beside the house. He had help from the people already living near the area as far as five miles away. They traveled by horse and wagon which brought all the hand tools they needed to work the land

and prep the wood for the house on the site.

When the farm was done in the summer of 1801, he found a bride and started a family. His wife's name was Catherin and she was just eighteen when they wed. Over the next twenty-five years, they had five boys, two daughters and all the family helped work the farm. As the family got older, the girls married first and moved to cities that were building up around the area. Four of the five boys struck out to move farther inland to help build the frontier. The last boy left at home, was the youngest, he stayed to take over the farm and help his parents. This boy's name was Jeb, born February of 1826 and he became strong and well educated from reading and self-study of nature.

Now, Jeb always read anything he could get his hands on, one day he found a strange rock in the woods near the river while on one of his strolls. After cleaning it in the water of the river, he found some picture type of writing on it. This captured his curiosity, so he brought it home and placed it in his room with the many other items he had collected through the years. He thought he could figure it out some rainy or snowy day when he had some spare time. However, once he started looking at the rock, this became a quest for him over the next few years, and with what little time he had that was free, it was used to look for the answer to the rocks strange markings.

One day his father became sick with a high fever and everything was done to help him get well. It lasted a week as he became very weak and then on the seventh day he passed away. Every one of the sons and daughters along with their families came home over the next few months to visit their mother and then the father's grave at the town chapel. They would stay at the farm to help their mother while there, then head back home after about a week.

Time went on, and after another several years, Jeb's mother caught a fever and just as his father did, after seven days she passed away. The people of the area came together for the wake, and the service to lay Catherin beside her husband Horton. As before, the family came over the next few months and again left after about a week. This time however they left with whatever was left to them from their parents last wishes.

The year was 1846, and Jeb now found that he was alone now on the farm that was left to him, with only the paid help as company and he figured that it was time for a wife. He traveled around throughout the area cities and found himself one day in Salem Massachusetts. There just by chance he came to meet a cute girl named Rebecca Mills over from England as a servant. She was just eighteen years of age, red hair, average height, with a very shy personality. She has been working for a jeweler to pay off her family's debt back in England for a few years. They met a few times, talked over the next couple of months on trips he made to see her, and then it was decided that they wanted to be together. Jeb made good on her debit contract to the jeweler and wed her within a week of her release from servitude. She was so happy that someone had taken a liking to her and was taking her away from a town that had stories of witches and demons.

Rebecca was a god-fearing girl with hopes of a good life and a nice family life. She found that she had strong feelings for Jeb from the first moment they met, so when he asked her to marry him, she felt she had to be with him. Along with documents of their debt release, she sent a letter back to her family in England. It told them about this nice man, and her new life, just before they left for their home in South Hampton, New Hampshire. This was the first time that she had sent such a happy letter home ever, she hoped that her family would now be pleased with her happiness and their release.

The trip was a little long by horse and coach but they were home in just one day. When they got there, she was welcomed very warmly by the help that he had working the farm with him. These were people that his parents hired who needed housing and work; they lived in the small rooms attached to the rear of the house like small apartments. They worked the field and livestock then would receive payment from the sale of produce at market. For Jeb this worked great, because he would have been completely alone working the farm after his parents passed away and there was always a vast amount of work year-round.

Now, Jeb having been well educated, worked at the small school in the town center by the chapel. There were few students but the job made a small amount of money and with the farm, he and Rebecca were well-respected and considered wealthy town folk. Rebecca was very knowledgeable in bookkeeping and the time she spent working at the jewelry store helped her run the farm. After having two children a boy first, Mathew, then a girl, Bonny, she found that she could not have any more children due to complications that nearly took her life. To both Jeb and Rebecca this was fine because they felt that god had a reason for doing this.

In his off time, Jeb still spent time studying the stone and the type of writing on it. He kept a large hide covered book of all the notes he made of the symbols on the rock, and to him, some of the markings looked like they would make a group of words. The problem he had was that they also seem to make up pictures and not words. This is as far as he got and it baffled him, he knew this all meant something but just could not put his finger on it.

By the year 1858, Jeb's son had become a little explorer and he would travel around the riverbanks and some of the woods in the area, marking the trails. He and his sister would sometime fish the river in different spots and the two of them would make maps of the best fishing holes and hunting sites. Their maps would have markers on them of large trees, rocks with hills and lookouts. Then one night, Jeb was going over these maps with his two children and he saw something that caught his eye. One of the symbols on the rock he was studying looked like one on his children's maps.

With a copy of one of the children's maps in hand, he used it to study the rock. Looking at this rock, its shape was not round but a little flat and was the size of his foot both long and wide on both front and back. It was only about two fingers in thickness with marks on the sides. Those marks looked like crosses and went in order around the stone in four spots. They also counted from one cross to four, clock-wise if you held it so that the one cross was on the top. Now on one of the stones faces, above the side that had two crosses, was a circle with lines coming off it. Across from it was a half circle with lines above the side with three crosses. Now he could see it, it was the sunrise and sun set. Now, when he flips the rock over he sees the crescent of the moon. This was the nighttime; it was showing the compass points where the sun and moon rise in the east. When he put the two maps side by side, some of the lines now made sense. He could see the river and a path from the river to a large rock, with a large hill just to the west of it. The path continued and then on the rock it ended at a large circle with a symbol in the middle. On his son's map, it shows a tree with writing on it. Now lines on the rock were coming from other areas. There were seven symbols around the circle on the rock, but he was never able to come up with what they meant. So far, he has figured out that the rock was at the start of a path and it showed the path to the circle, he felt that this was the next place he had to look. He came out of his study and informed his family that the next day they were going on a hike and would be using their map to guide them.

The next morning was the start of a beautiful clear day when the family headed off on the hike. They crossed the river on a fallen tree where they had cleared the branches on years before and set it up as a bridge. Once on the other side, they followed the path north along the river, then after a short distance the river bent to the east and the over grown path kept going straight. There was a small bend to the west, then after a short distance, it bent back north and then they were at the rock on the map. It was a large long rock, three lengths of a man long and one-man high in height. You could not see over it because of that height. It was set in a pine grove where all the trees were in line with each other as if they were planted. Jeb made a drawing of the area when he noticed some markings on the rock. After examination of the markings he made charcoal rubs of the markings and rolled them up to keep them safe when he put them in his sack.

They continued walking on the path away from the rock, following it as it twisted through the woods until they came to a large beech tree. It was not a clearing as he thought, the circle was a very large tree. Looking around he saw that all the large trees were at least ten paces away and small low brush filled in the area around this massive tree. He figured after a quick study of the site that at one time it was cleared around the tree. There was a small stream flowing just outside the circle, it was not big but enough to supply good water to the area. Jeb thought that this could have made some type of meeting area, but what did the symbols mean on the rock? He looked all around the area as his wife made a lunch for the four of them.

He moved around the tree past the branches just above his head, when he found a mark about ten feet up on the tree trunk. When he climbed the lower limbs, it became clear that it was one of the symbols on his rock. He made a charcoal rub of it and after he finished he rolled it with the rest of the rubs in his sack. He then used his left hands ring finger to trace out the lines of the mark. He used this finger for a couple of reasons; first was that he was keeping his balance with his right hand, second, the other two longer fingers on his left hand had hard skin on their tips from many years of farm work. He wanted to use the soft skin of his ring finger to feel the shape of the markings. However, while he was feeling the marks he cut his finger on a piece of stiff wood protruding from the mark, not bad but just enough to draw blood and give him a small splinter. What he saw next was unbelievable to him; he watched his blood as the tree absorbed it. This took him by surprise as he loosens his grip and fell from the tree, thankfully, it was not far. When he landed on the ground, he was able to land like a cat and not be hurt.

His wife came to him and he said that he was ok, that he had just slipped. He did not let her know what he had seen and sat there while looking at the tree as he ate his lunch. After he finished his meal, he walked to the tree and saw a piece of bark that was thin and peeling away from the trunk near the bottom. He did not see it before he went up the tree, so he used his knife, removed it, and put it with his rubs. He figured that they had seen enough and it was time to leave for home. They packed up their belongings then started back home after drinks of water from a skin pouch which his wife carried.

All the way home, it bothered Jeb that the tree had just absorbed his blood without leaving any trace of it on the bark, though he came up with some reasons why it had happened. It had been a little dry out and the dry wood just drew it in, or maybe the heat made it dry very fast and the color red blended with the bark. He felt that it was not anything evil in any way and joked while talking with his family on the way home about falling from the tree.

At home, they went about their daily routine and again gathered for a meal at dusk that day. However, Rebecca had notice that Jeb's cut finger showed no sign of a cut. He looked at it and assured her that it must have looked worst then it really was. He washed it just to be sure that there was nothing covering any mark but it was as if nothing ever happened. He just let it go, as if it were a bug bite, from the bugs around the garden.

Later that evening he retreated to his study with his rubs and information from the day. He studied the rock and the rubs and found that the rub from the tree matched one on the rock. He entered all the events of the day to the notes in his notebook with his quell pen and used ink from his inkwell. He mounted all his rubs into the binding of the book, which was bound with a wool string to hold it together. The last thing to look at was the piece of bark that he had cut off the tree trunk. He carefully lashed it on to a page using a needle and thread as if he was sewing a button on his clothing. Under the bark, he copied the symbol that was on the tree and he made sure all the ink was dry before he closed the book.

He felt that this was it for the night and went to sit with his wife and kids in front of the fireplace. He drew up his evening pipe then packed it with his favored tobacco, lit it, then sat back, and just listens to his children play a game. He listens to the fire crackle as he felt the warmth of the flames and every now and then, the wood would let out a squeal then a pop. It was relaxing just sitting there feeling safe and warm. He looked over to his wife who was sewing up some clothes, that was all he remembers until his wife woke him for bed.

When he got his thoughts about him, he stood, stretched, and then recalls that he had a dream about a blue stone in a ring. He mentions it to Rebecca and she asked if it was round and in gold. He thought that was odd that she asked that because it was as she described.

"Why do ask that," he asked.

"I had a dream about a ring with a blue stone in it just before I woke," she replied.

Now that seemed strange to him, but they have had like

dreams before about events of the day. However, he knows that he never saw a ring like that during that day or any other day. He went to the washbasin, cleaned up, and then crawled into bed. The entire events of the day ran through his head as he drifted off to sleep.

That night in his sleep, he tossed and turned all night and would wake up after each dream. A couple of times he tried to stay awake but found that he had fallen asleep only to be awaken by another dream. Before morning light came, he got up, made a fire, and sat in front of it in his chair. His thoughts were spinning around in his head but he could remember one thing in every dream, a stone box in a hole in a rock on the top of the big hill. He grabbed a piece of paper, a chalk marker and drew out a map from his dreams. When he finished the map, he put his head back in his chair and pulled the quilt over himself. As the fire went low, he drifted off to a more restful sleep.

Rebecca came down to the parlor and found Jeb asleep in his chair and she left him there. She had heard him dreaming during the night and felt that this was best for him. She made sure that the children and the workers did not disturb him until mid-morning, so he could get some sleep. When he woke, he was a little startled then jumped up saying that he had to go on a hike that day, to the top of the hill near the path to the tree. Rebecca insisted that he take their son with him, but he said he had to do this by himself, and that he would be back in a short time.

Jeb left for the short hike from the farm around noontime. He crossed the tree bridge and made the climb up the hill through the thick trees and bushes. He thought to himself that he has lived here his whole life and never knew about the tree or the paths or rocks. He got to the top of the hill and there was a clearing there that he had stood in many times in his younger days. He brought out the map that he had drawn that morning and looked for the items he drew on the map.

First, he found the tree line to the north and the hill face on the south side. He lined up the map by using those two items and now he could see the location where the rocks should be. He walked the field until he reached the area where the set of rocks indicated by the map were. He walked around a couple of clusters of low rocks, until he found a mark on a rock, it matched the one on the first rock he found many years ago and on the tree. It was very small and could be easily overlooked if you were not looking for it.

He began looking around the rock but did not find any holes in the rock. However, he sees that that rock seems to be sitting on top of another rock. He walked to the woods and got a long length of straight branch that he could use to move the rock. He returned with his lever, and wedged it between the rocks and started moving the top stone. As he slid it to the side, he saw the hole in the lower rock but he needed to move it more so that he could reach into it. The stones all around the hole had been here awhile with all the buildup of settlement around it he thought. He looked into the hole and saw what looked like a stone that somewhat was in the shape of a small box. He reached in, picked up the box, and found that it was heavy. Studying it, he could not see any seams or a way to open it. It just looked like a square gray rock around four inches square. He looked all around the area and there were no other items or marks around. He put the square rock in his bag then sat back and rested with the sun feeling good shining on him. He shut his eyes for what seemed just a few moments, took a few deep breaths, and stood back up. He felt stronger now and grabbed a drink of water, and then he started down the hill for home.

When he reached the river, he stopped and washed the box looking rock in it. Now that it was cleaned, he now could see that every side had the same marks on it that was on the rock and the tree; in addition, the sides were very smooth. He returned it to his bag and finished the trek to the farm.

Once at the house he was met by his wife who ran to him and hugged him. She kept saying repeatedly that she was so worried about him. He told her "I was only gone for half a day; there was no need to worry."

She replied with, "You have been gone a full day and one night."

"What are you talking about, it has only been half a day," he replied.

Just then, both his children ran to him along with some of the help, then all of them made comments about being gone so long. He now was a little confused about what happen that day. He went into the house, then directly into his study as the family followed him, while all were asking where he had been. They all sat around his desk as he sat rubbing his head.

He then asked them, "You say that I have been gone a full day, then why do I not remember it?"

"Did you fall asleep or get hurt," Rebecca asked.

"No, none of that, I found the area on the map I made from my dream and before falling asleep in the chair. I moved the rock that I found and removed this square rock," he said as he pulled the rock from his bag.

They all took turns holding the rock and he uncovered his notebook and showed Rebecca the cover. However, when he opened it, there was nothing inside it. He went through all the pages franticly repeating that it was all here. He shook the book and looked around the room looking for the items. After a short time, he sat back at the desk, winded, and all shook up. He placed the book on his desk and got the new rock from his wife.

"I am so worried about you Jeb," Rebecca said as she leaned down and hugged him.

Jeb was holding the rock and moved it over to his desk, then set it on the book. He hugged her back and he said, "I love you." When he looked back at the rock, he could see that it looked more like a box now than a rock. He held it again and he found how to open it with just a pull from both hands. Inside he found a golden ring with a large blue stone. He removed the ring from the box, placed it on his right-hand ring finger and held it up to admire it. Just then, the door to the study slammed shut and the windows closed. Everyone jumped to a standing position and held each other in the middle of the room. There was a light over the book now but it came from nowhere. The rock on the book now looked like a shiny jewelry box with markings on its sides. Rebecca and the children were now crying and Jeb was standing between them and the desk as if to protect them.

A woman's voice seemed to come from everywhere and said, "Do not be afraid, this is not an evil thing. You have fulfilled the many steps to earn the power of the Protectors. This is a group that watches over the meeting tree and helps humanity."

Rebecca cried, "this must be the devils work, let us leave here."

"Please do not fear, hold your family," the voice said.

Jeb looked at his wife as she was moving her head in a no movement but something said that he must do it. The next thing he sees is that they are all sitting in front of the fireplace and it is dark outside. The children are reading to each other and Rebecca is making a patchwork blanket. He however, remembers what had happen but also knows that his family will not remember any of it. He also knows not to let them be aware of it.

He lets everyone know that he is going into the study for a little while, then he picks up a candle in a holder and walks with it to his room. He closes the door behind him, then he sits at his desk. He knows the stone box is in his desk, so he rolls the cover up so that all items in the desk are visible. He opens the box and sees the ring is in the box, sitting there as if it was new. He picked up the ring and looked it over when he could see the symbol in the blue stone. He places the ring on his finger and a doorway opens in the wall, beside the wood door into the hallway of the house.

Jeb stood up from his chair and walked into the new doorway. Once through it, he stood in a room with paintings of people all around the room. It was not a large room, only ten by ten feet and was dimly lit from the light coming from the ceiling in the middle of the room. The light came from the ceiling but there was no flame. It shown down brightly onto his book now, that is on a wood reading pedestal. He stood by the book so that he could open it and when he did, all his notes were there. The book was now thicker and the pages after his, had writing on them that he could read. There was the history of the tree-meeting place and the symbols. Much of the writing also described a meeting place, where other people would meet to talk about the worlds events. The book seems to talk to him now and he is not afraid of it. The first rock that he found now sits beside him on a small square lower table.

As he reads, he learns more about how he must do what he can, to keep people safe and protect the meeting tree. He also is told that only he or someone of his bloodline, after this point in time can wear a ring. For now, he wanted to learn all he could, but he found much of it strange and did not fully understand all that was happening.

One thing he wanted to know was, "why did my family forget what happen in the study," he asked out loud.

The voice of the woman came back and said, "You asked us in your thoughts to make it easier on them because they are scared."

He asked, "Who are you?"

It said, "We are the tree, the house and the book, we are your guide and your friend."

He asked, "Are you alone?"

It replied, "We are here for you?"

He asked, "Who are we?"

It said, "The tree, the house, and the book."

He asked, "The house, do you mean the house is alive?"

"Yes, the house will protect you or whoever in your bloodline is wearing a ring like the one on your hand. As long as the book is in the house with the bark from the tree, the house lives to protect. It will also protect itself from harm from outsiders," the voice stated.

"Do you know why I lost a full day of memory," he asked.

"Yes, we do, when you retrieved the box from the hole in the rock you were tested. Only a person of good heart and nature can receive the gift, so your memory was tested through your dreaming," the voice said.

"So, what am I, some type of wizard or witch? He asked.

"In the history from the land across the water, that is what they were called, a wizard, not a witch. You can do things using your rings stone, but once you remove the ring you cannot access that power. The rings stone is your power with your blood that you gave to the tree. You can give this up at any time and only someone from your blood after you touched the tree can take your place. There are seven of these blue stone rings, each have different symbols in them, that stand for one of the meeting trees. Each tree is on a mass of land that has humans on it and the meeting tree was meant to pass on teachings to help them. You are now a teacher and can use your skills to complete the quest of the rings stone. Only a person that is not evil and is willing to learn will receive the stone. Anyone with your bloodline from here forward will receive the power, if they pass the test. The seven different rings can never be used by anyone else's bloodline; they are only locked to the first bloodline that they contact. You are the first, the only one for this tree and ring," the voice told him.

"Who made the rings and when," he asked.

"No one knows when, although it is said that a great one from the land of Welch, made and hid them, his name is said to be Merlin by some, but it has never been proven. Other lands know him as an off world being. However, there is no one that has ever seen him place the rings. We just exist and are here for you and the humans of this land," the voice finished with.

Jeb closed the book and headed out of the new room. When he returned into his study, he locked the stone box in his desk. He kept the ring on, then returned to the parlor to sit in his chair. Rebecca looked over to him and said his new ring looked good on him, then she returned to her work. The children had gone to bed and the fire was now low. He wondered what Rebecca would say about the ring and he now had his answer. Life was back to normal just as it was before they went to the tree. He told her lets go to bed, it has been a long day and she agreed, they cleaned up and turned in. As Jeb laid in bed awaiting sleep, he thought about what the book said about being a teacher. He felt that he could study the book and learn, then teach his children the lessons of the book. He then faded away to in to the world of dreams.

2

Life carries on

THE YEARS PASS BY AND JEB STUDIED THE BOOK to learn all that he can from it, however when the voice suggested areas to learn, Jeb always approached it slowly. He was still a god-fearing person, and he wanted to know all about this new thing, before he tried anything new with it. He still works as a schoolteacher as well as on the farm, with daily chores as Rebecca managed the farm and the house. She has managed so well that they managed to build up a very large fortune in their bank accounts, Jeb was proud of her; she has done well for the family. The children have attended higher schools in the city, where they have learned business, history, and Math. Bonny, their daughter met a banker, married him then they moved to England after he was transferred there. Happily, they started a family there. Mathew stayed around for a while, then built a farm at the base of the hill where Jeb found the ring. Farms were being built along the tree line and river, making a community within different towns.

It was now the year nineteen hundred, just after all produce was picked and winter was near. Rebecca now in her seventy-second year became ill; she had fallen to a fever and hives. They tried to help her but after several weeks she was weakened by her illness and passed away. This was a shock to everyone, because she was always so healthy. To Jeb though, it was a loss so deep that it tore him apart.

Jeb had kept the ring on since he first started studying it, he was never sick a day since finding the ring. He tried to put the ring on her but he feared it was too late for the house to fix her. He remembers that death is the one thing the house cannot stop if you are near it. One day, while she was sick, he was studying the book when he cried out that he could not find what he needed, and then the house spoke to him. Because he felt that he had powers, he thought he could save her, although the house informed him that both his children were born before he was part of the tree. If he had found the tree before they were born, both his kids and wife could have been protected with a sublet ring. From that day forward, he was hard on himself, every day he would walk the road up to the town square and visit her grave. He did not miss a day even on very bad New England weather days.

Time went by fast for Jeb, the house had made three other sublet rings at Jeb's request, and Jeb kept them in the box locked in his desk. He knew that he had no one to wear them but he felt that maybe someday, somehow that would change. He still had the help on the farm and now he had a banker keeping the records of the farm. He was wearing the ring less and less and spending less time at the book in his room. He would sit on the porch, watch the horse and buggies ride by while thinking how he could have done things differently in his life. Sometimes he would focus on the river on the other side of the road and see the fish jump for bugs which he found it relaxing. He could see Mathew's farm from the porch now, because they had built a crossing over the river just down from the house on the low area. People had built homes around the bend in the river and now, there was a junction of three roads at the low part by the river becoming part of the crossing.

He missed his wife and children, and now that he was not wearing the ring, he got older by the day. Then one day he gets some devastating news, Mathew had been crushed by a cow in the stall at his farm. Jeb ran to the farm and held his son as he laid on the ground. Mathew looked up at him and said with his dying breath "protect Bonney," then, he shut his eyes and passed away. Jeb was distraught and cried out loud for both Mathew and Rebecca. He held on to his son until the workers could pull him away and bring him home. He cried and paced the floors of the house as friends and neighbors came by to pay respect to his son and his son's wife. It was a long sleepless night and the thoughts went through his head that his family name will die with his death.

The next day he sent a telegram to his daughter, then waited at home to receive one back from England. However, they could not wait for her because even if she left that day it would have been weeks by boat and buggy to get there. They had to lay Mathew beside his mother on the family lot in the town cemetery. It was a very sad day and everyone around the area came to the home, as they had done for Rebecca. Jeb was now a broken man with all the money and power at his fingertips, but he could not protect his loved ones.

After everyone had left and traveled back home, he went into his study then put the ring on. The doorway appeared and he slowly made his way in. It had been many months since he had done either, but everything was the way he left it with a stool at the podium.

"Why, why did this have to happen?" He asked the book.

The voice informed him with, "There are many things that people go through, and death is one of them. We cannot help anyone that is not of the bloodline in the house and does not have a stone ring on them, it is the rule."

"That is not fair, I loved them and I need to be with them," he replied.

"We cannot change time or correct death. We can only teach and help you," the voice said.

"Can I have the ring keep all that I have learned in it, then when the next person puts on the ring, it lets them have that knowledge?" he asked.

"Yes" the voice replied.

"Then teach me everything that you told me to learn," he commanded.

"As you wish," the voice said and Jeb felt a pain in his head and everything went black.

Jeb awoke on the floor and had no idea what time or day it was. The voice asks, "how do you feel, can you move yet?"

"Yes, I can but I feel like I fell from a high tree," he replied.

"Sit in the chair so that we can test you," the voice said.

Jeb stood and sat in the stool chair. He was pulling himself together when the voice asked, "Can you tell me what is on the last page of the book without opening it."

"The page is blank but now I see that everything I am saying is being written on the page," he said.

"That is good, can you see the history of the meeting tree in your mind," they asked.

"Yes, I can, and I see the other ringed people that looked for the seventh stone and how it was hidden from them. This was so power would never be greater than the others in any of the bloodlines," Jeb replied

"That is correct and now you understand. You were the last missing piece and when you joined us, the seven stone rings and meeting trees now all have a single bloodline. If two different bloodlines are to join, only the male line will be passed on. If two of the same bloodline should meet, there would be no change. If a bloodline should die and disappear, then the line shall be done and the stone shall disappear forever," the voice said.

Jeb now knew that he had to do something, but was not sure how to do it. He had to find his daughter and pass on the gift that he was given. He was just turning seventy-four years of age, but because he had worn the ring, he aged only into his forties, but now he aged normally everyday he did not wear it. He knew that he had to go to England and find her. The book knows that she is in England near Stonehenge, but because she does not have a ring or the trees blood exchange, where exactly is hard to say. The book does know that there will be trouble in many areas, in the form of a massive war with many lives lost. Her last letter stated that things were changing and it was not safe for travel. That was the last he heard from her, even with the message sent about her brother which she did not reply to. He knows he had to go find her and leave the farm for a while.

Jeb set things up so there was a caretaker for his farm that kept it running. He also had a bank that will take care of all the taxes and bills, until he or his daughter or her family returned. He set up all funds to be invested for long term with investors. Then a way for identification of family, using a dual keyed bank box where he kept all the important papers. He packed all his belongings in a locked chest, including the four rings and placed it in the attic. He did not tell the book of his plan and he left for England, without a word to his friends. It was just after the turn of the century and he knew life was going to change, as he knew it. The two regrets that he has now are, that he wished he had learned what he knows about the ring now many years ago, but the biggest regret was that he was leaving his Rebecca.

3

λ New Life

IT IS THE MONTH OF AUGUST, 2015, and Seth and his mother Sue Hawthorne have been on the road for many hours, driving to their new house and home. They were doing this because they had left the town and state that had the Army base, where Seth had lived the first thirteen years of his young life. His mother had landed a job working at a school as a history teacher, near the town where she had bought an old house. Some of her family had moved to the area ten years ago, and she felt that this is where she needed to be. Since her husband died, she knew that life was going to change for her, but for Seth it was hard to be without his father, also to leave the only home he has known.

Their belongings were in a truck not that far behind them, so when they get to the house it would not be long before it is there. Sue had flown up weeks before this date when she bought the house and completed all the paperwork to be ready for this moment. She had done all that was needed so that she could just arrive, turn the key, and bring all their belongings in. People felt that she was getting into a money pit, because the house was abandoned after the last people that lived there for only one week then ran away from it. She could not beat the price because she paid the back taxes and it was hers.

As they arrived, Seth let out a groan when he saw the house. It was gray in color and looking at the outside, it needed a lot of work. Some of the wood siding was lifted and the molding was in bad shape. The yard was not like the neat yards back home, it looked a wreck and needed to be mowed, and the brush needed to be cleaned up. The barn was leaning to one side, and it looked like it needed to be torn down before falling.

"Come on give it a chance, it will look great with a little work," Sue said.

"Mom this place would only look great if it was to fall down," Seth followed with.

"We need to give it a chance and need to make it work. Let us think of it as an adventure and it is you and I against the task," she said as she gave him a little arm tap.

They got out of the car and she commented that it does not look as bad as when she first saw it. She reached for the door and before she touched it, it slowly swung open. At first, she took a step back then she went in saying, "The contractor that I hired to ready the house must have not shut it all the way."

The inside did not have any furniture in it and it was a little dusty. When she turned on the lights, they were very dim and few of them. You could see that the electric power was not in the house when it was built because there were wooden wire ways to the lights, switches, and outlets. The floor creaked as you walked on it and the smell of dust was in the air. Sue felt that the house was not very dirty and having the contractors clean it up would make it easy to move in when they arrived.

Sue led Seth around the house and explained that the front room with the fireplace would be the living/dining room, with the smaller room to the side as the den. The kitchen on the other side of the fireplace was small but had lots of cabinets. There was an island with a prepping top on it. There was a newer sink set up, which was made of stainless steel that Sue had installed. Across from that was the bathroom and it was upgraded per Sue's request. Moving up stairs there was two large bedrooms with the wall of the lower floors fireplace between them. Sue had the third smaller room changed to a full bathroom. It was an old house but the changes give it a newer house feeling with historic looking walls and molding.

There was a doorway to the attic and Sue told Seth that she had looked up there, and found that there is some old stuff still there. She said that she had some new lights put up there, but for now, we need to be ready to receive the items coming on the truck. Seth agreed and they went down stairs, brought in the stuff that they had in the car and put it in the bedrooms. Sue claimed the room on the front side of the house, which meant that Seth got the one on the backside looking out over the field.

After three hours, the truck arrived and the workers unpacked it putting large items where Sue wanted them. Any of the boxes that had items in them were placed in the proper rooms. The bikes, camping gear and outdoor items were placed in the barn. When the truck was unpacked, they left and now the two of them started unpacking the boxes placing items where they looked good. After many hours of unpacking, they realized that it was after midnight, they grabbed their sleeping bags and went to bed laying on the mattress as if they were in a tent, camping.

That night Seth did not sleep well, he thought he heard the house creaking on its own. He would listen for any noise that could be heard, then he would wake after drifting off to sleep. This happen to him several times, then before he knew it, morning had come. When he looked out his windows, he saw a group of deer grazing at the far end of the field. He watched them for a short time then cleaned up in the bathroom, then went down stairs to the kitchen.

Sue was already sitting at the table, she was looking around and making notes. Seth asked what she was doing, she told him that they will need to go to the store to pick up some food and supplies that were on her list. Seth got a drink of water, then sat back at the table and looked around with wonder of what they did to end up here.

His mother turned to him and said, "Did you notice the house does not smell like dust and the little that was here seems to be gone."

Seth put his nose up in the air, sniffed and said, "The house smells clean and a little like wood."

"That is what I thought, I think that keeping the door open, and bringing in our stuff off the truck changed the air around," she said.

Seth did not say anything, he just got up then went into the den. He started unpacking all the books and put them in the bookcases, they put in place the night before. They had a computer desk where he set all the equipment up, then setup the lamps so that good light was on the desk, also for the reading chair. After taking his time but working steady, in two hours the room was done. He then went to the living room, setup the entertainment center and the stereo, and turned it on when he was done, so that they could listen to one of the music disks that they brought with them. He placed the pictures on the table, so his mother could put them where she wanted them, then he unpacked one of his father and him. He held on to it tight, his mother walked in seeing him staring at it. She put her arm around him and hugged him. She knew he was hurting but all she could do, was kiss him on the top of his head and let him be. He set the picture gently on the table and continued unpacking.

It had taken four hours to finish the down stairs setup, and after it was done, they drove to the next town to some lunch at one of the fast food shops. On their way back, they went shopping for the items on Sue's list at a local grocery store and they found it very small compared to the ones on base. The car was packed now with plastic shopping bags, as they made their way home. Sue however, decided to take a longer way home, past some old farms that were now large open fields for the public to enjoy. As they made their way back into New Hampshire from Massachusetts, past the remaining farms and just a short way from the house, Seth notice a couple of girls around his age. They were standing on the little bridge just down the little hill from their house. They made eye contact as they drove by and stopped at the stop sign. He could see them watch the car as they drove up the small incline and turned into their yard. He could no longer see them once they were in the driveway, and as they got out of the car his mother smiled at him. She was thankful that there was finally a smile on his face.

They brought all the bags into the house then Sue told him, "Go find out who they are," and she gave him a big hug. Sue had wondered when this day would come, the day he noticed girls, this made her feel better about the move.

He said, "thanks" and he was gone in the fastest walk that she has seen him do in months. Seth was not an out spoken kid and was a little on the shy side, when it came to being in public, Sue had worked with him to bring him out of his shell. However, he was much more mature for his age then the other boys his age, people in the past have guessed his age to be as much as five years older by his demeanor. He was a sandy blond-haired boy with a taller than normal frame then kids his age. His mother was taller than the average ladies, and his father was tall at six feet two inches with sandy blond hair. Many times, in school Seth and his parents were told Seth had the build for a person that should be in sports, however he never showed an interest in any.

Seth walked down to the bridge and the two girls were now down on the old water cattle crossing beside the bridge. He stood on the bridge leaning on the rail looking down on them. "Hi," he said to them.

"Hi, are you the ones that moved into the old haunted house," the blonde girl asked with no hesitation.

"You mean that grayish yellow house just at the hills crest," he asked.

"Yes, that is the one, its the old Crocker house and no one has lived in it longer than a week since everyone left it in the nineteen forties," the girl with the dark hair said.

"That is great, I am living in a haunted house, thanks mom," he said while looking toward the house.

The girls made their way back up to the bridge where he was standing. The blonde girl, reached out her hand and said, "Hi I'm Kristle Blake, I live in the third house on this street just up that hill." Seth shook her hand then noticed that she was pointing up the road that still had the farms on it where his mom and he just drove past.

"Hi, I'm April Morse and I live a couple of houses past Kristle," the darker hair girl said as she shook Seth's hand.

"Hi, I'm Seth Hawthorne and I moved here with my mother from North Carolina just yesterday. My mother bought the house after my father passed away, we moved up here because she has family nearby. Also, she will be teaching history classes at the high school in Amesbury," he said.

Kristle spoke next, "That's where we will go for high school next year, we both have one more year here at the grade school. How about you, are you in high school?" she asked him with a smile.

"No, I have one year left in the eighth grade," he tells them.

April then asked, "You said your father passed away, what happen?"

Seth swallowed hard, he did not want to hurt them by telling them that he did not want to talk about it. Therefore, he agreed to talk to them if they sat on the porch of the house with him. At first, the girls were hesitant but then they agreed because his mom was home. They walked up the little hill, April called her mom on her cell phone to let her know where she was going, and her mom wanted to talk to Seth's mom. He went into the house, then shortly came out with her then introduces the girls to her. April handed Sue her cell phone, and the two mothers talked while the two girls and Seth sat in the porch chairs. After a couple of minutes, Sue came back and handed the phone back to April then told her that her mom will be stopping by in a half hour. Then she went into the house and brought out a pitcher of cherry drink and three cups. She set it on the little wicker table and went inside the house.

Seth then poured the drink into the cups and said, "It is a long story, do you still want to hear it."

Both the girls said, "Yes please."

Seth took a deep breath, looked up in the sky for a second and swallowed hard then started, "My mother and father met after he had joined the Army and became an officer. A few years later, I was born and we were living in base housing in North Carolina. Shortly after this, he was sent to Afghanistan to spend a year there. He came home and my mother started college while working at a local store part time, then a couple years later, my father was sent to Iraq for a year again. He came home for a short time, then he had to go to a base out west for some training that he would not talk about to mom or me. He was there for only two months, although when he came home, mom tells me that he was a little different in the way he looked at the war. I never knew this because I was so young." Seth stopped just for a second then continued.

"He went to work on the base then would come home to play with me as mom kept going to school, some work, and taking care of us. Then one-day dad had to go back over to Afghanistan again. This time, it was when I was just going to turn twelve while he was gone, it was hard to say bye to him, because I understood more of what was going on with the war. He left with his unit and went back to a very nasty area in Afghanistan, that required the special training he had finished years before. He would call and talk to us on the computer many times through the weeks, this time however he was there over a year.

Then one day after not hearing from him for a few days, we had Army officers in uniforms come to the door. My mother started crying even before they reached the house. A few of the neighborhood ladies came over when they saw the men, they stood beside my mom, holding her to support her while she got the news about my dad. One of the officers informed my mother as easy as he could in a military way, that my father had died in his Humvee during combat. They stayed for only a short time, and then we had people coming to see us for many days, to help us deal with the loss. They told me some of what happen, but I do not think that they ever told us the complete story of what really happen to him and the men with him.

We drove to the airbase to meet the Angel Flight and receive dad's casket, along with many other caskets draped with an American flag, that day the Army made sure he made it back to base. Then we had his funeral at the base and he was laid to rest in Arlington National Cemetery, by Washington DC. Mom and I then had to move off the base, so she worked on finding a job up here by some of her relatives. Because she now had her masters in history, she looked for a job teaching where she found one at the school in the next town over, and now here we are living in a haunted house." He looks up from the deck to see the girls were in tears. From behind him, he heard his mother sniffing from her tears. Both the girls came over to him and gave him a hug then they hugged his mother.

Just then, April's mom drove up and Kristle's mom was with her. They all introduce themselves and the girls went to their moms and told them a short version of what happen to Seth's father. The three moms went into the house while the three teens stayed on the porch. They talked about things to do around the area, then about the school that started in one week. After an hour, the mothers came out and said it was time to leave, they said so long as they climbed into the minivan.

As they drove off, Sue looks at Seth then said, "See you already have new friends and they will be in school with you."

"Yeah, new friends and a haunted house, this is going to be fun, yah, right," he said.

"What? That is just nonsense, people told me about it, but nothing has ever happened to the contractor or I. It is just part of what people say about old houses," she said as she went into the house.

Seth stayed outside and watched the water on the other side of the road behind the tree line. He felt like someone he knew had done this before from this same spot, but he or she did not have the newer house just to the left of his view. It was a strange feeling, as if, somehow this was the way it was with his past family. He stayed outside until late into the evening enjoying the peacefulness of the sounds he heard.

The next couple of days, Sue was cleaning and moving things around in the house the way she wanted it. Seth also had set up his room with posters of music groups on the wall and the computer for schoolwork and gaming. However, the cable internet service has not been set up yet, so he spent a lot of time on his cell phone. Then one night he was sitting in the den when some guest stopped in. It was Kristle and April with their parents. Sue had invited them over for just a little gathering to get to know them a little better. The parents stayed in the living room area and the kids went to the den.

At first Seth was a little shy but after a couple of minutes the three of them found something to talk about, their parents. The girls told Seth that they did not know that they were coming over until they got in the car. They both thought that they were going shopping down town but they stopped here.

Seth told them that his mother had not told him about people coming over either, and then they started to laugh about it. The girls started looking around the room, and pointing out all the fancy woodwork, and how it all looked so new. Seth told them that his mother was cleaning and was surprised how good the walls and trim looked being well over two hundred years old. April mentioned how the outside of the house did not look as scary as it always did. Seth said that is funny because they had not touched the outside at all. Kristle said in a scary tone that maybe the house is haunted and it is making it clean and nice for you. They all laughed and then the house made a noise like a loud creak. They all looked at each other with wide eyes and no sound, and then they started laughing.

"That was so funny, you should have seen the look on your face," Kristle said.

"Yours was just as bad," April replied.

"We hear sounds every now and then and it is just the house moving. Besides, there are still some old things up in the attic that we are going to go through some time," Seth told them.

"Oh, can we see it," April asks.

"It is really dusty with not much light up there after the sun goes down. Maybe you can help during a weekend, when we are cleaning it up. Would that be good for the both of you," Seth asked.

"Promise," asked Kristle.

"Let's ask my mom," He said and they walked to the living room.

When they got to their parents, April's mother was telling Sue about some of the known history of the house and area. The three of them took turns asking about helping to clean the attic and the parents just looked at each other. "Why, you are never this excited about cleaning your room or our house," Aprils mother declared.

"This is a little different than what you want to do at home,"

Kristle's mother expressed.

"I have no problem with it if its ok with your parents," Sue said.

"It will be like going to an old dig site and finding artifacts from the past," Kristle exclaimed. After she finished her words, the house creaked again.

"See even the house liked it," April said and they all laughed.

"It will be this weekend after all home work from school is done, how about just after noon time on Saturday. Is that all right with everyone?" Sue said as the parents were leaving for the night.

Everyone agreed and went to the cars. Seth turned around once everyone had left and looked at the house. It did look a little cleaner, and the grayish paint was a little brighter yellow now. He thought about it for a little bit and figured it must have been the rain the day before. It could have washed some of the dirt and old pollen off the siding. He did not put any more thought into it and he ended his day with the rest of a good night sleep.

The next day was the last day of school vacation and Seth was ready with new clothes and supplies. He got his backpack all set and made sure he had everything ready. He was going to be the new person in the class and he did not want any problems from the kids. At his last school, many of the boys would hang around in groups, then pick on the other kids just to show off. This new school had fewer kids in all eight grades then what two classrooms of his old school had for one grade. It was a much smaller school in both size and people and he hoped it is a much friendlier place then his last school.

In the afternoon, he decided to go up to the attic to see just what it looked like. He opened the doorway to the stairs then turned on the new lights that were installed, he saw that the stairs were steep and small; there was a trap door at the top, that he had to lift and latch. After he climbed the last step, he was then standing in the peak area of the roof looking down the length of the house. It was not dirty at all and there were a few wooden chests on one side and some wooden chairs, table and hutch parts on the other side. However, there was one chest that he could see, that had what seemed like a sheet over it, and he had a feeling overcome him that he had to open it. It was a scary feeling to him, he resisted it and went back down the stairs closing the doorways behind him. He went to his room and flopped backward onto his bed, and then put his arm over his eyes. He was wondering why he had that feeling and why is it gone now.

After a short time, he got up, went down stairs, and sat in the den. He felt that he needed a walk and told his mother that he was going to walk the street, his mom agreed then off he went. He walked into Massachusetts and up the hill into the more populated area, past all the apartments and the housing by Lake Gardner. He had gone about a mile before he turned around, and started walking back toward home. When he got to the top of the hill looking down where he now lived, he could see their house as well as the valley they were in with the hills along the river in New Hampshire. He was thinking how this looked like a dream he once had after he had a run in with one of the gangs in his school. He slowly walked back to the house down the long hill taking in the view.

Back at the house Seth and his mother had supper while talking about his walk, then about school the next day. After they finished they sat in the den, where Sue picked up the book she was reading, and Seth pulled out his phone and played with it. Just as they got all settled, there was a noise heard, the house let out a low rumbling snap noise. They both looked at each other and just smiled and went back to what they were doing.

After an hour, they said good night and went upstairs to their rooms. They got cleaned up for bed and set out their clothes for school the next day. Each of them got in bed, turned out the lights and just thought about the next day while in the dark, until the sandman got to them and they entered the dream world.

4

New school

IT IS THE FIRST MORNING AT THIS NEW SCHOOL and after Seth along with his mother arrived, they met his new friends April and Kristle at one of the doorways. They then had to check-in at the office where all was set to have Seth attend school, then Seth was given a map of the school and list of classes. When he went to his first class, he could feel the eyes on him from fellow students but he just acted as if nothing was happening. Both the girls were there in class with him so he felt that at least two people were not looking at him with curiosity.

The teacher welcomed everyone, then took attendance and when she finished she announced that there is a new student from the south. She asked Seth to tell everyone about himself, also where he lives in town.

Seth came to the front of the class and said "Hi," to the other kids when he faced them and added, "I'm Seth Hawthorne I moved up here from an Army base in North Carolina this summer. My mom and I live in the old farmhouse on Whitehall Rd just before the Massachusetts line. We have been cleaning the place up and here I am in school." These were short statements just as anyone his age would do anywhere in any school.

Just then almost every hand went up but the two girls he knew. The teacher called on the first boy and he asked, "Did you move into the old haunted house?"

"They say it is haunted, but nothing has happened there

since we moved in," Seth answered.

Then the teacher picked the hand of a young man that had a grin on his face, while waving his hand wildly. "You said you lived there with your mom" and with a sly nasty tone in his voice he asked, "where is your father."

The teacher jumped in and said, "That is not a nice question to ask someone."

Seth said, "That's all right," as he looked at her. He then looked at his two friends and he could see that they had the look as if they were going to tear up. "My father was a soldier in the Army and he did a couple of tours in Afghanistan. He died there serving our country, so mom and I had to leave the base housing. We moved up here near her family and her new job as a teacher in Amesbury," he told them with a slight cracking in his voice.

The room went silent and the kids were giving the boy that asked the question, a dirty look. Then April stood and looked at Kristle and motion for her to stand, and she did.

"We want to thank you for your father's service," April said and Kristle followed with the same. Then most of the kids stood and said the same but not the one boy, he just sat and looked at the floor. He knew that he had just crossed a line that made him look bad.

The teacher now in tears managed to get out a thank you Seth, then asked him to sit at his desk. She sat down and had to use a tissue to wipe the tears from her eyes. She said that was a very nice gesture on everyone's part and could not wait to tell the other teachers just what they had done.

From that point, she went over the class syllabus and requirements, then the day started. Seth knew now that this school was going to be very different from anything he had ever experienced before. For the first time, he was around kids that did not have a parent in the service, so not only was the area different, so where the families. This felt very new, exciting, and very scary all at the same time. He looked at his two friends and they smiled at him and gave a little nod of their head, to show that he was with friends.

After a few hours, it was lunchtime and he sat with April and Kristle in the lunch area. They had paper bag lunches as he knew them from the south and was happy to just sit and relax. The girls asked him how he was doing on his first day and all that he could say was that it is so different up here. They asked what he meant and he began telling them about the large classes and the different types of people there. He told them about the groups of kids that acted like gangs and how different groups stuck together for different reasons.

Now this was something that the girls had never seen or felt and they told him how awful that seems. They also hoped that nothing like that ever happened at their school or town. Just then, the bell rang and it was time for the start of afternoon classes. Some of the kids asked Seth how he liked the school so far as they all walked back to class. He told them that it was nice, people were friendly, and they told him that they were glad he liked it.

It was a Friday and this was the day before the Labor Day weekend. Schools used this day to get students and teachers ready to start after the summer vacation. All the students in the school seemed to be waiting for the last bell of the day to escape. At the end of school, April's mother picked up the girls and Seth, then after a briefing about what happen during the school day they made the mile trip to Seth's house. He thanked them for the ride and the girls told him that they would call him after suppertime to talk. He said that would be great and headed into the house as they departed. On the way in, he noticed the paint on the porch looked new, so he touched it but it was very dry. He wondered how it got so new looking, investigating for a moment then he went into the house. He was the only one home for the moment, so he headed up stairs to his room and put his books and papers on his desk and flopped into bed. For a few moments, he stared at the ceiling going through the day in his head. Both the kids and teachers and the way they acted were very different then back home he thought, he was very happy about it.

The next thing Seth knew, he was being awakened by his mother when she asked if it was a hard day. She pulled up a chair and asked him to tell her all about it. After a ten-minute short recap, Seth looked at his mom and she was in tears. He asked if he had said something wrong and she just shook her head and wiped her eyes. She said that she started losing it when he told the class about his dad. Now Seth was tearing up and just then, a long creak from the house could be heard as if the house was crying. They both looked at each other and for the first time they entertained the idea that maybe the house, was haunted.

Suppertime was a little quiet between Seth and his mother on this night. Sue knew that she had to talk to Seth about what happen in school where he was asked about his dad. She still had a hard time sometime with it but she had Seth to look after and it somewhat takes her mind from the loss. Nevertheless, it still was hard. She decided that she had to be the first to speak.

"Well kid-o, do you want to talk about it," she asked.

"No mom, I need to deal with it. Dad is gone and is in Arlington Cemetery and we need to live our life," he answered.

"Honey are you sure about it, the therapists told us there will be times that we need to talk about it. Maybe this is one of those times," she stated.

"Mom I do not want to talk about it now, there was so much that happen today and I need just to space," he said.

Just then, the house phone rang and Sue answered it. It was April and she wanted to talk to Seth. Sue called to Seth and he walked in from the den with his head hung a little low. His mom gave him a smile and said, "You have a young lady calling you," then she handed him the phone.

"Hello," he said.

"Hi, how are you tonight," April asked.

"I am ok," he said.

"You're real talkative," she said jokingly.

"I'm not much for talking on the phone," he said.

"Well, you are talking now," Kristle said.

"What are you doing on the line," Seth asked.

"We are not so backward up here; we are on a conference call. It is easy to talk to all our friends at once," Kristle told him.

Sue was listening to Seth from the doorway and she now knew that maybe this is best for him. Peer friends would help make life a little normal for him and it was safer in this little town. She walked into the kitchen, cleaned up all the dishes and put the left overs away, while thinking how happy she was for Seth.

Seth came in and was still on the phone when he asked her, "Are we still cleaning the attic tomorrow?"

"I guess we are, do your friends still want to help," she asked.

"Yes, what time are we starting," he asked.

"One o'clock," she said.

He smiled at her, gave a head nod, and walked to the den to sit on the couch while still talking to the two girls. Sue walked up to her room, picked up some of her papers for work and sat at her desk to work on them. Just as she started to read, the house made a soft noise as if it just relaxed. She said, "You can say that again," as if talking to the house, that made her look up not believing she had just done that, then she laughed thinking about it.

After a short time, Seth came up the stairs and said good-night then went into his room. After about an hour Sue got ready for bed and turned in after shutting off all the lights. It was the end to a long day.

5

House's Secrets

are Found

THE NEXT MORNING STARTED AS ANY OTHER DAY WOULD, by getting up, washing-up, and having breakfast. However, this day had the two girls coming over to help clean the attic and they were looking for an adventure. Sue could see that Seth was a little nervous, she wondered if it was because of the work ahead in the attic, or the two girls that were coming over. She thought about how her son acted around the two girls, as if they were family, yet he was still a little standoffish because they were girls. She felt as if she had known their mothers from somewhere in her past, but she clearly remembers all her friends and where they live now. This was a strange thing, she feels as if she belonged in this house and town all her life. She knows that she spent all her life in the midwestern part of the country or in the south after she got married.

Sue made up some sandwiches along with some flavored water, in case anyone got a little hungry during their adventure as the girls called it. She felt that making this a little family type meal was the best.

The girls arrived a little early and they were ready to go and dressed for dirty work. They all gathered at the base of the attic stairs and Seth headed up 1st, followed by April, then

Kristle and finally Sue. When the four of them stood together at the top in the attic and looked around, Sue made the comment that it was very clean up here.

"I came up here the other day and it did not seem this clean," Seth told her.

"The last time I was up here, I could swear that it looked and smelled dusty," Sue said.

"Maybe the ghost knew we were coming and they clean everything up," April suggested.

"No, the house felt bad that we would get dirty, so it made sure that everything was clean," Kristle replied.

Just then, there was a loud creak in the floor and everyone went wide-eyed and looked at each other. April was the first to speak, "I think we just had our first part of the adventure, the house just gave us the answer of who cleaned."

"No that is silly, we just added weight to the floor, and it moved. That is what it is, and I will prove it," Seth said. He then walked along the floor trying to get it to make noise but none could be heard.

Sue said, "I think the fun is over with, let us see what is up here." She then walked to the chairs and noticed that they were in great shape and she set up the three kids to bring them down into the living room. When the six chairs were gone, she saw that there was a matching table behind them and they brought it down.

Now down in the living room they assembled the table, then put it in the small area between the kitchen and living room and set all the chairs around it. The wood of the table set matched the woodwork in the area and it all seemed as if it was finished yesterday. Sue made the comment that now they have a formal dining set and said let see what else is up there.

They went back up and now they found a hutch that came apart in to four sections, they brought it down and reassembled it. They moved it to the corner of the dining area and it looked as if it was always there. The girls found a large box that had dining table items in it and they set up the table and the hutch with the items. The next box had dishware in it and the girls set it all in the hutch, where it seemed that there was a place for everything. The last box on that side of the attic had the silverware in it. They all had to help get it out of the attic, because it was extremely heavy and when they got it to the table and laid it all out, they were amazed. It was a full set of place settings and serving ware. On the bottom of each item was an imprint of the letters P.R. Boston 1775. This had taken about three hours and they all sat down and snacked on the food that Sue had made. They talked about the find then wondered what else was up there. Sue had found it odd, that none of this stuff was claimed by the town to pay off the tax liens. She however was not going to complain because the sale was as is, where is, to her.

They made their way back up to the attic and now it was time to move to the other side, to get to the trunks and items. Sue wanted to work with the smaller items first, so they started with the wooden boxes. They just fit through the stairway as they brought them to the living room. There were three in all, when they got them open they found paintings, in addition to some paperwork in an old leather portfolio with a string tie holding it closed.

First Sue laid out the pictures and after a short time, she realized that there were the same number of hanging hooks in the two lower rooms as the number of pictures. She decided to lay the pictures out against the wall under the hooks to see how it looked. Seth and the girls helped and in just a short time, every picture had a home. These were drawings of the area including the river and scenes from the top of the hill. There is also a painting of the original owner with his family, which fits over the fireplace perfectly.

In one of the other boxes was another family portrait and

it had a note with it that said Jeb and family. Sue noticed that Jeb looked a lot like the young boy in the first picture, she surmised that the one over the fireplace was the first family and the one with the note was the second and last family of the bygone days. Sue was now intrigued by the old tails of the house, because the rumors that she had been told seem to be coming true by paintings. She now felt that she had to research this and said to herself, that is just her thinking like a history teacher.

Seth and the girls laid out the portfolios on the table and Sue came over to join them. They were full of birth certificates, family tree history, land claims, and deeds. One had papers about the positions of office that people held and death certificates. Sue found that much of her work was now done for her research of the history of the house and its families. She refolded it all carefully and placed it all back in the box and decided to see if it fit in the hutch lower cabinet, to her amazement it fit perfectly as if it was built to be there.

Now back up to the attic and all that is left was the trunks. These were two wooden travel trunks, one with a white cloth over it. They used a tape measure and checked to see if they could get them through the stairway and found that they fit with a quarter of an inch to spare. They checked the handles and they were strong, as if both the chest were built yesterday. They put a soft blanket over the first one, the one without the cloth on it and lifted it. It was the heaviest thing that they lifted so far. They then checked to see if they could open it to take some things out but it was locked by the two skull key locks built in to it. They decided to take it down as is and carefully maneuvered it all the way to the living room. Once there they sat for a bit and rested. Sue looked the trunk over and felt that this was a lady's trunk with the designs of dresses and kids on it. The size of it was now clearer to see, just over three feet long and just less than thirty inches wide and tall, but still, it was locked. They now went up and looked at the other trunk with the cloth on it. It was the same size as the first one and there was a man on it with hunting scenes. It also had the same type of locks on it and it was locked. They went to move it and found that it was a lot heavier than the first. They placed the blanket on it so they would not hurt it or the doorways on the way down. They all found this trunk was the heaviest thing that they had moved today and they were glad that it was the last. They placed it beside the first trunk then removed the blanket, then removed the cloth that covered the last trunk. Sue saw that the cloth was a tablecloth with embroidery on it and wondered if it would fit on the old table they brought down. With the help of the two girls, she spread it out over the table and it fit with eight inches of overhang all around the table. On the edge of the cloth all the way around, there was a pattern on it that made it stronger as if it was made just for this table. She thought what a beautiful tablecloth it was, because the main area of the cloth was an embroidering of a large tree. Just then, the house creaked and she wondered if the house had heard her thoughts.

Seth and the girls were trying to open the last trunk but it was not giving in. Then Seth moved to the first trunk and pushed the locked buttons again and it opened with a loud deep snap. He jumped back and everyone turned to look in the direction of the noise. They were all focused on that trunk and you could see that both latches were open now, however the same thought was going through everyone's head, "It was locked." They all made their way over to the trunk and looked at it with disbelief. Sue was the first to reach for it and opened the cover.

As Sue slowly opened the lid, the first thing they saw was a white sheet that was folded over to protect whatever was inside. The girls along with Sue were now focused to see what was inside this treasure chest. Seth was just looking over the shoulder of his mother in anticipation.

Sue began to unfold the sheet and in front of them was a light blue dress with white lace around it. Sue easily picked it up and it unfolded before them. It was a full-length dress and the girls commented how beautiful it was. The dress was clean and smelled like it was new. Sue laid it out on the table and returned to the trunk where they found several more gowns and pieces of woman's clothing. Then there was a piece of the sheet again. Sue lifted this and found many pieces of jewelry, gold rings, and chains with stones of all types. Then under that layer, they found letters from this lady's family. They were addressed to Rebecca Crocker and some to Rebecca and Jeb. They now know whom these trunks belong to. Sue and the girls were looking at each item that came from the trunk until they were down to the bottom. Every item that was in the trunk was laid out on the table with care and the three ladies were looking over each item. The letters now interested Sue because this would make easy to see who these people are and where they came from. The two girls were more interested in the cloths and jewelry.

On one of the bundles of letters was a set of keys and Seth untied them and tried them on that trunk and it worked the lock. He now went to the other trunk and he first tried moving the buttons the same way but they did not move. He then put the key in the lock and turned it and the key turn all the way around in both locks. Next, he put his fingers again on the buttons and pushed. The locks snapped open and now everyone was looking at the last trunk. Seth easily opens it and found just as the other a sheet covered the items in side.

Sue stopped Seth from opening the linen and said that we should bring it into the den because there was no more room to lay everything out. They all agreed and lifted the trunk and placed it in the middle of the den on a coffee table. Seth then open the sheet and just as before he found clothes, a very nice suit, and other items of men's ware. He then found a rock with what looks like pictures etched in it, then he finds a stone box. He set both items aside as he found the papers wrapped just as the others in the first trunk. This time however, he finds a key tied to a note with the name of the old bank that is in down town Amesbury.

Sue reached for the paperwork and saw that the key looked like a bank key and she opened the letter. It read, "This key is to my bank box in the Amesbury Savings Bank. It is for my blood kin to have and open when they prove their kinship to the holder of the second key, which is the bank."

"Wow, this really is a treasure hunt," Sue let out.

"What do you mean," Seth asked.

"This is a key to an old bank box and whoever is a relative of the owner gets it. The bank is still there, and it would be interesting to see what is in it," Sue inform the group.

"Wow" the two girls said at once.

Seth picked up the stone box, held it up, and looked it over then he opened it where he found four gold rings in it. Three had a light blue stone on it and one had a dark stone on it with a note that read, "Put ring on while in the study."

"Mom, where would the study be in this house," Seth asked.

"I guess it would have been this room," Sue said.

Seth looked around and shrugged his shoulders, then put on the ring. A female voice from everywhere said, "Finally someone from the bloodline with a pure heart," All four of them look at each other with fear in their eyes. The den doors shut; the blinds come down, scented candles Sue placed around the room all light up. Seth, Sue, April and Kristle are now in a closed-in room and scared.

The voice says, "Do not be scared, we are the house, the tree, and the book, you are of the bloodline of the builder of this house and heir to the ring with all its teachings.

"Is this a joke," Seth asked.

"You are of the blood of the first person to wear the ring on your finger and you are the keeper and teacher of the meeting tree, Seth," the voice said.

"How do you know his name, he is just a boy," Sue cried out.

"Sue, mother of Seth, do not fear this that is happening to you. Please will each of you place a ring on your finger, it will not harm you in anyway," the voice pronounced.

The two girls were crying and holding each other but they felt that they had to do as the voice asked. Sue also placed a ring on her finger, somehow feeling she could trust the voice.

Once the rings were on the girls and Sue's finger they heard, "This cannot be, all four of you are of the bloodline! Sue, you gave birth to Seth and your husband was a direct descendent to Jeb who first wore the ring. By you sharing blood with Seth, you become part of the bloodline. When you first came to the house we could feel that you were somehow of this bloodline, so we did not try to make you stay away from the house. We gave you hints that you were not alone with the noise and wanted you to find the rings. However, April and Kristle are of the bloodline but are from Jeb's Granddaughter, Bonney Lee, who was Bonny's daughter who was also Jeb's daughter. You all are from the same family tree," the voice tells them.

They were all still a little unsettled and they just looked at each other. Seth tries to remove the ring but found that it will not budge.

"Seth, you cannot remove the ring until you all decide whether you want to learn more about this path that your ancestor started. Let it be known, that you can choose not to take on this knowledge and your memory will be wiped of this event. However, it also means that you can never talk about this to each other and will not be a part of this new realm you have found. Seth only you can decide this," the voice stated.

Now they are looking at each other and saying out loud

at different times the question, "we are related?" They are a little less scared now, but now curiosity has them with this one thing, they are all family.

"How can we be sure that we can stop this at any time and this is not an evil thing," Sue then asked.

"Jeb's family had the same thing happen to them, he asked us to make the others not remember so we did as he asked. From that day on, they never knew of any of the events, only Jeb stayed as the teacher and protector of the tree, until the day he left to find his daughter Bonny but he never returned. We knew where he was, what he had done but he left the ring here and we could never contact him. We feel that an enlightening problem happen between him and us. When we told him that the ring would only protect you if you were in the house, he thought it meant you had to be inside these house doors. It really means 'by in the house,' that you are taking part of the ring, the house, and the meeting tree. While you wear the ring no matter where you are, you are still part of the house. Now Seth you are the most direct of the bloodline therefore you are the head of the house. You are young however, Sue being the eldest will be your teacher and guide. April and Kristle, you are family but you are farther down the family line and you are sublets to the main ring wore by Seth. Sue, you also are a sublet but you are Seth's mother so you are his teacher. Do you understand so far," the voice then asked them?

"So, who are you and where is this voice coming from," Sue asked?

"We are the tree, the house and the book, we are here for you, to speak to you as one. We will show you more after we explain the rules. You must let us know first if you want to know more and become what your ancestor started so many years ago. If you choose not to become this you will forget that any of this has happen," the voice insisted.

"Mom I am willing to do this, how about you two," Seth,

said as he point to April and Kristle.

"I am ok with it," April said.

"Sure, I'm in," Kristle followed with.

"Well I guess we are all in, if we can quit at any time," Sue answered.

"Yes, you can leave at any time and if there are no other questions then let us begin. Seth's ring has all the knowledge that Jeb had learned and it can be given to all of you at the same time. Keep your rings on and sit down, it will not hurt and only take a short time. We will begin the teaching later," the voice said.

Then each of them said ok and next thing they remember is waking up. Sue looked at her watch and only a half hour had passed, by then each of them stood up and looked at each other. After they determined that they were ok, Seth asked, "Are you there."

"Yes, we are, how do you feel," the voice asked.

"We all seem to be ok but we do not feel any different," Sue said.

"This was just the transfer of information from the ring to you, now we must cover the rest of the teaching. Everyone answer the questions that I ask of you. What is the use of this knowledge to be used for," the voice asked.

Almost at the same time, all four of them answered, "To teach and protect the people, the meeting tree, and anyone that asks for it."

"What is on the last page of the book," the voice asked.

"Everything that we are saying," they said at the same time.

"This is how the rings work. They are your connection to the meeting tree, house, and the book; as long as you wear them, you can talk to us and us with you. With the ring on, the stone in it touches your skin and all the powers come through the stone, the ring just holds the stone in place. While wearing the ring the house and tree can protect you from harm, and sickness. Your body aging, after you have reached twenty-four of the suns full cycle will slow down. This means that you age one cycle of the sun to everyone who is not of the tree, five cycles. Without them, you are unprotected but we can keep track of you to an area but only you, not your offspring.

"Is this some type of magic and can we change the past," Seth asked.

"You cannot change the past and there are responsibilities that come with this power. You will learn this as the teachings continue. You must not at any time ever tell anyone about this power or use it for mass personal gain or any type of evil. It is late and April and Kristle's mothers are coming to the door" the voice told them.

Sue asked, "How do you know that."

"You will find out later, it is no trick," the voice told her.

After a few seconds, the knock came on the door. Sue opened the door to the den and then opened the front door. The mothers said hello and they walked to the living room where all the dresses were still laid out. The two girls join them and they were saying how much fun it was to find all this cool stuff.

Seth picked up the den, he put the rock box on the desk, and he removed his ring and put it in the box. He went out to his mom and the two girls and collected their rings and he put them in the box also. The rings now looked smaller then they first looked but he just let it go for now and joined them in the living room.

The girls, Seth and Sue went on talking about what they found and they found that it was easy not to talk about the rings. The only items talked about were what were in the first trunk, the mere thought of mentioning the second trunk was a feeling that it would cause problems. Therefore, it felt better to treat it as if it did not exist. Sue set out some snacks and the ladies went over the dresses and items laid out on the table.

The girl's mothers could not believe the shape of all the items and how nice the furniture looked. At that point, Sue decided to keep the table and chairs but she was surprised when she looked at the pictures. She sees that they are all hung on the wall in spots where they laid them on the floor. She however felt that the house must have done it and felt that there would be time to find out about it later.

As the evening went on, it was decided that the girls would be over the next day around one in the afternoon. Sue told their mothers that they were welcome at any time and then the girls and their mom's left for the night.

6

More to the house

AFTER EVERYONE HAD GONE HOME FOR THE NIGHT, Seth and Sue sat in the den and looked at the items from the last trunk. She got an I have an idea look in her eyes and expressed to Seth, "Let's put on the rings and see if we can get information on the family tree."

Seth agreed and gave her the ring that fit her then he put on his ring. "Welcome back and yes I can give you the bloodline information. It may be easier for you to see it," the voice said.

"Yes, it would, I could copy it down and get the formal paperwork needed," Sue added.

"There is no need for that, we can have all the papers ready for you, if you would like, Seth you just have to say, make a copy of all records of the bloodline," said the voice.

"Make copies of all records of the bloodline," Seth said.

Just after he said that, the doorway appeared in the wall and both Sue and Seth stood and looked at it with amazement. Seth walked to the house doorway that went into the hallway and looked behind it, but only saw that there was still a hallway there.

"Mom this is fantastic, the room is there but does not go beyond the wall," Seth declared.

"Seth, this is your secret room and it can only be seen if you have the ring on. No one else can see or enter this room unless you allow it. Come in and see what is in the room," the voice said.

Both Sue and Seth enter the room and they see a pedestal in the center of the room, with pictures of people all around the room. "These are the ancestors of Seth and the girls," the voice said. Just then, she sees a picture of Seth's father, her, and Seth on the wall. All the pictures were all paintings of just their upper torso, head, and face.

On the pedestal, they could see a very large book that is closed and to the side is a shorter pedestal with the rock that was in the last trunk that was open. To the other side there is a shorter pedestal with a pile of papers neatly stacked on it. There was also a stool behind the main pedestal, so someone could sit and read the book with out standing. There was a single light that shown from above, down onto the book, but it seems not to come from anywhere, although it seems to light up every surface of the room.

Sue walked over to the stack of papers where she found that they were in three separate piles. The top paper that she could see on one of the piles was Seth's birth certificate. When she looked at the other two piles, she saw that April was on one pile and Kristle was on the other. She lifted Seth's birth certificate and she saw her husband's death certificate. She let out a gasp and put her hand over her mouth, she then realized that this was the paperwork.

"This is all that you will need for Seth and the girls to reunite the family. Also, you and Seth are now the rightful owners of this farm," the voice informed her.

"May I take the papers out of this room to have," she asked.

"Yes, this is the paperwork for every birth and death as they happened. We have the ability to keep all that is seen, written, and said for each member of the family. However, we cannot react to or read the new item called a computer. We are able to recreate real items that can be held in one's hand or thought in one's head," the voice claimed.

"So, anything that is electronics you cannot interact with because it is not real to you," Seth asked?

"That is true, the thing you call a computer is a puzzle to us because we can see what you see but we cannot feel it. The same with the TV, your phone as you call it and your box that you play while using your TV. They or it puzzles us, we may be able to understand it in time, or maybe if you help us," the voice tells them.

"Why can you see all around the world, but not what is done by electronics? Is it because it is not human thought or nature through the air," Sue asked.

"No! There is a thing that exists called the Realm. All nature, all thought, and all that we know is kept there like a large gathering point. Only the stone on your hand and the tree can see, feel it, and learn from it. Because the book has part of the tree in it and the house has the book in it, we become one with your bloodline. However, you have part of the tree in you and the tree has your blood in it so you too are part of us. We are all part of us. Do you understand all the connections how we are one," the voice asked?

"That make sense but are we witches and warlocks, or something else like that," Seth asked.

"Your ancestor asked the same question so long ago and the answer is still the same. You are a teacher, helper of the tree, a wizard with powers given to you through the rings stone. However, you have knowledge from the Realm and the earth. There once was a master, who is believed to have made the first seven rings and hid them until the one could find it. Some have been in the hands of man since just after he set them out and many times the bloodlines clashed over land and wealth. The last one, the one you belong to remained hidden for many cycles of the sun until a worthy being could be found. Many of the other bloodlines with rings tried to find it, they somehow wanted to gain the power, but it was setup so they could never complete the task. What the master set in place was if they tried, their rings would lose its power and they lost the ability to search. That is because the stone, tree and Realm could read their thoughts just as I can read yours even without the ring on, now that you excepted the rings duties," the voice explained to them.

"If I wanted to do something bad, would you stop me," Sue asked.

"We cannot control free will, we can reject you from becoming part of us at first meeting if you put the ring on and we see it in your thoughts and memories. However, once you are part of us we cannot control you, but we can make your thoughts bother you, so you will be forced to leave us. We however have never done this, Jeb left on his own thinking, we know that. We did know that he set his thoughts on what he had to do and where to go. See, we could not read his wife, son, or daughter because they were born before the blood exchange with the tree. Therefore, his family at the time did not share life with the tree. He did not understand that but we can see that you do understand this, because of books that you have read and pictures you see both still and moving in your heads. See, Jeb's second son carried the bloodline from birth but Bonny's daughter was injured in an attack on their home, Jeb was able to give her blood and now she was of the bloodline. Her family tree leads to April and Kristle and Jeb's son Garry Hawthorne leads to Seth's part of the tree," they are both told by the voice.

"It is late and we do need rest, can we sleep with the rings on," Sue asked.

"Yes, you can, and if they will bother you, all you have to say is 'ring not be seen' and it will disappear from site to all non-ring wearers, it will feel as if it was not there. It will not fall from your finger, only you along with your sublets will see it. Seth only you can make a ring be not seen by anyone including a ring wearer, we will teach you that later," the voice tells them.

They each say the words, then ring felt as if it is not there but they could see it, only it looks transparent. They say good night to the voice, it responded the same and they left the room. The doorway closed and they made their way to their rooms, closing the house up as they did. Sue however had a pile of papers with her, which she planned to work on the next day to see the family history.

The next morning Seth wakes up, then heads down stairs to find his mother with all the paperwork, with it spread out on the table. She is checking each form, then logging it on a pad of graph paper. He went to the tableside beside his mother and he sat and watched her.

"Mom how do you feel this morning," he asked.

"I feel great like I slept for days," she says.

"You have slept only nine of your hours," the voice said to them both.

"Did you have something to do with that," Sue asked the voice.

"Yes, we did, as you were sleeping you learned from the knowledge that we have collected over the many cycles of the sun. You can test it at any time by having us test you," it tells them.

"Ok test me," Seth said.

"What is the Welsh word for magic," it asked.

"Hud," Seth answered.

Sue looked up and had a wide look in her eye, and said, "I don't believe it, I mean I do but this is unbelievable. Please say something in Welsh," Sue asked.

"Sut wyt ti heddiw," the voice asked.

"That is, how are you today," Sue said.

"Diolch yn dda iawn i chi," Seth said.

"That means, very well thank you," Sue replied then said,

"Oh my god we speak Welsh."

"Yes, you do, it is the main as you call it, "language" that is used by the Realm, but you will speak many tongues, as it is called in many books and writings. You can also read and write the tongues of all that you learn. As long as you wear the ring, you will always learn," the voice informs them.

"Can we do magic," Seth asks.

"What you call magic are tricks and ways of proving that you are greater than others. You will have abilities that other non-bloodlines do not have. However, there is one thing that you must always have and that is manners with stealthy ways about you. You are a person that can help and heel people and nature, however you can cause terror and harm. We want you to do good things in the world, the best way is to not let people know of your gift," the voice declared.

"Seth, we have been given a gift and we need to understand it before we do anything with it," Sue said.

Seth agreed with his mom and the voice helped them write out the family tree, all the way back to Horton Crocker. It had taken most of the morning, then April and Kristle showed up with their mothers. Sue told them that she had a file with all the history of the family and they were going to be surprised. Both the mothers had heard some years before, that they could have been related to each other, but never followed up with it. They were eager to see what the family line looked like for Sue and Seth, so they could do some research for themselves. Sue told them to pour a glass of drink for themselves and just sit and listen.

Sue started with the Crocker family coming to America, then settling around New England. In 1781, Horton Crocker moved to New Hampshire, in 1801, he then married Catherin, she was eighteen, and over the years, they had five boys and two daughters. The girls married first and moved to the city, four of the five boys move west. They married into those fam-

ilies that had also moved to the western frontier. In 1826, Jeb
was born, he was the last boy born and stayed on the farm.
After Horton and Catherin past away, he married 18-year-old
Rebecca Mills in 1846. They had one girl Bonny born in 1868
and one boy Mathew born in 1869. In 1888, Bonney weds
an English banker then moved with him back to England. In
1889, Mathew weds Joni and builds a farm just over the river
however, he died in 1901 in a farming accident.

In the year 1900 Jeb's wife Rebecca dies and he is left alone
on the farm. He then leaves as 1901 ends to find Bonny in
England and he only has an address that is near Salisbury
and Stonehenge. He finds his Daughter Bonny and meets his
granddaughter in 1902 after a long trip by boat and cart.

In 1905 Jeb meets Lady Sherry Hawthorne, then in 1906
they have a baby boy Garry Hawthorne but Jeb never knew
of his son because, Lady Hawthorne fearing a war moved to
upper Scotland. Garry Hawthorne grew up and became a pilot
in the Royal air core.

In 1918 during a night raid from zeppelins, Jeb's granddaughter was injured and needed blood, this is when Jeb used
some of his to save her. His daughter recovered also, but her
husband was badly hurt and lost both his legs. Having survived the bombing, they moved further outside the city where
they thought they were safe. Bonny and her husband put their
girl on a train to go live with her husband's sister in Scotland,
they were going to follow just as soon as her husband could
travel. On a fateful night in 1918, Jeb with his daughter and
her husband disappear, because the building that they were in
was destroyed by bombs and fire from the German zeppelins
during the night raid. A single gravestone with their names on
it marks the spot where their cottage stood. Lady Hawthorne
made the site a commemorative garden to all the people that
lost their lives. Lady Hawthorne then spent the rest of her life
helping the wounded from the wars, until her death during a

bombing of London during the second world war. She was laid to rest in the commemorative garden beside Jeb's grave by the people she helped.

In 1922 Garry Hawthorne marries Trisha French and moves to America. They have only one son Kevin Hawthorne born in 1925. Kevin grows up and marries Beth Simmons in 1951, where they have a son Kenneth who marries Mary Sanborn in 1975. They have a son Michael Mason Hawthorne, Seth's father in 1980 and he marries, Sue Berry, "me," in 1995 and Seth is born in 2002.

"This means that Seth is the blood related to people that built and left this house. He is the closest relative to the house," Sue said and just then the house let out a low soft creak.

"There is much more to the story, Bonny has a baby girl and her name was Bonney Lee, she marries American service man Chris Smith in 1925 and comes to the states. In 1930 Nancy and Jean Smith, the twins are born to the couple. Bonney and Chris die from an illness and the two sisters' move away from each other due to an adoption agency. By going their separate ways, they lose contact with each other, because they are clear across country. Nancy marries Tim Allen in 1953 and Jean marries Sandy Hill in 1954. Sarah Allen is born to Nancy and Tim in 1956. Then Phil Allen is born in 1958 and dies in an auto accident in 1978. However, Sarah marries Jim Michaels in 1975 and has June in 1976. June marries Jim Blake in 1998 and Kristle Blake is born in 2002. This now makes Kristle and Seth distant cousins."

Their mouths dropped and people are saying "what," with a surprised look in their eyes.

Then Sue said, "then remember Jean, she married Sandy Hill in 1954, well they had Michael in 1959, but he had no kids and passed away and Chrystal is born in 1960, who married Ted Sands 1979. They have Janet in 1981 who married Mike Morse, and then they have April in 2002. So now Seth is related to April and her mom Janet, also to Kristle and her mom June. You are all distant cousins. Here is all the paperwork to show it, I also followed up with the computer and it all matches the dates and people."

Now everyone was just looking at each other, not sure what to say but Seth was the first to speak up, "Well if that isn't a kick in the pants, I have relatives on my father's side."

It hit a funny nerve because everyone just started laughing. The two girls though looked at Seth and asked if this was all in the trunk with all the papers. Sue spoke up and said that some of those papers gave her leads and by asking the right questions, she found what was needed. She did not lie because that was all she did to get the papers. She also did this so that the girl's mothers did not get any ideas about the other trunk and the ring, because she was not sure how they would react.

It was now only two in the afternoon and the adults were going through all the paperwork and talking about it. However, in the den, Seth, Kristle and April were talking about their new family. They were in a bit of a daze, but they were joking about it.

April was the first to say, "Well that rules out dating."

Kristle followed with, "we are so distant that it does not matter."

Seth says, "That is just wrong."

Both the girls looked at each other and said, "Just like a boy."

They all laughed and continued to talk as teens do about their newly formed family.

7

More for the

Bloodline

Kristle was the first to say that their moms are also part of the bloodline, she wondered if they will need a ring. April also agreed and just then, a loud snap came from the box the rings were in on the desk. The two girls put theirs on and the door to the den slowly closed as if a small breeze was pulling it.

"I could have spoken to you in the open, however, your mothers would have heard us. I am speaking to you through the rings and to Sue also so that no one else can hear. Yes, April and Kristle's moms are of the bloodline, however before anyone else can be given rings the four of you must complete more of your training. Seth and Sue, you have already started, and your rings are hidden on your finger but April and Kristle are not. So, Seth this is where you must decide as head of the house, do the girls keep the rings with them and Sue your last word will allow his choice. If you say yes Seth, we can hide the rings all most the same way we hide yours but only you can do that so the ring cannot be removed from their finger or lost. Sue and Seth, you can talk between the two of you by just using your thoughts, only we can hear you and not the girls," the voice said.

"Mom, we could let them have the rings and they could learn just the same way we did," Said Seth.

"You can also control just what they learn," the voice said.

"I guess it is all right but if they say the words can they make the ring reappear," Sue asked in her thoughts.

"No, this will be Seth's first spell as you call it. He will hide the rings and only he can make them reappear. There is no harm to the girls or the rings," the voice responded to Sue.

"Then let's do it," Sue thought.

The voice then explained to the girls how Seth would be the head of the house and that they can never let anyone know that, they will have a hidden ring. It also told them that they are being given a great thing, that it will help them with their life as well as the people around them.

The voice tells Seth, "All's you have to say is what you want to do in Welsh, so just say "Hide ring from sight," and look at the ring without blinking. Then make a motion with your body, as a hand wave or finger point and it will be done. It is reversed by the same way."

"Ok, here we go," he said as he looks at Aprils ring and says, "Cuddio neilltuo o'r golwg," quietly, so the girls could just hear him, then he waves his hand.

April's ring vanishes and the girls let out a sound of Aw. He looked at Kristle's ring, repeats the words, then the wave, then her ring does the same thing. Unlike Seth and Sue's ring, which can be seen by their sublets and Seth, the ring is not visible to the girls at all, but Seth can see it as a transparent or ghostly item on their finger.

"That was awesome, can you do it again or make something else disappear," April says.

"This is not to be fool with, as we said this is great power and you will learn about this as you sleep. We also will be with you now through everything you do in life. We can help you answer questions and do things. However, we will not interfere with your schooling unless Sue allows us, she is the teacher for the three of you now. Remember you cannot tell anyone of the ring and power," the voice informs them.

The three of them opened the door to the den and went into the living room, where their mothers were going over all the papers while Sue was making copies for them. April suggested that they walk down to the rivers bridge and sit on the bank for a little bit. The mothers said that it was a good idea and they would call them when it was time to leave.

They walked out the front door and turn right at the street where they made their way down the little hill to the bridge. They climbed over the guardrail and sat on the rocky dirt area and watched the water flow slowly by. Since they left the house, none had said a word, but Kristle was the first to say something.

"Do you think that this is how they came up with the idea for the movies that we like," she asked.

"I don't know but I don't feel any different, other than knowing that we are all related through a house that we use to think was haunted. This is very different than anything I ever dreamed about," April Said.

"I would have never thought that something like this would ever happen to me. I wish my father were here because this is his side of the family and he would have loved this. He used to sit with me and watch all those movies about wizards and magic and we would kid about changing the world so that people would not hate each other. Because of just what we wanted to change, he is not with me anymore," Seth said as he picked up a stone and threw it into the water.

Both the girls had sat so that Seth was in the middle, they leaned into him and gave him a hug. He pushed them away gently and said, "Thank you but that feels a little weird."

They sat for a little while and heard some cars go over the bridge, then stopped at the stop sign before going in one of the two directions. Some ravens could be heard off in the distance at one of the farms. The girls commented that they were probably raiding one of the fields or holding court over one of the birds doing something wrong. Seth asked how they knew that, and they told him that the birds are around all year round, always talking in their groups; sometimes they would attack the trash that was put out for pickup.

Seth told them that he had never seen that, because when they put out their trash back on base, it had to be in containers with a lid on it. A truck would come along the road and it would pick the container up and dump it into it. He also told them that this place was so much quieter then the base. There was so much noise from aircraft, trucks, and the large amount of people there. There are more trees and wooded areas here with a lot more hills that are taller than the ones there.

"How can people live like that," April asked.

Then from behind them they heard Seth mom say, "When that is all you know, its part of living."

They all turn around to see all three of the mothers standing on the bridge. The girls looked both surprised and pissed. "How long have you been there," Seth asked.

"We just got here and we talked the whole way, guess you just did not hear us," Sue said.

The other mothers started pointing out the different homes, telling her who lived there and a short history of the house. It seemed now to the kids that the three mothers have bonded, and they just looked at each other and smiled. The three kids climbed back over the guardrail and joined the moms as they walked around the neighborhood. They walked down to the second bridge, which was just a few hundred feet away up the road, which headed to the town's center on the hilltop. They stopped at the single rail bridge; they could now see how the river flowed around the back of two houses making a bend like a horseshoe from bridge to bridge.

They all decided to head back to the house and from there

they would call it a day. When they reached the house the girls mothers got their copies and notes and loaded up the van. The girls said good night first then said that they would call Seth later. The ladies told Sue they would keep going over the papers and would call if they find something wrong. They started the van, and drove off as Sue and Seth went into the house.

"Well that went good," Sue said.

"I hope so, we have not been here very long to have people that don't like us," Seth said.

"They do not hate you; in fact, they are happy that they have found a long-lost part of the family. They think that it is going to be wonderful that they have family in the area," the voice said.

"Are you going to start the girls teaching to night?" Sue asked.

"Yes, but you must let me know just how much to let them know," the voice said.

"How about the basic information and then we will decide from there as we learn more," Sue said.

"That will work well, you can keep track of all the youths training," the voice said.

"Can their mothers be taught the same way," Sue asked.

"There are many things to look at first. We can do it but it would be best done at different times to answer questions that people have. The girls will learn the same things that you learned on your last sleep and we will stop there. Both you and Seth will be one-step ahead of the others and you being the teacher will let us know of any problems. We mean that, if you find the ways of the past may have problems with the ways of today, you can inform us of the problem. When the old one went out into the world, the lands had kings and chiefs that led the people. There was also medicine men and advisors or as some of your writings call them wizard to the leaders. Many of these soothsayers used knowledge or as you call it, magic to help the leaders gain an advantage over the people or their enemy's. It seems to us that these days are not like that and the old ways could be harmful to the person who uses it," the voice told both Sue and Seth.

"Can we hold teachings in the hidden room just like a classroom, just as we have in school," Seth asked.

"That is your space or room as you call it; you can use it as you need it. However, only a person of your blood with a ring can enter it, with your presence being there. This is your secret place from the world and the Realm," the voice tells them.

"You keep telling us about the Realm, can we go there?" Seth asked.

"Yes, when you are ready, that is a place where you will be tested again. Not because of the reason we test you but because of power. That is a very different place then here. There will be many sublets in the meeting place seats, along with a table with seven chairs at the front for the wearers of the seven meeting tree stones or rings. You will be challenged to prove yourself even though you do not have to per the way things are intended to work. Man has made it a place of conflict at times and not of peace. We will teach you this tonight," the voice informed Sue and Seth.

Being Sunday night, Sue wanted Seth to start getting ready for school as if it was a school night even though the next day was the Labor Day holiday. She wants to start getting the routines in place so that the start of the official school days will be easier. She had Seth layout his clothes and set up his school bag in his room so the next day they could relax with a cook out.

The phone rang for the house and Seth knew it was for him. He answered it and it was April and Kristle laughing on the other end. "What is so funny," he asked.

"Well Kristle's parents are having a cook out at her house and my mom and her mom want to have the family that is in the area come to it. Now before we met you, neither of our families had anyone in the area and now we have the three of our families as families, does that make sense," April said to Seth.

"Say what, ya'all confusing me," Seth told them.

"See I told you that I could get him to say it," April told Kristle.

"Now you are making fun of me," Seth exclaimed.

"No, we were talking about how cool you talk, you have a strong way of getting your words heard, and you are so polite. It is so nice to talk to you," Kristle told him.

"Thank you, I guess," Seth replied.

"There really is a cookout tomorrow and I believe your mom told ours that you are coming so we will see you tomorrow around noon, ok," Kristle said.

"If that is the plan then I will be there," Seth answered and the three of them said good night and hung up.

Seth went to his mother and asked about the cookout and she acknowledged that they were going and she said it sounded like fun. She also said that everyone from her side of the family was going to other relatives, so it would be nice to be around people from the neighborhood. Seth agreed and said that he was headed to his room for the night and needed some rest. Sue acknowledged him and said she would be going shortly also.

Sue however was now working on the papers; she got all the timeline written down and papers in order by dates. She also had the bank notices and bank box key all set up so she could go to the bank Tuesday after school. Both Seth and her will find out what was in the bank box and find out if the deed to the farm was all set, even though she got the house through a tax lean. She did not want any problems, so she also hired a lawyer who is part of her father's family. When she had it all in order she bundled it up and headed to bed for the night.

The next morning Sue and Seth met at the kitchen table. After some good morning gestures, they fix a bowl of cereal and sat reading parts of the newspaper on the table. The voice was the first one to speak. "How do you feel after the teaching last night?"

"I feel rested and ready to take on the day," Seth said.

"I feel no different than yesterday," Sue said.

"What is the fifth rule of the council," the voice asked.

"That all who possess a trees ring must meet on the third full moon after the winter solstice, however the Realm has a gathering every full moon for common things," Seth let out.

"What is the first rule of the council," it asked.

"Only a bloodline ring may sit at the council of seven," both Seth and Sue said.

"Who heads the council of the seven," the voice asked,

"The bloodline with the shortest family tree from the first time the blood was exchanged until the present time. It holds no power over the others, just the position of Chancellor of the meeting. This is rule three of the Council," Seth said.

"How many sublets can one tree ring have," the voice asked,

"An infinite number but only seven have seats and voting privileges in the Realm, per rule four, section two, of who may attend a meeting," Seth exclaims.

"Wow, there are a lot of rules, as you asked the questions I could see them come up in my head," Sue said.

"This is the important one, rule six, every member of the seven can have one advisor to assist them, but that member must be of direct blood meaning father, Mother, son or daughter. See a ring wearer can pass the ring forward in the bloodline and become a sublet as long as the tree passes them. Or if there is no one beyond the current person, the next closest can become head of the meeting tree. So, Sue you are Seth's advisor and he being young will need your help," the voice tells them.

"I have just one question, why is it a tree," Sue asked.

"It is a living thing, reproducing life, and it stands high so that it can be seen from a distance. It is on all but one continent and there it is too cold to live now, so it is on the tip of the large land mass near it. You call it Antarctica but we know it as the land of snow. The meeting tree is on the tip of what you call South America and we know it as land of peeks and forest and have the smallest of amount of people visiting it of all the trees. South America's tree is in the city Paititi, which is a so called legendary city and refuge in the rain forest; it is at a boarder of three countries.

Asia's tree is in Shambhala, the mythical kingdom hidden in inner Asia. Many people know of this city but it is kept secret so that the monks can teach in peace. Australia's tree is guarded by its indigenous people called the Aboriginal people. With help from their spirituality known as the Dreamtime, it places a heavy emphasis on belonging to the land. Africa, the tree is located at the base Mount Kilimanjaro and protected by the Chagga people. In Europe, the tree is located on the British Isles where they say the great one lived. There are many stories and none can be proven but when you follow the age of the stories, they start around five hundred AD, however we believe we are older than that. We know of over five hundred sun cycles for this tree. It is the twentieth tree in its place and here in North America, or as we know it Markland. The tree has moved from the top of the hill down to the side by each rebirth, because its seeds would fall that way. Here we know that both Natives and Norsemen visited the area. Then Europeans settled and changed the land," the voice informed them.

"Why, are we not taught this so that everyone can live in

peace," Seth asked.

"We are the land, the forest, and the creatures, but the humans are a different thing all together. Nature as you know it can go onward without man and it changes as the world changes. Man, however came and brought his ways and ability to change things that he sees fit. Man is ruled by another that we do not have knowledge of, and now man has control of things that we do not understand. The boxes that you handle and talk into, the thing you call computer also the picture box. We cannot feel them or read them but we know that they are energy of some type," the voice tells Seth. Seth sat for the rest of the morning thinking about this, and before long, it was time to leave for the cookout.

Seth and his mom walked up to Kristle's family's house on West Whitehall Rd. It was not far just over the bridge and a few hundred feet up the road. When they got there, both Kristle and April met them at the road and started introducing them to everyone there. Kristle's mother had taken the snacks that they were asked to bring from them, allowing them to mingle with the group. There were around twenty people there and most were the neighbors from the street, the rest from different parts of the area. As they were introduced to the people, they would all ask, "You're from the haunted house?" and give a little laugh. Seth kept thinking to himself, "If you only knew" and he just smiled.

They were then introduced to a couple that owns a farm on the start of the street near the bridge. The voice told both Seth and Sue that was Jeb's son Mathew's farm before he died. Sue thought it would be a good time to bring that fact up and stated, "You own the farm that was built by Mathew, Jeb's son. Jeb Crocker was the son of the builder of our farm."

The wife of the couple said, "I believe that is right, he was killed by a cow and his wife remarried, sold the farm, and left the area. Most of these homes around the area are tied together somehow it seems."

The husband said, "You can follow the trails along the river and through the woods. These were all the old logging roads used to get wood used in the houses and barns. You are welcome to walk out through there but you should do it before the hunting season."

"That is great, maybe we can take a walk tomorrow or next weekend out through there," Sue answered.

"Go next weekend and April and I can go with you. We have walked out there with our parents and we can help you," Kristle said.

"Well, I guess that will be great because neither of us have ever been in any woods. We'll just follow the paths around the river area for now," Sue said out loud for the neighbors. However, between the four of them and the house she was saying in her thoughts, "we can walk the trail and find the tree, so that we know exactly where it is."

"I agree," Seth said.

"We agree and we can help you get there by showing you the maps in the book," said the voice.

The rest of the cookout that day had the adults all-talking together about town politics and families. The kids had some outside games and some video games setup in the garage. Every so often, Sue checked in with Seth and she saw that he was finally having fun with kids his own age. Sue was watching him and remembered the so many times that he would come home hating being in his school and wanting to leave the area. Many days he had bruises from being hit by the kids that would pick on him. She would go to the school without him knowing it and talk to the school officials but they said they could not control the gangs.

Sue made the decision to finish her degree in education, so that she could start home schooling Seth. This would start in the eighth grade so that he would not have to go to the high school with all the gangs and problems that people seem not to deal with. Seth's father and she had decided this before he had deployed on his last mission, then they got the bad news of his death. This changed everything; she was losing her home and the main support for the family, worst of all was the loss of Seth's father and her husband. The Army had some support but their life had to be off the base, wherever she could get reset up to work. She had just finished her education and got her teaching certificate, so she made the decision to move to the northeast where she had some relatives. It was not what they wanted, however, it is what they had to do.

She had lost both her parents just before she married her husband. Both had died in a car accident on the Massachusetts Pike, just west of Boston while coming home after her brothers' game at college. At the time, she was taking classes in North Carolina, where she had met her future husband who was station at a nearby base. She stopped taking full time classes after they died, she married which started a family, but kept working on her education part time. She never gave up her dream of teaching, just added a family into her life. She felt that having a son was the best thing to happen to her. To see him now having fun and acting like a kid was the greatest feeling to her right now. Many of the adults asked her how Seth was adjusting to the small-town setting and she would tell them that time will tell.

The night was on them, they had a small fire, and people were toasting marshmallows. The crowd was thinning and people were planning to meet at the next holiday, which would be Halloween. Sue wanted to leave before it got real late, because they had to walk the dark street home. They said their goodnights to everyone and almost everyone said that Sue should hold the Halloween party in the old house. She told them that maybe it is a great idea and said they all will have to talk about it, and then they waved good-bye and left.

The walk was only a short one down a slow curving road then over the Powwow River bridge. Once over it, they turned to the right and up a small rise and they were at the house. Once inside they put away the items they brought back and they got cleaned up. When they retired to their rooms, they each got on their computer, Sue was cleaning up some work for school; Seth was adjusting his music and loading it to his phone.

8

What does the key unlock?

THIS WAS THE FIRST FULL DAY to start a near full week of school, the morning was warm with the sun bright in the sky. Sue dropped Seth off at the front door and when he was in the school, she headed off to work at her school. Seth went to his classroom when it was time to start and got set to start the day. Both April and Kristle meet Seth and they started making small talk about what was ahead for the day. Some of the other kids came over to talk to the three of them adding to the topic they were talking about then. After a short time, the bell rang and all the kids sat in their seats. Their teacher came into the room, took attendance, and started the class. April said in her thoughts, this going to be fun and both Seth and Kristle answered her without making a sound. The three of them looked at each other and smiled knowing that no one in the room knew what had just happen.

"Ok you three, play nice," Sue, said to the three of them in their thoughts.

"Mom, aren't you at school," Seth asked.

"Yes, I am, but when you use your thoughts as a group, I hear you. I think that it is by design, it keeps track of the three of you, so you don't do anything wrong," Sue told them.

The voice speaks, "Yes we did this because you are their teacher and we do not want anything to go wrong. There is a lot that we do not know about school and groups in this day and age. Each of you can turn it off, if you do not want the others to hear you. It becomes active only if you think about any of the powers given to you. We can make changes as everyone learns all that is taught and can control their powers."

"Ok, we will be good," April said.

"Can we talk in other languages without sending messages to mom," Seth asked.

"Sue that is up to you," the voice said.

Sue thought about it for a few seconds and said, "That is fine with me."

"It is done," the voice said.

From that point on the three of them would greet each other in Welsh or Spanish and hold conversation in one of the two forms. When others asked how they learned it, they would say that they picked it up by hearing it.

Many of the kids were dumbfounded by the fact that the three of them are related when they are told. Some of them had a smart remark or two but that was just from the boys. There were a couple of girls that commented that April and Kristle were not competition anymore on who can date Seth but the girls reminded them that they are just distant relatives. The day finally ended, Seth was driven home by April's mom when she picked up the two girls. Seth thanked them for the ride, walked into the house and started working on the little homework he had. He found that it was a breeze and had it done within an hour.

Sue arrived home and when she came in to the house, she told Seth that they were going to the bank before it closed for the day. She grabbed the folder that had all the paperwork that the house left her as well as the paperwork that was in the trunk. They drove to the old bank in the center of Amesbury and asked to talk to a bank official about an old account there.

They were met by a young lady in her late twenties and she asked what she could do for them. Sue told her that she has a key for a safety deposit box that was set up one hundred and ten years ago. She also told her that she had all the paperwork that shows that her son is the heir to the box. She told her that they are welling to have them copy all of it but only in their presence. The young lady looked over the paperwork and looked at the key then excused herself and left the office in a bit of a hurry.

After five minutes, she returned with an older gentleman who introduced himself as one of the bank officers Kendell Solara. "This box is part of the old bank and it is locked away in the vault down stairs. The bank updated the boxes some thirty years ago and they had to remove the box from its former spot. It was cut away from the other empty boxes but it was never opened," he exclaimed.

"So, can we open it or is there a problem?" Sue asked politely.

"My assistant tells me is that you have all the birth and death certificates that go back to the original owner. The big item is the key and you have that in your hand, therefore, there should not be any problems at all. If you wait about ten minutes we will have it in the viewing area for you," he said.

"Thank you, I think that will be just fine," Sue said in a kind southern manner.

After a short time, they came and retrieved the two of them, then led them into a bank box viewing office area. They were given some paperwork that they needed to sign which stated that the bank was no longer responsible for the content of the box and it would be closed out once it was opened. Once the paperwork was completed they were then taken into a small room off to the side and on the desk, was a large black item that looked like a small safe. You could see the cut areas and the door with the two key holes in it. The girl that met with them as they entered the bank, told her to place the key in the lock, then turn it. Sue did as she asked and the key fit and it took some strength but it turned. The bank rep put her key in, and it turned just as hard then it made a loud unlocking sound as the door broke open but just very slightly.

The girl removed her key and said that if they needed anything she would be at the desk in the other room. Sue said thank you as the girl walked out and shut the door.

Sue turned to Seth and said, "Well, let us see what we have in this part of the treasure hunt." With that, she opened the door and it opened very hard with a loud creaking noise. Sue could see that there was a covered tray in it and she slowly pulled it out, then saw that it was closed with no locks. She laid it beside the large part of the box and slowly opened it, being careful not to disturb anything in it. There were several large envelopes that were tied closed with a string using a bow, also some smaller envelopes with handwriting on the front. One was marked 'the house,' when she opened it, she could see that it was a letter. She read it out loud: "To whom it may be that opens this box, this is to let you know, that I, Jeb Crocker am leaving all that I own to the first relative that opens this box. Good luck" and he signed it, there was also a seal and signature of a lawyer on it.

"Well that is a type of will, let us see what is in the other two," Sue said and she opened the next one and it was full of money. They were Bison ten-dollar bills and Seth started counting the bills. Sue then opened the other envelope, it was also full of money, again it was bison ten-dollar bills. They both stopped and just looked at the bills for a minute and then at each other with a wide eye look.

"What did we just get," Sue asked.

"Mom how much is there here," Seth asked.

The two of them went on counting the bills when Sue

noticed that they all were dated 1901. There were twenty bills in each envelope and Sue put them back in and looked at Seth.

"These are very old bills and can be worth more than the amount on its face. We need to get these to a collector and find out the real value of them. Until we find out everything about the items we have here, we cannot tell anyone about what we found. The letter is the only thing we will let out to anyone that asks," Sue told Seth.

Sue put all the paperwork in a satchel that she had with her, this also kept it out of view from anyone they may run into. When everything was packed, they called the bank employee back in to the room. They told her that there will be no use for any security box any longer and that they will be on their way. The girl asked what was in the box and Sue told her that there were letters about the property and the family accounts. The young girl told them that it will be good to get rid of the old box finally, it was awkward and took up needed space. She guided Seth and Sue out to the main office area and the bank president was standing there waiting for them.

"I hope that whatever was in the box is going to be of use for you," he said.

"We need to get the papers to a lawyer and see just what they mean to our family," Sue told him.

"Do you have one, if not we can recommend one," he told her.

"We are all set and we will be seeing him near the end of the week. I want to thank you for your help offer and for keeping this for my son," Sue told him.

He looked at Seth long and hard but Seth just acted as if he was one of the bullies looking at him back on base. Seth just ignored him and went on his way and Sue followed him out of the building. He made his way to the car, which was just a short distance from the door of the bank, parked along the street curb. He got into the passenger side and Sue handed him the satchel then closed the door. She walked around to the driver's side, got in, and closed the door very quickly.

"What is bothering you," she asked Seth.

"That man gave me a bad feeling, like he was trying to read my mind or something," he said.

"I did not feel that at all, are you sure that you feel ok," Sue asked.

"I feel fine but he acted like he was trying to read my thoughts," he said.

"Seth is right he was trying to see if Seth had any secrets but the ring hid Seth from his thoughts. He must be from another bloodline and has figured out that he has some ability but he does not have a ring that we could see. We felt that he has never had a ring on or maybe he has it hidden in some way. When you hid your rings, there is a part of the spell that only allows members of that bloodline to be able to tell if a person is wearing a ring. If the person removes the ring a part of the spell stays with the person for their protection and it will keep anyone else from seeing a connection to a meeting tree. That can never be removed from a person, only by death can it disappear. We will train all of you, how to block and see this before something bad happens, because of this event," the voice informed them.

"But, if he was from another bloodline, why did he not get all the information in the lockbox or just take it," Seth asked.

"Jeb did all this without his ring on and we knew what was happening but did not log it into the Realm. Jeb did not know of the Realm as much as you do, so information that he fed back to us was still at the stage of development. We knew what was in the box, as things, but what they meant was new even to us," the voice told them.

"But who is the man," Sue asks.

"He could be a couple of things. One is, he has no power, other than what he discovered about himself without any knowledge of the order and he uses it to gain power. On the other hand, someone wants to get into the meeting tree from outside the bloodline and gain the seat on the Realm. He maybe a person that was placed here as a watcher for someone with a connection to a meeting tree. We will need to follow up on this," the voice said.

They started driving home and talked about the trip at the end of the week where they would be going to see her cousin in Massachusetts. She would pick him up at school before noon and drive directly there for the rest of the day. It had just been five minutes and they were now home when Sue noticed that the house looked much better now on the outside.

"Is the house happy now because of us being here," She asked.

"Yes, and the barn is now all set for you to have your car in it," the voice said.

The doors slid open and Sue drove in so she was just clear of the doors. They got out and walked out of the doors and they slid closed. As they got to the front door, they heard it unlock and they went in, then the door closed behind them and it locked.

"We think that the two of you need to be protected even more now because of what happened today," the voice said.

"How can we do that," Sue asked.

"We will teach you this as you all sleep. It seems that there may be people around that are from other bloodlines. They may have evil on their minds and we need to have you ready if something does happen," the voice informed them.

Sue went into the kitchen to make dinner and the two of them talked about what to do with all they had found. The voice would ask a question every so often and Sue would answer the best that she could. When evening came, Seth went into the den, sat, and played on his phone. The evening passed away and they headed to their rooms for the night.

That night as the two of them slept, along with the girls, the house taught them how to hide thoughts and keep an expressionless face. In addition, they taught them how to keep calm when faced with confrontation and how to read people in a situation. This will help them with people they deal with every day. Seth however was also learning how to use the power and access it when needed, this was because he was the head of the group. Almost all of it was pure thought control to stop a confrontation or be the aggressor when needed. Every night more learning was accomplished without disturbing their everyday life.

Seth had learned that he could put a spell of protection on everyone that wears a ring in his bloodline. It would make it so there is a space around the person that no one could enter, if they had a different bloodline then theirs. However, there would be problems with it in public, because it keeps others away, the action could be noticed by people.

He also learned that he could make it so that the wearers could feel an event just before it happens. This way they can avoid being hurt or put in a harmful situation. They had to be careful with this because it could spook people if they do things that they see as magic.

Now as the four of them learned from the training at night, the house, tree, and book learned from their thoughts. Up until this point the house, tree, and book only knew what was in the ring. This only from the time it was made and the information from the tree since it became a meeting tree. Then when Jeb came in to contact with them, what little knowledge he had was passed on to them. It also received information from the Realm that was common to all wizards.

After some talk about what happen at the bank both Seth, Sue, and the voice decided that, they should put everything about the bank box under wraps. This meant, it would be kept to them only, and not involve either of the girls or their parents until all training was complete. Although the house, tree, and book are part of the Realm, they knew and felt all its rules, but they did not know of all its people and animals. They knew of the people that had the six other rings but not their sublets

They knew there is evil in the world but how far it went into the Realm has never been proven. The house taught them how to feel evil that is nearby but how to handle it will take more training. The girls will get this training without known any of what happen to Seth and his mother, for now.

The school days went as schedule and the kids were being kids, and making friends, also learning who the school groups would be. Seth kept any thoughts about what they had found, out of his head, while he was out in public. He did find that he could tell if any of the kids in his school were going to be friends with him. He could also tell the kids that were going to be a challenge like the one who asked him about his father on the first day.

Both the girls found it easy to feel which girls, were just going through the motions of being nice and those that were real friends. They found it odd that kids that they thought were friends were just really snubbing them. Seven years of thinking, they were good friends but they were just putting up with them. They felt odd about this but then Sue's voice came into their thoughts and told them that real friends would not do that. However, some of the kids that they did not always hang around had a friendlier demeanor toward them and they felt that they were the ones to be-friend. This was all new to them and it was a bit of a surprise.

Sue went on teaching her history classes and looked out over the classrooms to see if anyone of her students gave her a bad feeling, none were found. She however seemed to get a feeling of who would do good in class or who was a wise guy. She could never pick this up before and felt that these feelings would help her be a better teacher. It also allowed her to feel if any of her kids were having trouble with any of the classes that they were taking and could head them in the right direction for some help. This was helping her to become a well like and trusted teacher in her school.

Back at home, Seth and his mother talked about what to do if anyone ever approached them and tried to get information of any type out of them. They planned to play it so that it seemed that they had no idea what they were talking about. They were new to the area and found that if they played it this way they were not taking any sides and could act as if they had no feelings any way. With everything that they went through with the loss of Seth's father, they could use that feeling to their advantage. A deep sad thought could give the feeling to the person that confronted them that they were to hurt to talk. In a way, they both felt that it was not a lie and they did not have to practice it because it was already real to them.

9

Who would have thought?

THURSDAY WAS HERE AND SUE AND SETH SET OUT for a road trip to the city, after picking Seth up at school. They left very late in the morning and had to sit in traffic to keep an appointment with their relative's law office in Cambridge Ma. When they arrived, the meeting started as an informal family friendly meeting until Sue and Seth removed the papers from the envelopes. Their relative's eyes went wide, and he started examining each piece shaking his head as he looked at them. He called in some of his assistants and they started making copies and writing information on work sheets. Sue asked what is wrong and all he would say was, "not a thing for you and Seth, just bear with us and you will love what you see."

Now Sue had a confused look on her face and Seth noticed it and rolled his eyes at his mom. She returned the motion and they just sat and watched as the people looked like a busy bee-hive as they moved throughout the office. After about an hour of fast moving people with both Sue and Seth having anything they want to eat or drink, as the office personnel had it delivered, Sue's cousin sat down with them. All the papers were spread out on the table in front of them with notes attached to them. "Sue this is unbelievable, you two have fallen into something that people have prayed for since money was invented. Seth, you are the wealthiest young man that I have ever met. These bonds are still good and have split and gained in value many times over the last one hundred and fifteen years. If you were to sell them all now after taxes you will be worth around fifty million dollars if not more." Sue's face went white and within seconds she passed out, Seth held her to keep her from falling off the chair and keep her seated while calling out "mom, mom" over and over.

When Sue regain her wits, there was a group of people around her with damp cloths, a drink and anything that she needed. Seth was trying to talk to her and when she became aware of everything, all she could say was "Are you kidding us?"

"No, I am not, you have a lot of funds, and now you need to decide what your next step will be," he said, then followed with, "If I were you I would hire a lawyer."

"Ah, do you want the job, I cannot think straight but do you have all the knowledge to deal with this?" Sue asked.

"Yes, but Seth you have not said anything, what do you want to do," he asked him.

"I want to make sure mom's ok," he said. When Sue looked at him, he had a scared look on his face.

"I'll be just fine, that was a lot to find out all at one time," Sue said to Seth as she was running her hand along his face.

"Mom I thought I lost you too," he said as he had tears running down his eyes.

"Seth, I am here for you and am not going anywhere for a while," She said to him with a smile on her lips.

Nicolas, Sue's cousin the lawyer also had tears and had to wipe his eyes. He knew at this point, Seth did not care about the money, his mother was his world. He cleared his throat, then they turned toward him and Seth reached for the bag he had held until his mother fainted.

AWAKENING

"We also have these, can you tell us about them," Seth asked.

Nicolas opened the two envelopes and he fell back into his chair. "These are Bison ten-dollar bills, they are no longer in circulation but they are worth much greater than they were while in circulation as currency," he said as he turned to his computer. He typed in some information and it came up to an auction site that dealt with old coins and currency. He checked what the bills were selling for there and the common value shown on this site was six hundred and forty-nine dollars each. He turned in the chair he was sitting in and faced Seth and Sue with a look of disbelief and thought for a second or two before speaking again.

With an inquiring look he asked, "Do you have any more of these."

"No, that is all we have," Seth said.

"Well," he said in an informative tone, "these could be worth around two hundred forty thousand dollars to a collector. The two of you need to make some decisions, like what do you want to do with all these funds."

"Can we turn some these into tangible funds and reset up accounts with up dated names," Sue asked.

"Yes, we can, and the first thing to do is log all the accounts and have a contract set up between us. This way we will have all the paperwork with names, account numbers and give a paper trail so there will be no problems between us. The first thing we are going to do is give you a log of all that is here. This is a very large fortune and no one wants to mess this up," Nicolas declared.

The office personnel worked on copies, logs, and pictures then it was all put together in a portfolio with Seth as the owner and Sue as executor. Now it was starting to come to reality to Seth, that his mother and his life will be changing again but this time for the better. He however, still thinks how much he misses his father and wishes that he were here to share in all this.

After some time and a lot of paperwork checking, it was time to leave for home for Seth and Sue. Nicolas had a person from the office staff escort them to the parking garage and their car. That person made sure that they got on their way back home safely.

They made their way out of the city and the house's voice asked if they were happy with the outcome. Sue asked if they knew about the money and funds and the voice told them, that after Jeb removed the ring there was no way to hear his thoughts. Nothing, that he had done, was logged into the book so there was no way to know. Value of objects does not mean much to the meeting tree, only the value of life.

Once home Seth and Sue sat in the living room just looking into the small fire, that Sue had started in the fireplace. There was a long period of neither one speaking, but then Sue spoke first. "You know we now have funds so that we could leave here and move closer to your father."

"Mom what good would that do? We cannot bring dad back and we will live the pain over again," Seth told her with a scorn look on his face. His answer was quick and meaningful and she knew he had reasoned this out in his head already.

She watched him and looked to see if there were any tears, but none were showing. That statement by him seemed so grown up and she felt that it should not have come out of a fourteen-year-old. This worried her a little because he was acting many years ahead of his age level. She then said, "Well, we have money for you for school and maybe we should just live normally like other people around us. You have a few more years before you need to decide anything about school."

"Mom, do not get me wrong but I have new friends here and I want to finally have some fun. You have money from your parents and from dad and you just wanted to live in a quiet spot and teach. That sounds good even to me after being around angry kids in my last school. Its new here and who knows what else we will find," said Seth.

"Then we will have Nicolas set up all the funds and accounts so you can draw some out at times and save the rest for a later date. Let's have some holiday parties for our family and friends," Sue said and Seth agreed with her. They continued talking into the night making plans, even made plans to give some to the girls for school and their future. Before they ended their day, the one thing that they were sure of, was that they were not going to change because healing was still the needed thing right now for them both.

When Sue finally got to bed she could use the quiet of her room to sit and think. The events of the day went through her head and she tried to place it in an order so she could make sure that they were making the right decisions. She thought about the money that she already had in her bank accounts, that she had received from her parents after they passed away. Also, with what she had from funds that she and her husband had built up in savings. She had used a large amount of it to buy their new home but there was still a large amount left to live with. Then there was the money from Seth's father's life insurance, which she was saving for Seth's education. However, it all seemed so small now compared to what was just handed to them from the items left from her husband's ancestors. She was happy that Seth could do things if he wanted but the question is what does he want to do? Eventually sleep came and she was off in dreamland.

The next morning Sue was making breakfast when Seth came down, he quietly made a plate, and only spoke two words, "morning mom." He sat at the table eating very slowly and looked as if he had something that was heavy on his mind. Sue got her plate together and sat with him. After a couple of bites, she asked, "What are you thinking about?"

Seth looked up from his plate and almost had no emotions showing on his face. "I can't stop thinking about dad and what we could have done together, the three of us with all this money."

Sue felt her body shake and a large sad feeling hit her. She was holding back the tears that just want to flow from her eyes while thinking about how to answer him. She could only find one thing to say but she knew that it was not going to answer the feelings he was having. "He will always be with us, no matter what we do, both together and apart," she said to him.

The emotional looks on Seth's face lighten a little bit but she knew it was still on his mind. Just then, the horn sounded from April's mother's car that was picking Seth up for school. He finished his meal in one gulp, kissed his mom on the cheek then out the door he flew. Sue placed the dishes in the sink after rinsing them off and she went off to her school. During the short drive, she kept thinking about Seth when the voice asked her, "do you always worry about Seth like this."

"Yes, he needs to find his path in life and I am his only parent now, but I also am not over what happen to his father. He was a big part of my life also but I know that I have to be strong for Seth, without having him see how bad I am hurting," Sue tells them.

"We are here for you but we do not understand what you are feeling, we cannot make it better because we cannot change the past," the voice tells her.

"I know, I need to get ready to start class so I am going to put it out of my head," she tells them as she is getting out of the car, to head into her school.

Both Seth and Sue continued through their day doing what was needed to finish the day. They both had thoughts of their loss, which brought them to this point. The new money that they now have, was the last thing that they were thinking of, however the two girls were making Seth smile and laugh and Sue could feel that and it made her happy. She knew that this will help him but her feelings were deep and she missed her husband so much.

10

Μεετ τhε Τρεε

IT HAS BEEN JUST UNDER A WEEK since the Labor Day cook-out and it was a nice end of summer weekend day. April and Kristle walked down the street to meet Seth and his mother at the bridge, then they walked along the fence then turned into the field where the old trail started at the gate. You could see a well-worn old road type path following the river until the river bend then it keeps going straight. It was blocked after a few hundred feet by a new house set into the woods that had been built with its driveway coming from the other road.

There was a path to the left just before the blocked area, and they followed that for just a short distance of two hundred feet. This was a smaller path now used by walkers during the summer and snowmobilers in the winter so it was clear of brush. It came to another path that you could follow into some fields, or turn right and follow it farther into the woods. They turned right and went into the woods following along what seems to be an old logging road. It went by a large rock sticking out of the ground that looked out of place, when they walked around it, they found a carving on it. Seth told them, "It is the symbol that is on the stone and written in the book."

They spent some time at the rock and when they were done, left it then continued following the path past small ponds, then over a short stonewall that came to an area where the path split. They walked down the right path and there they were, at the tree. It looked like much of the path was changed by the house that was built in the woods and from time letting trees grow back in place. It is now taller than when Jeb was there and it is older with many carvings into it from people visiting it. At one time, this was a place called, "lovers lane," which had started at the other end of the old logging road that was closed off by tree growth. The area was grown up around the tree but now there were many little off springs of the big tree that circled around it. It is now growing its replacement that will come in the near future. The tree is now on the property of a neighbor of the lands original owners' lot, because the land has been divided up by the different owners over the century. They walked around the tree, which is now many feet across, being amazed by its size. They looked at the carvings and saw many names of people that came to the site. Some had been there for many years and only show as a big scar on the tree. The carvings were not deep as they were only on the bark, after many years they were almost gone but the bark showed it as a black mark.

Seth climbed up the lower branches of the tree and as he made his way up it, he could see the very old marks on the trunk. He had made it to an area where he saw a symbol that looked just like the one that he could see inside the stone on his ring. He traced it with his right hands index finger and it did make the shape but it was very dark, deep, and old looking, however it was perfectly shaped as if it was not carved but grown in place. Then just as he was pulling away, he felt a prick on the finger. He saw just as Jeb did the small amount of blood absorbed by the tree. He did not fret because he remembered from his night teachings that the tree does this to know if the person should be there.

He made his way back down the tree and rejoined the group as they were cleaning up the area, moving branches on the ground to the outside of the ring. There were many very old dead branches already outside the circle as if someone had been doing it but had left no trace of whom they were. However, it could have been people coming there to have some type of gathering not having anything to do with the powers of the tree. Looking around they saw what the training has stated, how you can see the land was being changed and houses are getting closer to the tree. There may come a day when the tree itself will be endanger and will have to be moved by growing one of its off springs in a safe area.

They gathered their things together and followed the path back that they had walked to get into the woods. Making their way back to the road they could see how man had been in the woods moving things. When they walked in, they had the view with the woods behind what they saw ahead of them. However, on the way out they now could see the fields, the many buildings, and the road through the trees.

They walked out of the woods into the field which brought them to the road through the field's gate. They proceeded over the river by the bridge and then walked the last hundred feet to their house. Seth was thinking during the last part of the hike what it would have been like a hundred years ago, when they did not have to worry about cars and trucks hitting them on the dirt roads there. The voice answered him and said that they could show him during one of the dream trainings if he would like. He then asked if it could show everyone just how it looked in the past so that they can understand more about the land. The voice agreed and once they were in the house the group proceeded to attack the refrigerator for snacks and drinks. When they had their required snack, they sat in the den and talked about the tree with the voice filling them in on the history, as they knew it over the years.

"Man has been here for many cycles of the sun but only until the three hundred of your years has the tree been in danger by man," the voice said.

AWAKENING

"Why," asked Seth.

"Man used stone and dirt to build caves and huts to shelter and live in when they first came to this land; however, they use trees now and mix dirt to form blocks to build shelters now, like this house. For the last three hundred years, they have been using many trees to build houses and to keep warm. Although the tree is protected, it offspring are not and many have been removed by man. Someday it fears it will have to protect itself and hurt man to survive. This is against all that it believes and it has never had to do this during any of its lives. Teach and protect is its mission given to it, from day one," the voice informs them.

"We will do what we can to help," Sue said and everyone agreed.

They ended the day by saying good night and everyone headed to their own little getaway in their homes. Each person in the group, Seth, and his mother along with the two girls now had the tree on their minds. They now look at the tree as a leader in this group and the known start of the adventure that they are on; nevertheless, the voice tells them that there is a starting point even before the tree. There are other trees out there, in the world that have people like them. More questions come now, such as 'are they young or old? Do they feel the same way as we do about our gift? Where did this all really start?' So much to think about as their learning continues as they sleep.

11

Training for the Realm

A FEW WEEKS GO BY; both Seth and his mom have set up a routine in their daily lives, that match the life style of their new home. Seth and the girls have become very close, somewhere between family and best friends during this short time since meeting. They have learned many things while they sleep and while they are at the house, talking to it while building their friendship and family ties. Their schoolwork has been easy to them and the three of them are at the top of their class without using any of their hidden training.

The house and tree informed them that it was time for Seth, his mother, and the girls to now train for the meetings in the Realm. They are told that there are meetings every full moon but the third full moon that is after the winter solstice is the big meeting for the Realm. That a head of the meeting tree, cannot miss the yearly big meeting after they have started attending meetings in the Realm. The rules state that if this meeting is missed, then voting by the sublets for that group does not count for a year. This can change the power and rules of the Realm in favor of a couple of groups. Up to this point in the time of the Realm, this meeting tree has had an open seat at the meetings and no one is to fill it or vote on its behalf.

AWAKENING

The voice starts the training with, "The Realm is in disar-
ray, because of a couple of groups that want to change the old
ways. The order of the Realm was never setup to have power,
only to help stop man from destroying the earth and themselves. There needs to be a check and balance in all things or
one side will over run the other which has happened many
times in the past. The earth is a living thing and it is always
changing with weather, volcanoes, and just age. Every living
thing on the earth depends on each other and people are no
different. Nevertheless, there are some people, which will stop
at nothing to have it all. Because of their greed, false beliefs,
their blindness, they want everyone to follow them and only
their way of life.

As of right now, there are people sitting in the seats of the
Realm that belong to you and your bloodline, even though the
seat should be empty. They have forced their way in through
false claims and trickery over the years, and you and your
bloodline must confront them but not in such a way as to have
a fight. Understand this, you are an innocent and do not have
the feelings that you want to run or control everything. They
will try to provoke you but you must make a stand without
being seen as the aggressor. You are also younger than they
are in both your age and family tree, so they will argue those
points and try to use it to gain the power. However, here is
how you will overcome them. Rule number three gives you
the position of Chancellor, which means, you sit in the center
of the table and your sublets sit at the same color chairs in the
meeting room directly in front of you. Your job is to run the
meeting using your other officers, one that reads the rules,
also a scribe that logs all notes, there is also a herald to enforce
your call to meeting and voting. These officers are just people
from any of the groups of sublets voted on by the group to help
you. The three that are there presently have been doing it for
many years and are from the Europe, Australian and the land

of snow groups. The Chancellor position is the least senior family tree and he has no more power than everyone else does on the head table; however, he has the power of the Realm to control the meeting. Wizards however have tried to make it a seat of power and that is against the rules of the Realm, it is a position of service. Some have held it for centuries and some for decades, as groups came to be in the Realm. You are the last to join and the last meeting tree to serve as Chancellor unless there is a rule that we missed that changes that. No one knows what will happen after all the seats are filled at the head table; there may be rules that are meant to change when all seats are full.

We still do not know how the ring wearers can block the meeting trees thoughts in their minds. We told you if you were going against the training and rules, we would be in your thoughts making it uncomfortable and force you to give up the ring. The thought of doing this to you brings great sadness to us because we are so fond of you.

The other way is to be forced out by the Realm but this has never happened. We have lived in peace for the most part but sometime lands go to war and meetings can be very harsh. You may be heading into one of those harsh meetings, so every one of you will need to know what to do. We will show you how things should work in a meeting of the Realm," the voice informed them.

All this training is happening while everyone is asleep and allowing them to have regular dreams. During the days that the girls are at the house they would go to Seth's secret room, which now had more seats, to have lessons with the book. However, there were many days that the three kids would just gather and have teenage fun together. The mothers used the time to chat as a group while they planed the next parties and gatherings in the future.

Seth has been picked up for school by Kristle's mother and Sue was getting an early start to her days. One day she walked out to her car and there was a Snowy White owl sitting on the hood of her car. She tried to scare it away but the owl just tilted its head and flexed its wings once. She walked around the front of the car and the owl just turned its head around until it had to turn it back around to see her on the other side. She again went to scare it away and it just hooted at her.

"Don't be scared of the owl, she is here for you," the voice said.

"What do you mean she is here for me, it is just sitting on the hood of the car and will not go away," Sue said.

"She is here for you because she chose to be your friend and helper. If you hold your arm out, she will jump up on it. We must let you know that her talons are sharp and it would be best to have a sleeve on your arm. Just relax and ask her to join you," the voice said.

"Ok, but is she, friendly," Sue asked.

"Yes, she wants to be with you," the voice told her.

Sue puts out her arm after putting on her jacket and the owl walked over to her and stepped up on her arm. She then lifted it up and held it away from her face then asked, "You want to be my friend"?

The owl made a series of chirps and Sue answered her with, "Really you want to stay with me," she said. Then she realized that she just understood what the owl said. "Can you understand me?" She asked the owl.

The owl chirped several times then walked up her arm and stood on her shoulder. She then began to preen her hair and was gentle with her talons so not to hurt Sue. Sue however understood what she had said and now knew that she could understand and talk to her.

"Ok little girl I have to go and I will be back a little later, so you have to go now," Sue said.

The owl let out a small chirp as if to say ok and flew up into the big oak tree in the front yard. Sue said so long and got into her car and started shaking her head and repeating that she could talk to an owl. The voice came back saying, "Each member of the house will have a friend of some type of an animal. It will represent their personality and job each wizard has in the Realm. Yours is that of a wise owl, a teacher and she will stay with you all your life. She is your friend, eyes and your relay of information to other animals," the voice told her.

Sue started the car and told the voice that she will need to learn more about this. The voice told her that it would be in the night learning but she had to do all the talking to the owl because the owl would only respond to her. From that day forward, she will be there when you call her or when you need help.

When Seth got home, he started doing his homework so he could have some free time that night. His mother came home and could not wait to tell Seth about the owl. She told him step by step what had happened and Seth kept saying no way. As she finished the story, a pecking came from the kitchen window where Sue had put a bird-feeding ledge. When the two of them got to the window, the owl was standing there looking into the window. Sue walked over to the window and opened it up so the owl could step in. Sue put out her arm and the owl walked up to her shoulder and began preening her.

"What the heck! That is so neat, will she come to me," Seth asked.

The owl chirped a couple of times when it turned it head to talk to Seth. "Why," Seth asked then he just realized that the owl said that she wants to sit only with Sue. He just talked to an owl and understood what it said. He took a step back and said, "This is getting very scary now."

"Seth, do not be scared, if humans would listen, they could understand animal's expressions but they are too self-centered," the voice, said.

Then a large black raven landed on the ledge, it made everyone jumped a little but the owl kept on preening Sue. The raven stepped in and stood on the sink, let out a few chuckles, then what sounded like a purr and it kept looking at Seth. It would turn its head so that one eye faced the ceiling and the other the floor then rotate its head so the eyes changed position.

"I understood what he said, he wants to be my friend," he said.

"Wow, you have a raven as a friend," Sue said.

"Now this is awesome," Seth said.

The raven let out a couple of caws and some purring and jumped down to the floor. Seth and Sue both knew that it said to follow him. It walked with a waddle out of the kitchen, made its way into the den, and jumped up onto the arm of a chair. He made a couple of purrs and a caw and Seth knew that he said open the doorway to the book.

"The raven is asking you to open your room, can you do it," the voice asked.

Seth raises his hand and clears his mind and thinks of the room and it opened by the wall fading. "Can the raven go into it along with the owl," Seth asked.

"Only the person they attach to can allow them passage but for the safety of the house we will check them before they enter this house. Remember this room is the heart of the house where your book is kept. We do not want anyone or thing in it that can hurt us or you," the voice tells them.

The raven and the owl looked at Seth and Sue as if to seek

permission to enter, then when Seth said, "go ahead," they walked in. Both the birds flapped their wings, then flew up to a stand that was made of wood beside the podium with the book. Seth and Sue stood beside the book and it turned its pages to an area that showed a drawing of the birds and the two of them holding them on their shoulder. It was not a camera picture but more like a painting done with pencils.

"You must formally name your bird, Sue, we will start with you," the voice stated.

"Snowy," Sue said with no hesitation and the owl chirped that she liked it.

"Snowy it is," the voice said and the name appeared under the picture.

"Mason, after dad" Seth said, and his name showed up after a couple of purrs from him.

"You are now logged into the history of the meeting tree and this house. In the very near future April and Kristle will meet their animal mates and they will be logged into the next two pages," the voice told them.

They left the room and when everyone was clear, the room disappeared and the four of them sat and got to know each other. During the evening, Sue and Seth sat in front of the TV to watch a movie and they brought out some popcorn. Both the birds had a small dish of it and when they were done they walked to the kitchen, flew up to the sink and out the window they went. Both Sue and Seth were still a little overwhelmed by the fact that they could talk to the birds. Sue came up with the best answer to the events of the day, "only in New Hampshire," then they retired for the night.

The next day at school, Seth was telling both April and Kristle about the owl and the raven when they were interrupted by the boy Mike, he had asked Seth about his father on the first day of school. He heard that the two birds had come to them and he insisted that no bird would ever come to them.

The three of them tried to walk away from him, but he kept coming after them with remarks. After a short time, Seth had enough and turned to him, he stood tall, quiet, and looked at him straight in the eyes. He in turn stopped in his tracks and could only look at Seth and could no longer move or say anything.

A teacher saw this and walked between Seth and Mike, then told Mike that he had to stop teasing Seth and the girls. Mike still could not move or say anything and was now trying to forcing his body to turn away. When Seth turned to check on the girls Mike found that, he was able to move again. He turned, ran away, and could not understand what had happen to him. He found himself in a cold sweat and now fearing Seth.

The teacher asked Seth and the girls if they were ok, and Seth said that they were fine, that he had worst happened to him at the old school with the gangs. The teacher told him that if it happens again, to let her know but Seth told her that it is unlikely that it will.

The girls were not saying anything but they were confused about what happen to Mike. They each stood on one side of Seth and April asked, "What happen to Mike when you stood up to him."

"It looked like you froze him in time," Kristle exclaimed.

Seth swallowed hard and said, "I thought of him as a stone statue and he stopped and did not move."

"That is just what happens," the voice said to the three of them and followed with, "You used your power to stop him without hurting him."

Just then, Seth heard his mother in his thoughts, "Are you ok honey, do you need me there."

"No mom, I dealt with the problem and now I just want to forget about it," he answered her in his thoughts.

Seth turned back to April and Kristle who had no idea that his mother just spoke to him. "Let's get our lunch and forget this ever happened," he said, and they sat with their bags to eat. They ate in silence and went back to their class work to finish the day. Seth kept his thoughts to himself but it bothered him that he had to do that. Mike was only keeping his eyes at his desk, never looking toward Seth or the girls. Seth was reminded of the days back on the base school when kids would face him down. He did not want to become like them or even hint of having power over anyone in any way. He was feeling bad that he scared Mike.

After school, both April and Kristle came to Seth's house after they completed their homework and sat with Seth on the porch. Seth's raven was sitting on the rail and was watching the girls. Every so often, he would rotate his head from side to side to see the girl's movements. Seth started the conversation with, "I hated doing that in school today to Mike, and I think that I really scared him."

"Well he should not have jumped into our conversation uninvited and he should have not followed us when we walked away," April said.

"Maybe I should not have been talking about the birds," Seth exclaimed.

"It still was rude of him to do what he did, he always was a bit overwhelming to people for as long as I have known him," Kristle said.

"This is something that I need to think about and see if I could have done something else," Seth said.

"Like fight him," April asked?

"He was the bully toward you, not you bulling him. Besides, you protected us, thank you," Kristle said and she hugged him.

Just as she did that, Mason, the raven gave a caw and then two other smaller ravens joined him on the railing. The girls could not believe that they were so close to the three birds but they did not dare move. They watched the girls and made little sounds between them as if they were laughing. After a couple of minutes, they walked around the rail and jumped onto the chairs arm that, the girls were sitting in. Each made a couple of squawks and some purrs and the girls were fascinated that they just understood what they said.

"Well it looks like your time is here for you to choose a friend. They are here so you can decide if you want them or not," Seth told the girls.

"Hi girl, how are you?" April asked the bird on her chair.

It answered with some purrs and then she jumped on Aprils shoulder and started preening her hair. She had a small white patch on her throat area and April named her Star because the white spot looked like a star in the dark sky. Kristle was doing the same with the other raven and it too jumped on her shoulder and preened her hair. She had some white on the tip of her bill so Kristle named her Tipper.

Both the ravens purred that they like their name and the voice said, "Their names and pictures are now in the book."

The ravens stood on the girl's shoulder for twenty minutes as the kids talked about how cool it was to have them there. The birds then got together on the porch rail and sat side by side while watching the kids. After ten minutes, a snowy owl came down to the rail and sat beside the three other birds.

Sue walked out of the house with drinks for the kids and said hi to her snowy owl, in return, it said hi with a couple of little chirps. Sue sat in the chair on the other side of the porch and she asked if the girls like their companions. Just then the voice said, "If any of you are unhappy about your companion they will leave and another will come in its place."

"I love her," April said.

"She is so cute," Kristle declared.

"They are so funny when they watch you, the way they twist their head," Seth said.

"They will be your eyes, ears, and friends. They will follow you wherever you go and watch you and things around you to be sure that you are in no danger. They will also be the look-out for the house and the tree. They will stay here at the house when you are in it and their friends will watch the tree as they have for many years. They will always be there for you," the voice tells them.

"Do all the trees have the animals protecting them," April asked.

"The earth and nature will protect it," the voice said.

"We do not want anyone to enter the land or the house that can harm you or the house. If anyone that intends harm enters the land, we will make him or her feel scared and believe the house will harm them. This is how we got the people in the area calling us a haunted house and it kept people away. If any-one from the Realm or other bloodline nears the house, we will lock everything and go on the offensive to protect. Our animal friends will also help in the protection of the house, and you. The tree is always protected and it will allow people on and around it but no device, can ever bring it down. The tree will also protect itself against weather and storms, but it someday will succumb to age, but not before passing on its power and knowledge to one of its offspring," the voice exclaimed.

The afternoon turned to evening and the girls went home with their raven's flying above them, until they were safe at home. Both Snowy and Mason flew up to the old tree in the yard and stayed there after Sue locked up the house. Both Seth and his mom said their goodnights and they turned in for the evening. Seth spent his last moments awake, thinking about what happen at school with Mike. He still felt bad that he scared him, even after what April and Kristle said. He had a thought, that maybe he would confront Mike on a friendly level when the time comes to make up for it. He knew that this stance he did with Mike is what will be needed when they enter the room at the Realm. He must be ready if he is chal-lenged or needs to prove a point. He also thinks about how much his life has changed in the last year, then he drifts off to dreamland.

Part of the training is how to use the power they are given, so the four sat at the living room table many times with a set of cards and some coins. At first, they would have all fifty-two cards face down and each person would ask one of the others to pick up a specific card by its suit and value. Next, they would pull the called card out of the deck without touching it. With them face down each person would think of a card and have it slide itself out of the deck and stay face down. When all four had a card pulled out, they would flip it over with their thought.

When they got tired of cards, they moved to the coins. They would make them float in air, stack, spin like a top and flip into cups. This was much more than slide of hand, they also talked about how to make it look like a hand trick. They were all finding it easier to use the power with this training, with the help of the voice. They were learning how to focus and think quickly with these little techniques.

They talked about how to hide their new power and how to act with it, because magic was not real in society and people would react badly to people that had it. Sue knew that she could hide it easily, but the kids will be in situations that will make it hard for them. Impulse will be their worst enemy while being young with all the different kids in school; she also knows it is difficult for the average kid with a simple secret never mind a secret like they have. The voice told Sue that she would know when each of the kids were going to use magic, and could be the voice in their head to guide them.

All three of the kids felt that it was a great idea and this surprised Sue a little. These three teens are acting more grown up then most adults that she knows. She could also feel that the kids trusted her more than the kids trusted anyone else in their group of friends.

However, Sue feels that she needs to have some time with people her own age doing the same thing. Somewhere in the future she knew that she would be doing this with April and Kristle mothers and hopes it is sooner than later. When this day comes, she feels that it is going to be a big surprise to the two of them and they will need some adult time together.

12

ḥalloween party

practice

IT WAS DECIDED, everyone including the house felt that the Halloween party for the neighborhood should be at Seth and Sue's home this year. A week before Halloween all four of the group started practicing the tricks that they were going to use at the house party. With the help of the house, they were working up many tricks that looked great with the costumes they were wearing for the party. In reality, it was real magic made to look like store bought or common slide of hand tricks to the average person. One of the items was an eighteen-inch crystal ball that would activate and glow when asked a question. In the middle, a red dot would expand into a 3D twelve-point star which would then rotate in multiple circles to answer the questions. This was April's illusion with her cute young witch's outfit.

Kristle had a floating ball illusion where the ball would float above her hand. She could change it from hand to hand as if there was a string or moving it with a hand held magnetic ring, also the ball would change colors with sound made by the people close to it. She could also levitate cards and coins on a table, just in case if anyone was to look under the table there was a large magnet taped there. She was dressed as a female wizard with a white gown and robe with ice crystals on it.

Seth was dressed as a wizard with a black vested outfit, with a long black cape with a red lining. He had a staff made from plastic, and finished to look very old. On the top, there was a six-inch plastic ball, which would glow a faint yellow color. This would happen when he tapped the base on the floor, then it reacted with a bright white single flash. It would trigger other balls around the room that would flash at different times and with each flash of the staff. He could also move items around in the room such as chairs, lamps, coins, and doors. However, he was not happy with the costume staff that worked the light effects. Therefore, he was going to see if he could build a better one, from some ideas that he found on the internet, he wanted it to look more real with real wood, he had plans kicking around in his head.

Sue will dress as an old scary housemaid, manning the house and would bring people from room to room, to see the three acts before getting them into the party in the barn. However, as she moved the guest around she had stories to tell them of evil and mischief. Many of these stories were from old tales and lore in books that she made fit the part of each room they went to. Each room was decorated to match the costumes worn by the three kids and the stories would build up sensations before entering the room. Seth's room is the den and there is a large wooden chair behind a pedestal with a fake spell book on it. The book's cover was made from old leather from a chair with the pages made from old newspapers. When the cover is opened, a puff of fake smoke would rise from it. The lights around the room were flickering candle flames lights. Kristle's room was the dining room and it was set up to be dark, with only a single chair in the middle and her small table. She would be sitting in the chair and the smoke machine would be putting a heavy fog out with a multi colored light that would change with noise.

April had the living room, where there is a table set up with a large chair for her to sit, also there was a black cloth hung to divide the dining and living room. There were four other smaller chairs at the table in front of hers. A black tablecloth covered the table and only went halfway to the floor so people could look under the table. The house set it up so that it could move and shake the table when a question is asked.

The four worked on all the voices, costumes, and each room. The outside of the house was fixed up with small decoration until the day that would normally be trick or treat. All the big webs and scary trees would be brought out of the barn and set up to make the house look extremely scary, fitting the holiday.

The night of the full moon was coming for the month of October, it was just before Halloween, however it also meant the first trip to the Realm for the group. The four of them were a little nervous about it but they also bordering on being scared. Although they have been receiving training in their sleep, they were still new to this and have never seen the place in real life. Memories of movies and books went into their thoughts but it still had the fear of the unknown that kept them on edge.

The four of them have come together as friends and family and the teenagers had fun doing just about anything together. Sue sees a big change in Seth's outlook on life now and hopes it keeps getting better. When he lost his father, she saw him pull into himself and hold back all his emotions, just as he had also done when the other kids in the last school he was in, started picking on him. He never really recovered from that, then his father's tragedy added to his problems. Even after the loss, the gangs of kids were ruthless in their treatment of Seth. Sue never wants him to know this, but she is happy that they are not living on the base anymore after seeing him miserable from school.

A few days before all the big events, Seth was researching

how to make a lighted staff for his costume. He researched how to set up some electronics to give his staff a fancy light show using a coil, and spark setup. He figured that if he could use the same items that makes a grill lighter work, it would make it work without batteries. Seth had learned that different quartz crystal creates a vibrating frequency that makes electrical charges and fields. With a large crystal and some diodes and capacitors, he could make a light stick that would work when he struck the quartz crystal and allowed it to vibrate.

Over the next couple of days after school, he worked on his new project. He found himself a hollow piece of one and a half-inch wooden pipe used to make a large spring pull down shade that was six feet long. On the top, he fastened a piece of tree fork that could also hold a crystal ball. For the bottom, he made an electronic coil using copper wire wrapped around a small tube. Between each layer, he had a layer of insolated tin foil, that was wired to a circuit, which was wired to the light emitting diodes which light up the crystal ball. He used two quartz crystals he got from a museum that he had visited a long time ago in Washington DC, to strike each other. They would vibrate while hooked to wires going to the coil and electronics, this made him large amounts of power in a very short time. All the electronic parts came from an electronics lab that his parents had bought him years ago, that he played with on rainy days.

He tested the unit by striking the staff's bottom on the floor and then there was a large flash and the smell of plastic burning. Now he had to make some changes because the first test had so much power it burned out the light emitting diodes. He had to install some larger resistors on the next set to make them work. He then put a wire on each side of the crystal ball so that it would make a spark to drain the power from the staff. The next several tests works great with a couple of adjustments to the wires to make a good spark. He wired in the little transmitter that triggered the lights from the costume staff, and when he tested it, the lights flashed just as they did with the old staff. He assembled the unit to look like a wizard's staff with some stain and clear coat, added some leather and lacings and made a handle where he could hold it. It looked like something out of the movies and it was ready to use on Halloween night.

13

The Realm

ALL THE MEETING TREES WERE IN TIME SYNC with each other, so that the meetings in the Realm could be held at the same time every month. The full moon was the prompt for the meeting and a special meeting could be called at any time, but only by the Chancellor if needed.

The day was here and it was time to face the other wizards of the Realm. The four of them met in the afternoon and waited for the time to come to proceed to the meeting hall, when announced by the Realm. When the call came, the voice directed them to the den, all the windows shades were lowered and the door shut and locked. "Seth, you need to open the doorway to the Realm and only you can open it for this group. Think Realm and raise your ring hand, then draw an arch," the voice told him.

Seth cleared his thoughts and thought only about the Realm. He then raised his ring hand and very slowly made an arch with his hand from left to right. As he finished, a doorway appeared with a blue mist filling the frame from floor to the top of the entry. They all readied themselves and Seth led the way through it. As they went through the mist, they came into a small room and they now were dressed in robes. They were black and made of heavy cloth with a colored frill around the neckline and the sleeves end. Seth's were dark blue, Sue has a medium sky blue with red stars, and the girls were light blue, almost a robin egg blue. Seth also had a pendent with a dark blue stone on it with the marking of their tree etched in gold on its face.

The room was only about fifteen by fifteen feet and behind them was the doorway with the mist in it. On the walls, there were paintings of the four of them dressed in robes with wooden benches under the pictures on the two sidewalls. In front of them was another doorway and a meeting hall could be seen with people dressed the same as they were. The doorway however looked as if there was a wall of water filling it but you could see through it. From across the crowd there are other door frames just like theirs. They were gray doors that looked like mist and people just walked out of them. The ceiling was white and the light that lit the room came from it. The floor was wooden and you could see through the door that it went all throughout the meeting room.

The floor of the meeting room had a slight slant to it so the people that sat behind someone could see the head table without any obstruction. The seats were all wood frames with cloth cushions and they were in groups of seven and in seven different colors with one chair of the seven at the head table matching each color. The main room was all wood with a medium brown wood finish color. All the woodwork was old medieval design and looked new with no hint of its age.

The four of them looked at each other and Seth asked if the voice was still with his thoughts. It came back and said yes and any time they were ready they would help each of them. Seth gave the two girls a nod and then looked at his mom. She gave a nod back then he started for the door.

Inside the Realm meeting room, people were talking among each other and the seven people at the head table were having a heated discussion between themselves. Seth was the first one to step out of the gray doorway mist, everything stopped in the hall then all the people were looking at him. Then his mother walked through followed by April then Kristle. People were whispering between each other but the head table stood up and some of them rushed to Seth.

"Who are you and how did you get here," one of them demanded and followed with, "you do not belong here."

Seth stood his ground and said, "I am from the seventh tree, from the land formally known as Markland but is now known as North America."

"That bloodline is dead and there is no one alive that follows that line. Jeb Crocker's family was lost with their deaths. Nothing could have survived when the zeppelin bombed the building and Jeb, Bonny, and her families were all killed," the person wearing a light-yellow stole with ravens on it pronounced.

Seth answer with, "Jeb had a son in England with Lady Hawthorne, and he never knew of him but his son follows the bloodline. His daughter Bonny had a girl, Bonney Lee and Jeb used his blood to save her during one of the raids. They sent her to live with relatives in Scotland. Lady Hawthorne also left England and moved to Scotland to keep her son safe. The rest is logged in paperwork and blood."

After a stare-off and Seth holding his ground, he asked the question, "Why and how did the people in the Realm know or think this was the end of the bloodline? Do you not trust the information passed on in the Realm? An empty seat should be at the table, which is for the tree that I am connected to with my bloodline. When I came through the door, there were seven people at the table and the entire sublet seats were full. Who is not where they should be," he was staring into the eyes of the person with the stole on and not blinking.

"That is perfect, keep doing it," the voice said in his head.

"You are too young and cannot hold office," the wizard said.

"There are no rules that keep me from the position and I do have a proper advisor," Seth informed him. Just as he finished his last words, the stole that was on the wizard disappeared from him and reappeared on Seth. People throughout the hall now were ablaze with words about the switch of the position of Chancellor, which is now Seth. He made his way past the others and walked to the center of the meeting table, which had a red chair and sat in it. The girls sat in the red sublet chairs, which were in the front middle of the rows of seats, after the people that sat there vacated the area. They only filled three of the seven seats there, so four were left open. People were still talking among themselves and Seth picked up the gavel, banged it twice, which means sit, and come to order per the meeting rules.

Just after Seth banged the gavel, a sublet from the group of the wizard's chair color to the left side of Seth, came to the front of the head table. She turned to the sublets and banged her staff on the floor once. She then said, "Come to order, the Chancellor has started the meeting." She then gave a nod of her head to Seth, then returned to her seat and stood waiting for her wizard to sit.

The Wizard who had the stole prior to it appearing on Seth sat to the far-left end seat and still had a bewildered look on his face. His sublets filled the seats that matched the color of his new seat and they looked to him for guidance. The other wizards noticed this and had short remarks and hand gestures between themselves.

The other sublets waited for the head wizard of their groups to sit in a seat color before they sat in their seats. They made their way to the head table and one of the ones that was yelling the loudest was left without a seat. Seth looked at him and did not see a pendant on him and he had on a plain black robe. He and the seven others whom were in the sublet seats quickly walked to a doorway and left the room. Everyone in the room came to order and turn to Seth waiting for his next words.

"The first order of business is the reading of the Realm's

rules," Seth ordered.

A man got up from one of the sublet seats that matched the color seat to the right side of Seth. He then walked to the podium between the head table and sublet seating and he set himself up to read from a large book that was on it. The book was so large that he had to stand on a wooden stool and leaned over the book holding his body with his hand off the lower part of the book. It was very thick with many bookmarkers throughout its pages of many different colors. He read all three hundred and forty-five rules, which had taken almost an hour. When he finished, Seth asked for a motion to accept the rules as read. A voice came from the middle of the seating with a hand raised and the scribe made a note of the name. Seth asked for a seconding, a hand came from behind the girls and again the scribe logged the name.

"All in favor," Seth asked and all the sublet raised their hands as well as the six others at the head table.

"All opposed," Seth asked and the room was quiet.

"Motion passed," Seth said and he banged the gavel once. The hall had a loud applauds and after about two minutes, everyone was back sitting and looking at Seth.

The scribe was catching up with the writing and when he was done, he looked at Seth and gave a nod of the head.

"Now introduce yourself and your family to the group, but be humble while doing it," the voice told him.

My name is, Seth Hawthorne, and I am here with my advisor, Sue Hawthorne my mother and cousins, April Morse and Kristle Blake. Thank you for welcoming us to the meeting. I am looking forward to meeting each and every one of you. Thank you," Seth declared and the hall again rose in applauded and sat at the end.

"Now on to new business and by the rules of the Realm only the head of each group can bring an item to the floor. Let us open the floor" and he banged the gavel once to start it.

One hand at the head table rose and it was the last Chancellor. Seth acknowledged him and motioned him to the podium. Seth noticed that he was a fair tanned skinned person and that most of his group was the same way, he had the walk of arrogance about him when he went to the podium.

The wizard introduced himself as Akmal Mustalph Kiral, from the African continent and he would like to propose a change, to the number of sublets that can be in the hall and vote. There was a lot of grumbling within the sublets and some head shaking from the head table. Seth bang the gavel twice and said let him talk. Kiral stated that they have had the same number of sublet since the beginning and it is time to change. There are more people in the world now and less area that is uninhabited. That the world needs more guidance to help, the countries that are isolated. He finished and walked back to his seat and looked out over the people with the look of leading the charge. Seth asked for anyone else with a comment on this change. A hand came up on the other end of the table and Seth acknowledged the person. She walked to the podium and gave her name as Sonia Pastel from the Land of Snow.

"We have been through this before, the seven-sublet rule, is so a single country cannot put in runaway rules that will change the balance of power. Not only for my area but for a couple of others," she said and she walked back to her seat.

Seth asked if there were any other comments and no one answered. Seth then asked for a motion on the item in front of them. From the sublets came a motion to kill the item and Seth asked for a seconding on the motion and it came. He gave the scribe time to write it all down, he received a nod from the scribe when he was done.

"All in favor of the motion to kill the proposal raise your hand," he said.

After the count he asked, "All opposed to the motion raise your hand," he said.

The scribe saw the tally and there were fifteen hands opposed, that were counted out of forty-five voting sublets. Seth seats were missing four of the seven spots; there are a normal forty-nine.

"The proposal is defeated by a 45 to 15 vote", and he banged the gavel.

"Are there any other items to come forward," he asked, but none came to be voted on. "Then that closes the meeting business, are there any other things to be brought forward for the group," he followed with.

"I motion to close this meeting" came from the room and then a seconding and the scribe nodded to Seth.

"All in favor," Seth asked and every hand came up.

"All opposed" Seth said and no one responded.

"This meeting is closed," and with a bang of the gavel, the first meeting and his new position of Chancellor was done.

Some of the other wizards left the meeting hall and went into one of the seven rooms with the gray doorways of mist. A few stayed and came over to talk to Seth and the girls. Sue stayed by Seth's side as if to protect him.

"When did you become part of the Realm," one of the other wizard's sublets asked.

"We just became one with the tree a few months ago but our ancestor started the bloodline over a hundred years ago," Seth, told them.

"You may have trouble from the group that left. They have been pushing for a vote to change the Realm from the seven to more seats. They say they found a way to increase the number of seats but they would not share the information," the Wizard from the Europe tree said. He is also the person that sat to the right of Seth at the head table

"Where are they from," Seth asked.

"No one knows, and they come through everyone's rooms but never did they get into their own room. Somehow, they convinced the Realm that they were the missing meeting tree, and were always at odds with the Antarctic wizard. Other people try to stop them but when they go into the mist, they are not in that room. This has been a problem for many years and sometimes they are a problem during the meeting," the wizard said.

Then one of the other wizard said, "It was once believed that there were eight trees and maybe even more. That tree was said to have been on the lost continent of Atlantis but that means the Realm as we know it is older than we think."

The wizard from England expresses, "It would explain some of the facts about some of the other trees. The tree for the Antarctica is not on its land mass but there are tree stumps on the land mass of the Antarctic. Our history of the world shows how the land has moved over the years but just where Atlantis is, has always been a mystery. The legend says that Atlantis was an island continent and they had the power of the crystal just as we do. They were doomed and there are many tales of why. However, there is also a legend of how they knew of their doom, and sent out into the world many people with skills and powers. Could the great Merlin have been one of these people, even have been the one who had the power of the crystals?"

"So, some of the stories that are only mentioned in school could be true," Seth said then added, "What if there was an eighth tree that was Atlantis and the tree and family bloodline were wiped out? Could the Realm eliminate his room and seats and only show the seven?"

"That could have been, because we have never seen a loss of the line only a fulfillment of the last line, we do not know what will happen. Then we do not really know how old the great one was because, stories build their own stories, as time and people move on in time. There are many great sites that have been linked to old groups of mythical people, such as the many wooden and Stonehenge's around the world. Even where you come from in the northeast of North America, in Salem New Hampshire is a Mystery Hill, now called American Stonehenge. There are many others in your land, some in the southlands and even one said to be at the bottom of one of the Great Lakes. We have many in Great Britain and there are sites in France, South America, the Middle East, and some yet to be found under ice and in the seas.

There is still much that we do not know and when we search for the knowledge, something stops us from it. We have had many people researching the history stored in the Realm but when we get close to the answers that we seek, something bad happens and people are hurt or disappear. From what we can tell, it is not the Realm itself that does it, it is from the outside." The wizard from Europe informed them.

The voice in Seth's head tells them, "Lets end this meeting and do some research from your room. End this gathering on a good word."

"Well, this sounds like it is going to take some research and study to get some information. We must end this meeting but we look forward to our next meeting here. Thank you for working with me and good day to you and your people," Seth said as the girls made their way to their waiting room. Seth turned and followed with a polite wave of his hand to the other people then proceeded into his room through the mist.

In the waiting room, they all stood there watching as each of the other groups also made the exit into their rooms. When the meeting room was empty, the lights dimmed and the room could only be seen as a chamber of shadows now through the doorway mist.

"I can see that we need to fill the other seats for voting," April said.

"I think we need to find out more about this Realm and be ready for any questions and problems," Seth said.

"Seth, you did great, the class on how to run a meeting you had at your last school help to run this one just fine," Sue, told him.

"He is a born leader and a very mind strong young man," the voice said and followed with, "Come back to the house and we can talk about the next meeting at a later date."

April and Kristle went through together and Seth and his mom went next into the mist. Once on the other side they found themselves in their normal clothes and the doorway of mist faded away. The shades slowly rose on the window and the door opened.

"Everyone sit and rest for a little bit and we will explain what happen," the voice said.

"Ok but let us get something cool and have a drink before we start," Sue said.

"Yes, that would be good," Kristle said and went to help her.

Seth and April sat and just looked around the room until they returned with glasses for everyone. They sat with their drinks and waited for the voice.

"What you saw has been happening for many years now. Someone has been breaking up meetings and trying to change the Realm, as we know it. You took control of the meeting and ran it as it should be run, your knowledge from your school has worked well for you. Your training as you sleep, comes from the knowledge that we have given to us from the history of the Realm," the voice tells them.

"Is there more to the history then what is known," Sue asks.

"That is what we do not know and cannot seem to find out. We believe there is more but we cannot find it in the Realms written history. All that is said and done is kept in the Realms notes and is protected, but timelines seem to start differently than history in the notes. Written history says we started just over one thousand years ago which is when stories of the great one start. However, there are legends long before that and old ruins in our history that have been abandoned," the voice told them.

"This sounds like research on the computer and some road trips coming in our future," Seth said.

They talked about the Realm until the early evening and when the girl's mothers showed up, they talked about the upcoming party. When it got a little late, good nights were said then the girls and their moms went home. Seth and his mom clean the dishes up and turned in for the night, but both sat on the computer and started to do some research and creating notes.

The next day all four were researching history, stories no matter how small, and logged them on to a thumb drive. They now had a common goal, to find information and each night using the computer, they would share information and leads, to each other to follow up on. As each received the others data, they would look over the area on the web and build on what they may have found. Some leads would end because it was found that it was made up and only about five percent of data found was viable. Sue being the teacher she is, made sure that regular schoolwork was done first with the kids. She being a history teacher found this fascinating and enjoyed the research for this type of information. Both Sue and Seth had turned their loss and feelings into the energy of finding something that may or may not exist without realizing it. The girls found this exciting as if it was another treasure hunt.

13

ḣalloweeN NiġḣT

THE TIME HAS COME, it is four pm on Friday October 30th and trick or treat begins. There are several housing units just over the line in Massachusetts, and the kids are walking down the hill to make the houses the last stop. They are coming by the groups of four or more and are lining up to see the show. There are few kids who live in the local area of South Hampton, but they all come to see the show. The town is not having a trick or treats night where kids go house to house this year; however, they are having an event at the town hall that starts later that evening. There are also parties on this Friday night at isolated homes where it is safe for the kids to have some fun.

Here you can hear scary sounds playing on a sound system which adds to the experience for the people touring the house. The house looked like a scene from a movie and the kids came in all types of costumes. Parents that had come with their kids were taking pictures of their little ones to share later. Older youths and teens that came out in groups were having fun both in and out of costumes. People were amazed at the work done on the effects and the tricks that were happening right in front of them.

The neighborhood group of friends had gathered in the barn for a party style cookout and evening of scary fun. The barn was all dressed up and had some colored lights to both add to the mood and to bring out the colors in the costumes. They had games that consisted of apples hanging on strings, floating in water, ring toss over pumpkin stems and many others fun events. It was a fun filled evening with Halloween themes snack foods of many types and on many tables. There was also a person from a local restaurant working at a grill in the back yard, cooking up hotdogs, burgers, and strip steaks with peppers and onions. There was cider, soda, and water of different colors for drinks if you dared try it. It is a fun night for everyone that comes to the house to enjoy the holiday.

After some time, there was a group of four people, which walked up to the front of the driveway. One of the people, a man, started into the driveway and the person was stopped in his tracks as if he walked into a clear glass wall and could not get past it. People that were around the front of the house and barn saw it happen, then started to laugh at the person as he kept walking into an invisible wall. The people thought that they were mimes that were performing. Then one of the people stepped back on the road, put both his hands together at his wrist in front of him and a flash came from them. It hit the surface that stopped the first person and it lit up in light blue, to show a dome all around the farm. People were pointing to it and clapping as if it was part of the show. Just then Seth, Sue, April, and Kristle came out of the front of the house in time to see the light show. The voice told them that someone from another bloodline was trying to come into the house's protective area.

Seth cleared his thoughts, then he thought about a lightning bolt to land at the feet of the intruders, then he tapped his staff on the ground and pushed it forward. With a loud crack, a lightning bolt came from his staff and hit the ground in front of the four people with a flash, then they were gone. People in and near the barn, clapped and whistled because they thought it was part of the show. Sue went to Seth and told him that was fantastic, both the girls followed her saying how wonderful he was. The voice was saying that it was good that everyone thinks it was part of the show. It told them to say that it was all a light show and say that they cannot tell anyone how it was done.

"We will have to tell them that this was a special effect that we set up just for tonight. Once used it cannot be done again. This will make it more believable for them," Sue stated.

"Will they be back," Seth asked.

"I do not believe they will tonight because you showed them that someone here has power," the voice said then followed with, "Now we must get you back to the Realm and claim all the seats that are yours. Someone tried to get in tonight, that means that there is an evil wizard out there, which the Realm and its meeting trees cannot control."

They went to the people in the barn, and they were congratulated for a fantastic show and party. As people walked past them, they would tap on their shoulders and say well done. They had no clue just what happen between the two groups and they wanted to keep it that way.

At the end of the party and after everyone had gone home or to the town halls party, both Seth and Sue went into the secret room. They sat at the podium and started asking questions. Sue asked the first, "Just what happen tonight and will it happen again?"

"There have been times before you came here, that it had happen!" The voice told them.

"How have you fought them in the past?" Seth asked with a look of being concerned.

"The shield as you know it has been in place on the house since the day Jeb put on the ring for the first time. The tree has had it since the first day the great one put the mark on the very first tree for this land. The meeting tree has had many leaders of different people from vast distances, try to hold meetings around it and they even tried to destroy the tree. However, it never found someone with pure intentions and kept itself safe. Then came Jeb, now protection was needed for him and the house once he visited the tree and shared his bloodline.

It is said that the great one had knowledge of the power of crystals. He came from a long line of people that learned to use them for both good and bad things. However, history has many tales and legends that have dates that change with versions of story. The only people that know the real meaning are long gone and time has removed much of the writing and pictures from the stones," the voice informed them.

"We have covered some of this before, but where are the crystals he used and how does it apply to us," Sue asked.

"First of all, your rings are crystals that are the conduit of your powers from us. The tree is connected to the earth where it gets power by crystals in the soil. It is said that the great one has his domain in a crystal realm and can receive all that is gathered by the trees and the rings. Many humans have searched for his realm but have never found it. There are many stories and legends about this place but we do not know where it is or how to get there. It would be a wonderful place if ever found," the voice informed them.

"Can we look for and find this place," Seth asked.

"Anyone can look for anything they desire in their lifetime. This is freewill and we cannot interfere with that as a rule. You can travel and search for anything on this planet, but if it is in the Realm only a wizard can search that area. We only know, what the Realm lets us," the voice replies.

"This may seem like a bad question but is there more to the Realm than you can tell us?" Sue asked with a serious tone to her voice.

"We will tell you all that we know because you are part of us and we are part of you," the voice replied.

"How much do you know of the other meeting trees," Seth asked.

"Only what they let the Realm know. Some are very open to everything they do; they are as you know them England, Australia, and Antarctica. The ones in South America and Asia let some information go to the Realm, however, Africa has been very guarded and confusing, as are some of the sublets and even the wizard has confusing thoughts and information," the voice said.

"Sounds like being drunk or high on drugs," Sue said.

"We will share that with the Realm if you want," the voice asked.

"Only to the ones that give all their information, let's see what happens at the next meeting. Also, let's not mention it again until after the meeting, let them also know that," Seth said.

"It is done," said the voice.

"I think we need to bring Aprils and Kristle's mother into our group now and give them protection just like the girls," Sue said.

"Seth, it is your call as the wizard of this meeting tree," the voice said.

"If I understand this, we can bring in their mothers but their father will be unprotected," Seth asked.

"You are correct, they do not share the bloodline, however let us see if there is a way to cast a spell on them to protect an innocent," the voice replied.

"I think we need to ask the girls if it is ok," Sue added.

"Ok that is for another day, I am tired, it is after midnight, and I am headed for bed," Seth said and they left the den then closed the house.

This night outside the house two birds, an owl and raven, sit in the tree on guard. At each of the girl's homes, a raven also is on guard just watching and listening, with this nights attack, the four are watching for the smallest amount of trouble.

14

The Dream

SETH CRAWLED INTO BED AFTER GETTING CLEANED UP, however he found it hard to get the event of the night out of his head and let his mind relax. He tried thinking about different thing, like what was happening in school or people he knew. It all came down to the fact that he could not relax because of the excitement earlier.

He went down to the kitchen and got a drink of water with a couple pieces of bread. He thought that this would help with his stomach acid if he had any, and let him start to relax. He returned to his room and laid back down hoping to have a visit from the sandman. After a short time, he decided to put on his headphones and listen to music that he had recorded on his phone. It was not long before he found himself drifting off, he removed the headphones, and then laid on his side and he was asleep.

Seth was awakened by a noise from the kitchen, he thought that maybe his mother had the same problem. He got up and made his way down the stairs to the kitchen, where he found that no one was there. He walked to the bottom of the stairway when he noticed a light coming from the den, it was not a house light, it was a radiant light from everywhere. He carefully made his way through the doorway and there were two people standing there, but he could not make out their faces, he could only see their dark figures.

One of them stepped forward, then Seth saw that this gentleman was dressed in clothing from the late eighteen or early nineteen hundreds. When he could see his face, he saw that it was Jeb, the man in the paintings. Seth gasped and went to call for his mother, but Jeb motioned for him to be silent with a movement of his hand to his mouth. Seth felt that he had to do as he asked.

He lowered his hand and he spoke, "Please do not be afraid. You know who I am because I can see it in your eyes. I am here to thank you for carrying on our family's heritage. I did not understand what was given to me and I made many mistakes with it but you can use it to make life better for people. There is so much that you need to learn but be aware that not all is as it seems. People are not always who they say they are and will make it hard for you. Yes, you are young but you have more knowledge than many people in the world and your mother and father have taught you well."

"I have seen many movies, shows and read many books about wizards and magic but I always thought it was a story. This all is so real and not a dream, and I ask myself if I can do it almost every day," Seth replied.

Then from the other dark figure he heard, "Yes you can do it and I have faith in you and your mother."

Seth recognized the voice instantly of that of his father and he called out in a very sad tone, "Dad?"

The figure stepped forward and he could see that he was dressed in his combat uniform, as he spoke. "You are doing better than I could have ever hoped. I did not know the complete secret of our family but if you remember, we use to get a special feeling when we saw any of the movies about magic. We would talk about how we felt, and that we could do what they did and we even played like that when you were very young. Remember those days because it will help you do this and make it easy for you."

Seth was in tears while slowly easing his way toward his father until he was able to hug him. As he reached around him, he felt that he was real and he squeezed him. He felt his father put his arms around him and give him a squeeze. "Dad I miss you so much, why did you leave mom and me," Seth asked.

"That is not your mothers or your fault and never think it is. Everyone has a set time on this earth and you must make the best of it and live your life. You have been born into a life that you can do what you loved so much with all the movies and books that you read. Use all of that to help you and your mother live this life. I will always be with the both of you," his father said.

Seth replied, "Dad don't leave me, stay with us here." Just as he finished those words, the bright lamp lights came on in the room.

"Seth honey are you all right," he heard from his mother behind him in the doorway as he regained his sight.

"Mom, he was here, dad was here, and I was holding him. Where did he go, he was standing right here," Seth was saying as he franticly moved around the room looking for him.

"Son, it is alright," she put her arms around him and held him tight, telling him that it is ok now, she was there.

Seth started crying saying he was here, repeatedly, she continually held him tight as he finally put his arms around her and just cried. After several minutes, she asked if he was ok and when she was sure that he could stand on his own, she dropped her arms. Seth then dropped his arms, said that he was sorry and stated that it must have been a dream. Sue eased him into a chair and sat beside him.

"Seth please do not get excited again but look in your right hand," Sue told him.

Seth held up his right hand and he was holding a small piece of cloth about four by four inches in size. It was the same as the uniform on his father's image. He gasped and held it to his face and with tears filling his eyes said, "He was here"!

"Yes, he was," and Sue pulled the same type of cloth from under her nightshirt, that hung on a piece of string around her neck. "He came to me a few days ago and I thought I was dreaming, but when he left me I had this in my hand. The house cannot explain it and just as you did, I held him. He was real and he could not explain how he came back, just that he had a message for us to enjoy our life. We need to remember him as he was, when he was home with us, and never forget that." She put her hand under his chin and lifted his head so that she could look into his eyes, then she said. "He will always be with us no matter where we are," Then she hugged him and held him for several minutes.

The two of them got up from the chairs and left the room, shutting off the light. Seth looked back into the room but there was no one there so he turned and went up to his room. He said goodnight to his mother, shut the door, and laid back in his bed. He thought about what just happen, and he started to tear up, and that was the last thing that went through his head as he fell asleep.

Sue stood looking at Seth's door after he went in, she knew that he was going to have a rough few days coming. She walked into her room and laid on the bed clutching the piece of cloth that hung from her neck. She was thinking how she feared that this would also happen to Seth, and had wondered what would happen to him. She thought of many things that they could do together to take his mind off what happen, however she knew that he had to deal with it in his own way. Whatever would happen, she would be there for him.

The day after Seth saw Jeb and his father, he just hung around the house and the yard picking up after the party and packing away decorations. April and Kristle along with their mothers came by and helped in the cleanup. The girls asked Sue if there was a problem with Seth and she told them that he had some things to work out about his father. She asked them not to ask him anything until he brings it up. They agreed and knew somehow that this was the best for him, just to let him be.

After a couple of days, Seth walked down to the bridge, sat on the riverbank, and tossed small stones into the water. Both the girls met him there and sat with him, then after a half hour, he started to talk about what happened to him.

"I had something happen to me the other night and you are going to laugh at me," Seth said.

"We are friends and family and if you need to talk just ask," April said.

"My father and Jeb visited me the other night and I held my father," he told them.

"What," Kristle said.

"They came to the house and stood in the den after I came down to get something from the kitchen. Jeb started talking and then my dad joined him. I walked up to him and held him and he held me. My mom came into the room after a very short time, turned on the light and he was gone," he told them.

"You must have been walking in your sleep and dreaming," April said.

"I was left with this piece of his uniform, which looks like it was torn off the one he was wearing at the time," he said as he showed the girls.

"How did that happen," Kristle asked him.

"I don't know but the same thing happened to my mom and she has one just like it. He told both of us to live our lives and be happy. I miss him so much," he finished with and both the girls sat close to him. With one on each side of him, they both put an arm around him and held him as they sat.

"I believe you," April said, then she added, "Think about it, we thought this house was haunted but found that it is so much more, so why could that not have happened."

"Yes, it seems that we need to believe that what we once

thought of as just fantasies and dreams could now be real," Kristle exclaimed.

"Sue could feel just what the three of them were thinking and she knew that Seth was in the hands of safe friends and they could help him. "Ok house please disconnect me from the three of them so they can have privacy," she asked.

"Yes, we will until you ask us to do it again," the voice said.

"Can you send their animal friends to watch over them for me?" She asked.

"It is done" the voice said.

After ten minutes, all three of the ravens showed up in the trees above the three youths and kept a close look out of the area. She asked this to be done because of what happen the days before with the strange people showing up. She knew that with all that has happened; their lives were now involved with a world that up until a few months ago was a fantasy to them. She finds it fascinating and knows that the three kids do also, but she knows there is danger all around them now.

15

Αpril aΝδ Κristle's

μothers joiΝ

τhe house

SUE HAD THE GIRLS OVER FOR DINNER ONE NIGHT and she had a teen's favorite meal, pizza. There was a reason for this meeting, after dinner the girl's mothers were coming over for a snack. They started eating after the pizza was delivered from a local shop and sat around the table talking with the girls.

"April, Kristle, we have a question for you and only you can decide this," Sue tells the girls.

"Do you want your mothers to join us with the Realm and the things we can do?" Sue asked them point blank.

"What about our fathers," Kristle asked.

"Their bloodline is not part of the meeting tree and they cannot do what you do," the voice tells them.

"That means that they could be hurt if someone comes for them from the Realm, right," April remarked.

There is a way to stop that from happening, something that we found out from the Realm's history," the voice said.

"How is that possible, you said that only the bloodlines can be protected," Seth asked.

"Seth, you can put a spell of protection on them so that they will not be harmed. They will be in a bubble and will need to have a reason to explain it away. The question is can they do that and can they deal with their slow aging wife and kids," the voice informed them.

"Let's have our mother decide," April said.

"I think that is best," Kristle followed with.

"Ok, when they show up, let us break it to them by showing them some magic tricks. Then tell them that they can do the same if they put on these rings. When they do, let the house talk to them just like it did with us," Sue said.

Seth gave the girls a ring that looked like theirs before he hid them. They put them on their finger and agreed to give them to their mothers as part of the plan.

They all agreed and went on eating pizza and joking around. Sue made some snack plates for the mothers and some adult drinks. After an hour, they came to the door and the house opens the door for them. They walked in laughing and asked how they did that and both the girls said at the same time, "Magic." The mothers laughed at that answer and sat at the table with their girls.

"Want to see a magic trick mom," Kristle asked.

"Sure, go head, do your best," her mom said.

April had a deck of cards and shuffled it, and she passed it on to Seth and he did the same. Seth passed it on to Kristle and then told each mother to do the same. They did as he asked then April told both the mothers to remove nine cards each and put them in three different piles of three each in front of them face down. The mothers did as he asked, joking as they did it. April then told them to look at the piles without show-ing each other or them and arrange them in any order they want them in. The mothers did as they were asked and made fun of it by saying that this will mess them up. When they finished they sat there waiting for the next thing to happen.

"Mom don't freak out until we show you how it is done," April told her mom.

"You also mom," Kristle told her mom.

"How about you Sue," April's mother asked.

"Oh, I know how it is done," Sue tells her.

"We are going to tell you what each card is before you pick it up and show everyone," Aprils said.

April told them to each select a pile for one of the three of them. After they finished that, Kristle started with her mom, "The top card is a seven of diamonds." Her mother flipped it and there the card was, "The second is a two of clubs and the third is a Jack of hearts." When the cards were flipped, they showed she was correct.

April read off her pile with her mother and they were all correct. Then Seth called his pile with Kristle's mother and then without stopping calls out Aprils mothers pile for him. Both the mothers look at each other in amazement. April then called her pile with Kristle's mother and Kristle called the last cards with April's mother. Both the mothers looked at Sue, she told them it is very easy and calls the top card of the undealt cards.

"Ok, you need to tell us how it is done," Aprils mother tells them. Seth asked them both are you sure you want to know and they both answered with a yes.

"We have two rings that will help you do this and you need to put them on and keep them on," Kristle told them and the girls handed them the rings. Both the mothers looked the ring over then eventually put them on and were amazed that the rings fit.

Just as before, the shades lowered in the living room where they were and the front door locked. April said, "Please mom, do not be afraid."

"Welcome Janet and June," the female voice said. "Please do not be afraid and do not try to remove your ring, it cannot come off until you make a decision. This is not an evil thing and you can decide whether you want to learn more or never find out what this is. Talk with your daughters, they will let you know that we tell the truth," the voice informs them.

Both the mothers had the same look of fear and surprise that everyone has had when they first hear the voice. Both girls tell them that this is harmless and if they decide that they want nothing to do with it, they will never know it happen. They can return to their regular life without any problems related to this. The mothers both asked if they were part of it and both girls said yes for several months now.

Both the mothers looked at each other and then at Sue. She told them that she also is part of this and it is a family thing. They asked her if it was a trap and Sue said that the voice tells the truth and it is well worth hearing about it, and if they want, they can quit at any time.

"So, I can quit at any time," Kristle's mother asked.

"And we are not going to be harmed," Aprils mom asked.

"You are both correct," the voice told them.

"Let's go into the den, sit, and talk about this," Sue said as she led them in and the door shut behind them by itself.

"You both are part of what we call a bloodline that was started by Jeb of your family's history. The girls, Seth, and his mother are part of the house and meeting tree for this land. They also can quit at any time but have chosen to remain. Seth is the most direct of the bloodline and he is the head of this group, and his mother is his advisor and she is the teacher for the youth here. Both the girls are sublets in the bloodline just as you can be. Seth is a wizard with powers from his ring and bloodline that are part of the house, the meeting tree, and the Realm. Both April and Kristle have powers that are granted to them by Seth and is monitored by Sue. None of the power can be used for vast personal gain or evil. If you choose to stay with the group, you will learn while you sleep and you will not feel any different. However, while you keep the ring on it will protect you, slow your aging, and keep you healthy. You must decide now if you want to stay," the voice tells them.

Both of them had wide eyes and the look of mass surprise. They tried to speak but they were at a loss of words. Sue then added, "Do you remember the stories that you told me about the house being haunted? Well you were not far from the real reason the house did what it did. It was waiting for someone from the original family to return and continue to protect and educate the people of the area. I am part of the bloodline because of Seth being in my womb and his father being part of the old family's bloodline. It is like a dream of being in a movie but only this is real. It is up to you but I would welcome some adult company along with the kids."

"Well I guess I'm in if you are June," Janet said.

"Well it sounds different and if we can leave at any time, then I am in," June answered.

"Please stay sitting and it will be over in a short time," the voice said, just as Janet was going to ask "what." They both went limp and then in a short time, started waking up.

"What just happen," June asked.

"You just were made part of the group and you will start learning while sleeping at home, your daughters do this same thing every night. Now we will have Seth hide your rings and make it so that they do not fall off. It will not hurt at all," the voice said.

"Ok, here we go," Seth said as he looks at June's ring and says, "Cuddio neilltuo o'r golwg," he then looked Janet's ring and said the same. He waved his hand and both rings faded from sight.

"What did you just say," June asked.

"Hide ring from sight, in Welch," Seth said.

Then the two girls started talking in that language then Seth joined them. Janet stopped them and asked how they learned the language. They told her that they knew many tongues as they call it and they will learn them as they sleep.

Seth then pointed at the wall and opened his secret room. The mothers had a look of amazement and followed everyone else into it. Now on the wall were pictures of the mothers with their daughters. They walked to the pedestal and table and the voice told them the history of the house and family. Any questions that either of the mothers had were answered until they understood fully on the subject. The night ended around nine and the group headed home after everyone said good night and hugs were given all around.

Seth and his mom sat in the den and talked to the voice. They went over the amount of training and power that each mother would have. It was also decided that a block would be put in place so that none of the sublets could hurt each other in any way with their powers. In addition, they would be brought up to date with the girls before the girls learn much more. They then turned in for the night.

The next day they all were meeting at the house, after Janet, and June's husbands headed to the sports club for a meeting. The husbands do this every month as their night out with their friends. Sue felt that this would be a good time to cover what they learn to see if they could handle a faster training. She let the kids gather in the den and the three ladies talked in the living room. Sue was amazed that they had learned so much and they did not feel tired. However, they had many questions and the voice of the house answered them as they asked them, no matter how small or funny the question seemed.

The house then asks Janet about a memory that she had, about giving blood to a local hospital. She told them that there was a shortage of her blood type and she could only give that one time. She had a hard time giving blood because of her low blood pressure and that she was told never to do it again.

The voice then stated that there is someone out there with

the bloodline because it was transferred to them, and they need to follow the trail of paperwork if there is any. However, Janet could help even more then they knew, because she found out who got her blood. She was thanked by the parents of the two girls that needed her blood, after special permission was given by the hospital. They send a holiday card to her every year since it happened. The girls are, Elizabeth Miller and Sarah Simpson, both live in Newburyport Ma.

After some discussion, it was decided that Janet would send an invite to meet them and see just who they are and learn more about them. They could come to the house and be checked by it to see if they had any evil, to also see if they would be able to be part of the group.

With the group now getting larger, Janet and June were told about the Realm meetings that day. Also about the need for the two more people to make up the seven sublets for voting. Over the next couple of weeks, training and meetings were the agendas of the two new moms to the group; however, this brought everyone closer together as a family.

Seth with the help of the house, found the spell to help protect the girl's fathers. It was like a bubble spell, you could touch them as if nothing was there. However, if something was going to harm them it was like an outer layer of steel skin. They still get knocked around but nothing could penetrate the layer, only medicines, food, and doctors. The girls and their moms could also lower the shield for touch. It was put in place one night when everyone was there for a dinner. As the two fathers were sitting in the dining room, Seth put the spell on them from the room connected to it. The voice made sure that it was worded correctly, and helped Seth put it in place. Both the fathers had no idea of what had happen and it was planned that both their wife and daughter would test the spell with small accidents. They would then convince them that they were just lucky lately; this way it looked like bad things were near misses from then on without them knowing that there was a spell.

With the two new mothers in the group and the protection spells given to the dads, everyday events and school was the same for the two girls but for Seth, he was still learning how to become part of the New England life style. He did not miss the schools back on base and the gangs, but the large number of students back then made it so he did not stand out. Here he is still the new kid in the school with the southern drawl, and very polite manners. Some kids wanted him in projects for school and some would shy away from having anything to do with him. Sometimes kids changed between the two sides but Seth really felt that this was typical and had no problem with anyone changing their affiliation. He played along with however people were and with his new powers, he could read them long before they would ask. Being a polite person, he just let people be people.

16

a find on the Web

SUE, SETH, AND THE TWO GIRLS were still spending time on the computers, looking for any information and leads leading to the Realm. A few times, there was some reference to events and old conversations found, strangely some things were removed after any of the four looked at it. It was as if someone was watching their every move on the internet, nevertheless, each one of them was setup to look for different things and log the information.

Sue used her history background to find anything on past cultures with reference to a Realm of magic. She found that everything seemed to come back to a lost civilization from the Mediterranean Sea or the Atlantic Ocean. Some leads led to old stories, about a story that was passed down many times. Some led to old books written for entertainment or that had been rewritten to meet a religious creed.

Then one day she found an old book that was written in a very old form of Greek dialect. It told a story of an island that blew-up in a day and all its people were killed that stayed on the island. Those that tried to escape by the sea had lost their life by a hot cloud from the volcano or a giant wave from when it disappeared. It mentioned that for a long time before the disaster they sent teaches out to far off lands to work with other civilizations. They would come home with new inventions, information, and new foods that could be grown in their volcanic soil. Some of these lands were years of traveling away, and many could only be reached by sea travel.

The culture had advance knowledge of heating by using vents from the earth. They could move water using these vents to heat inventions to lift it so that it would flow downhill. They had mineral enriched soil to grow vast crops in their warm environment and use it for trade.

They also had crystals that would make power and a special group of people that worked with that. She also found a reference to a group of people that polished these crystals and used light to destroy, not to create. They used them in a way that went against the leadership of the island and there was a war. Many lives were lost and when the island was again under control of the leader, these people were forced to leave. They also found no friends or lands to welcome them anywhere within vast travel distance of the island. It was also known that while they were searching for a new home, they looked for a place where they could continue the work using crystals.

Sue found this information but it stopped as fast as it was found. By all accounts, the crystal technology that we all use today did not start in the 19th century, by the words in this book it was thousands of years before the computer age.

One night when the girls, Seth and Sue were together, they talked about a show on TV. It was about theories that also hinted that Egypt, Mayans, Aztecs, and many more have carvings, objects, and history of advance beings. They talked about how some of these shows were based on entertainment but as they said, so was magic and here they are deep in a new life with that. The group did agree that this sounds like the path that needed to be followed and decided that Sue would continue this.

With all the information Sue found, much of it quoted that Plato was quite explicit in his period and location for Atlantis, he said it was around, "9,400 B.C. and in the Atlantic". In addition, to travel there you had to travel through the Pillars of Hercules, which has been known for many centuries as the Straits of Gibraltar, which is the entrance to the Mediterranean Sea from the Atlantic Ocean. Again, this is known detail, with little hints that many of the cultures along the shores out to the Straits have been started by Hercules and many other figures from history.

The last reference of the book was that people were sent out to all corners of the known world to teach what had happen to them, to be able to survive their near extinction. They would use tricks from the crystals to win over the people respect so that they could tell the story. The book was written as if it was to be continued but it ended. The images that she was reading, were very old pictures of the writings that was really a scroll parchment. Someone just after the camera was invented took glass plate images of the scroll and put it into a college library. The library put it into a research book form, then on microfiche when it came out, then it was put into digital form for the computer age. However, if you want to see the original images you needed to read it in old Greek dialects to see the first hands view of the story. Sue however sat back and thought about a large library that had scrolls from that time that could have held this information. This library, is the great library of Alexandria Egypt, which was destroyed by attacks from foreign lands and the earth itself, by earthquakes and floods. She thought about the knowledge that was there and how wonderful it would be to be able to read from it, to learn what time has forgotten.

She saved all the stories to a remote drive and she made a printed copy of it on her home printer. To many times, things that they find and did not save would disappear off the web, so they made new plans to copy everything in the safety of the house. She felt that this story talked about what the base of the meeting tree was all about. However, it did not cover that the crystals where a source of information. This was something to ponder over with the rest of the group.

Seth had put a block on all information learned by anyone in his bloodline, from going into the Realms writings. The house, voice, and tree are forbidden from giving up any information from the group to anyone outside this group. This was the best way to figure out just what is happening in the Realm he felt. If the troublemakers, knew what they were up to they would try to stop them and they had no idea what they would do to do that. They even set it up so that if you are doing research on the web you also have a game going at the same time on the computer. Trying to show that you are casual about this may keep anyone that was snooping on you from seeing just what you are doing, like acting like a kid.

Seth was looking over documentaries and stories of vast crystal lands, areas, and caves. He has found many mines and a reference to a vast crystal cave in Mexico that was recently drained of water and researched. There are many areas where there are crystals but nowhere does it talk about finding a livable area.

He did however find that there is a tale about Merlin and his cave realm where he would disappear to at times. He did this to recover after his power was drained from use for the kings that he advised during his lifetime. It told of how he went to a stone structure, said a few words, and tapped his staff for entry and he would just disappear. There was also a reference where he approached a great tree, made a motion with his hand and a doorway opened for him. This sounded just like the way Seth himself makes his doorway for his room and the Realm. He found this very interesting and he saved all material to a remote drive and printer.

He made notes and followed up on the creating of doorways. He found that there are many tails and stories of wizards, Leprechauns, fairies, and even little girls finding doorway or holes. He notices however, that most stories mentioned accessing it by drawing, air drawing, or tapping to gain access to a door. He decides to follow this path, looking into everything that gives reference to the subject. One of the biggest areas that he finds leads in, are movies and shows about wizards. He knows that someone got the idea from somewhere but how accurate the information was could never be relied on. Just logging it with the information to be checked later is all he could do.

April is looking into anything that is mentioned about how to make mind control possible. She has found an unlimited supply of sites on the web that give reasons for it. She then added the word magic and the list gets smaller, however, she found that there are computer games and videos involved. She worked with Kristle on this the next day and they came across a common practice used by many civilizations in the past and even now. The common word in many of its different names or references is 'preparations.'

They find in their research that both drugs and alcohol has been used, even in some of the video games that kids play. Depending on the games realms, there is a way to keep a mind control or mind reading person from hurting or using you. Simply, take a drug or get drunk to inhibit the person or thing from controlling you. In the game, you do not suffer any after effect or illness but it works, that is, on the game.

April and Kristle look further into it but it seemed to them, that this is the easiest and simplest way to achieve what they are looking for. They asked each other several times, if it could be that simple, by just using different circumstances and the answer always seemed to be yes.

"There is only one way to try this," April said.

"How can we do that without hurting ourselves," Kristle asked.

"The adults are going to have to test it, I mean, that they need to see if alcohol can work and if it does then we have the answer. That is, that they use drugs to keep the Realm and meeting trees from keeping track of them," April told Kristle. They looked for other ways and found silly mind control from space aliens to creatures from some made up land, but the use of chemicals or alcohol was mention to have happen all through known history.

The girls brought their findings to the next meeting with Seth, and all three of the moms. The house was not sure how a substance could keep it from seeing one's thoughts but felt, that it was worth trying. That evening the mothers sat with some glasses of wine along with the two girl's fathers. The kids stayed in the den and played a game on the computer using the same thing to see if it showed the same outcome.

As the evening went on, the kids had their outcome, that some drugs changed the outcome of the games. This of course is just the way whoever wrote the software made it work. However, with the three mothers, the house found it harder to read their thoughts and at one point, they could not interact with them at all. This is where the kids then talked to their moms to find out just how much the wine had affected them. They had them write something and repeat things that they heard, then to walk a straight line. The girl's fathers thought it was a game, so to them there was no sign that it was a test.

The kids relayed the information to the house and Seth reminded it, that this was not for the Realms information. The house found the information interesting and found it hard to see that the wine could do that. This part of the test was done and now it was time for the second part. The kids then whispered into their mother's ear that they were done. With that said, the ladies stopped the wine and now waited to see when the effects ware off. Sue wrote down on the pad of paper she had, just how she felt and how much wine she had to drink. Seth was also doing the same from his prospective and he was keeping a close log of the time line for the event.

Sue and Seth had setup one test that was not seen by anyone around the room. She was using her power through the ring to write things on her note pad in her room. They wanted to see if they could use the power of the ring, which is the power of the crystals. To their amazement, they could still do things using the rings without the house knowing it.

The end of the evening came and the house still could not read any of the ladies even though they seemed very aware and normal as they walked home. Seth was sitting at the kitchen table with his mom and they talked about the test. She told him that she has had only two glasses of wine and did not really feel inebriated at all. However, after she finished half of her second glass the voice of the house got softer until it was gone in just a short time.

She tried to talk to the house but she could not hear or feel it. The house also tried to talk to her and Seth at the same time but only Seth could hear the house's voice. They stayed up for many hours and tried the interaction, but it was the same each time they tried. They finally turned in for the night and Seth made notes on his pad of the time. As he laid in bed, he thought about how he and the girls worked as a team to solve this problem. He thought about how nice it was to have such great friends and people he trusted.

The next morning Sue woke and said good morning to the house, and house returned the greeting. "When could you start to hear my thoughts," Sue asked.

"Only just now, it seems that you have found how the

people get around the bloodline connection to the tree," the voice said.

"Does Seth know this," Sue asked.

"Yes, he does and he has been up for hours working on his computer. He said there must be something out there about the Realm and its location. He wants to find it," the voice tells her.

Sue got dressed and went to his room but he was not there. She went down to the den and saw him there on the computer, typing. "What are you doing up so early," she asked him.

"Well if there is truth in how a drug works on people in the Realm, I thought maybe there are hints to where the Realm is in some of the games. I am setting up a new account with fake names to see if I can find anything. The computer will log anything it finds and it will play on as if nothing happened. It is so simple and someone else wrote the program that is doing this, so it is not me looking," he tells her.

"That is, all well and good, but I want you to have some fun away from all this stuff. Let's take the day off and go shopping," she tells him.

"Mom, last night April and I made plans to watch a movie at her house today. Can I do that instead of going with you," he asked her.

Sue was a little surprised by this because he never wanted to go with other kids before this. She instantly said yes to him. This was what she wanted for him for many years. While they were on base he spent many years just staying home not wanting to leave the house. This to her was a great sign that he was happy again.

Seth's computer was now playing all the games that he was online with, Sue thought about how young he is and wonders how does he know how to do this. On the other hand, when she was at his age, computers were a work item mainly and not commonly used by youth, as they are now. Back on the computer she could see any mention of Merlin or cave and/or power would be logged so he could check it later. As he and Sue watched the printout on the screen, it seemed that there was a pattern but time will tell.

16

Janet and June meet their Animal friends

SUE HAD THE GIRL'S MOTHERS over for a friendly gathering, for a coffee and Danish on a Sunday afternoon at the house. They sat on the porch, admired the warm November day while spending time talking about their kids. Along with the stories of their kids, they swapped stories about their lives growing up and added some comments about their husbands. It was a good gathering for just the three of them with none of the kids around. Without warning, Snowy, Sue's owl lands on a railing and begins making a series of sounds. To the ladies it seemed like a song out of chirps, while she was looking at the three of them in an owl bright eyed look. Then out of nowhere came two different types of owls, landing on the railing with one on each side of Snowy.

"This is different, I have never been so close to owls before," June exclaimed

"Looks like the two of you have a couple of new friends, if you want them," Sue said to Janet and June.

"Oh, they are so cute," Janet exclaimed.

"Will they bite and who is who?" June asked as the birds made their way to the table between the two ladies.

"They will come to you then you will need to accept them,

if you want them to be your animal companion. If you do not want them they will leave and someone else will come," Sue told them.

"Will they hurt us," Janet asked.

"No, they will be your eyes and connection to other animals," Sue tells her.

Just then, both the birds jumped on the lady's shoulder that they were watching, without even a prick of their talons, they began to preen their hair by their ear. The owl on Junes shoulder was an eastern Screech owl which was about a foot in height, with many colored feathers of gray, tan, black and white. The one on Janet's shoulder was a Barred owl, which was about a foot and a half tall, tan, and white in color. They made a very faint chirping and something that sounded like soft giggles. Without a human word being spoke to them during that time, both the ladies said, "Yes, thank you."

June then turned to Sue and Janet did the same a split second after her. "I understood what she said to me, she asked if I liked this," June said.

"I cannot believe this, she asked the same thing to me," Janet exclaimed.

"They will be around for you when you need them and they will watch to be sure things are safe for you. Both the girls have small ravens and Seth has an alpha male raven. It seems that this is part of who we are now. Each of the birds will follow the person who they are attached to, and watch everything that goes on around where you are located. You can also ask them to be your eyes and ears to see and hear things that you may not be able to. They also can be a good one to keep around if you are by yourself, if nothing else but to have someone to talk with," Sue told the ladies.

"What about when there is bad weather, do they need to come into the house," Janet asked.

Just as she said that, her owl let out a series of chirps and

Janet looked at her and said "OK"

"See they are all set and will let you know if they need something," Sue replied.

"Could you hear what she said," Janet asked Sue.

"I understood her," June said.

"Our animal friends will let people around either understand them or not, depending on what they have to say or what they want heard. However, they are loyal mainly to the person they team up with first and their group second," Sue told them.

The ladies talked to their new friends and Snowy joined Sue by sitting on her shoulder and gently pruning her hair. They talked as a group and got to know the owls, then at one point the moms were asked if they wanted them as friends. Both ladies without hesitation said yes, and at that point were told to pick a name for their new partners. For almost an hour, the group tossed around names, then they were decided. The owl with Janet was to be called Hoot because of his call sound. He let June know that he was happy with her choice with a loud call that sounded like he said in human language, "Who will cook for you"

June decided on the name Bright Eyes because of his large yellowish colored eyes. "He may be smaller than Snowy and Hoot but his eyes make him stand out with the three of them sitting side by side," she said. Just as she finished making her statement, Bright Eyes made a sound that sounded like a gray tree frog but much louder and longer.

The group finished their gathering; as it was getting to the time when Janet and Junes husbands would be showing up at the house, coming from the sports club. All three of the owls flew off to find a good tree to have a vantage point, to watch their new partner and do some pruning on their feathers. Then June out of the blue asked, "Why owl's and ravens?"

The voice from the house answered her, "These creatures

choose you at random so we had nothing to do with who will come to you. The tree lets the animals know that there are two humans, that need animal partners and when they feel that they like you after watching you, they come to you. We find it easier to do it here at the house so you and they are safe, also we can provide protection at this delicate moment. See the animals are not protected until they become part of you; we then protect them once you say yes. We do not need their bloodline to do that because they are already part of the meeting tree, it is just a natural part of it."

"That's great but again why birds," June expressed.

"Birds do one thing that others cannot, fly. Each bird has a couple of things that others including you cannot do, sit high in trees, see from the air, move without paths, and see in low light. Owls are smart and watch with great tolerances to stay where needed. Ravens are also smart and able to fly; however, they have a cunning way about them that acts as teacher, watcher, gatherer, and aggressor if needed. What better partner is there for the youth in a world where they will be challenged? We do know from the Realm that not all the wizards as you call them have partners in the animal world. This is by choice but it does not include why they chose this, it may have something to do with what you and your children have discovered," the voice informs them.

The two girls and Seth showed up at the house after a day of walking around down town Amesbury. It was not a long walk just about a mile and a half each way but it was up and down the hill on White Hall Rd. They walked a short cut through a couple of side streets, which brought them to the center of the store front area. They had stopped in a few stores that were open on this Sunday, and made it to a pizza shop, which has been a stop for many kids through the decades that it has been in business. Because they went to the school, in South Hampton, they did not know any of the other kids there but they managed to talk to a few. These kids went to one of several town schools which had different age groups in them, some were public schools, with a few small private ones in the area. However, kids being kids, they talked about age related things. The one thing that did stop some kids in their tracks was when Seth spoke and the southern drawl came up. The topics then switched to him and they wanted to know as much as they could find out about him.

When it was time to move on, they all said their goodbyes and the three of them went on to their next stop. However, from a high point there were six eyes watching them and their every move. To the average person the ravens look like one of the local crows that are always around the town, however to the trained eye, you could see the larger feathers around the neck area that made it look like a bad hair day. Their tail feathers had a triangle appearance instead of the rounded fan look, or the wing tip flight feathers, that look like fingers were much larger than that of a common crow. They moved around as the kids moved, just watching and ready to help if needed.

Sue also knew what was happening with the kids, because being the teacher of the group as well as a parent, the meeting tree and house kept her informed. She could also turn it off so they had their private times but at the first sign of trouble or if they went outside their safe zone, she knew it.

Now they were home safe, they already knew about the new owls to the group, because the link does work both ways. April and Kristle were happy that their moms had their partners now; however, they had to make sure that their fathers would not chase them away. In a way they both wish they could have their fathers in on the secret but they understood why it was like this. They both relate to a modern movie that they like, where the kids have the power but not some of the adults.

Both the girl's father showed up after they had stopped at a local Asian food restaurant. They had picked up a few common group items and the group decided to eat in the house. There was a football game on with the New England team playing. They all sat around the living room and watched it, and like any other fan across the world helped their team by yelling at the TV. When the game ended, everyone decided that it had been a long day and home they went, leaving Seth and Sue to close the house up. Neither minded doing it, because to them it is part of being a family and they were both happy to have one again. Then outside as the girls and their parents made their way to their houses, there were two more sets of eyes watching their homes in the dark.

The next day everyone got up and got ready for their day to start. The girl's fathers headed for their jobs and the girls got ready for school, with Aprils mom dropping them off after they picked up Seth. Sue had already left to reach the high school, so that she could get her display board's setup for her first period class. She really loved teaching and now with her abilities to read the pupils better, she could help them understand history so that they learned more. There was only one thing that bothered her, after all the research that she was doing about the history of the Realm she was finding conflict with the school's history books. She however was not going to let any of the information go to waste, because she was familiar with doing research and writing papers from her many classes that she had on the base. She decided that the different information and its facts will be saved, and then she will use it to write a book or paper on it to be published later, matching new information against real or false facts.

As her first class was coming in before the late bell rang, she was reminded of all the evenings that she would sit and go over her information and try to keep the bad thoughts out of her head. These could be anything from hearing of Seth's run-ins with the kids at his school to the fear of something happening to her husband. She found a way to turn that feeling into a learning tool and it worked well for her. But it was time now and she had to turn her attention to her students and do what she loves to do, teach.

The day for everyone went just like many other days without any problems. Time either moved slow because of the subjects or fast when things were interesting. Home work was finished just after they got home from school for the kids with help from each other. However, for Sue sometimes it went into the night with test corrections or setting up next day's work. Every day was a new adventure to everyone, life was not boring.

17

holiday and
the Realm

THIS WAS A VERY BUSY DAY FOR SUE AND SETH, with School, then the meeting of the Realm that evening, also Thanksgiving preparations for the holiday meal. Sue went shopping for the last of the needed items for their Thanksgiving meal. It was just after school let out and she found the stores crowded with kids picking up snacks. She was strapped for time while trying to stay sane while in the mad rush. Seth and Sue were only going to have a small meal for themselves, but they had invited the girls and their family over for a late afternoon/ early evening sandwich and drink. She was not ready to have a large family meal yet and she needed to see how Seth was going to handle the day. Both Thanksgiving and Christmas were a big holiday for them as a family, but now with Seth's father not around she was not sure how Seth was going to act. She was herself already having troubles with it, with her feelings. She was finding it hard knowing that she was not going to hear from her husband either by phone or a letter as had happened when he went away before. She just kept herself busy and hoped that Seth was going to be ok.

The voice had also asked many questions about the holiday and Sue did her best to answer them. The voice said that they have no knowledge of the holiday and could not find it in the history of the Realm, and found that strange. Sue however, filled them in on the meaning, how it is a United States holiday and nowhere else. She said that they should just listen and watch what she and Seth do, as well as the girls and their family and do not ask anyone about it. She told them that they could learn what the holiday means to each person because it means a little different thing to everyone. Sue also asked that they leave Seth alone so that she could see how he will feel this year during the holiday. The voice said that they understood and they will just watch and learn unless they are needed. She thanked them and said that it was also a test for her also, and she needed to be a mother this holiday.

Seth's day at school was all about learning some of the New England traditions on this holiday. Many of the kids in his class including the two girls wanted to know what it was like to have the holiday down south. He told them the many different dishes that they have with the turkey and how many were the same as there, in New England, but the spices and herbs were different. In addition, some of the drinks and desserts were different and he found that some of New England items sounded better then what he had on base.

When he got home, he and his mom talked about what they were going to have the next day. To his delight he found out that his mom was going to keep what they like best during the meal. However, she will also have the regions common fixings like cranberry sauce, butternut squash, New England style apple and pumpkin pie. Seth jumped in and gave her a hand making things and when he could, he tested the taste of each item. They worked together and had the TV on a cable channel that had some shows and movies about the holiday. Some that they had seen before but some live shows that talked about the real history of the holiday. They were both surprised how much different it was from what they had learned in school and down south. They found this interesting and it passed the time very quickly, then before they knew it, the work was done; much of the preparations for their meal were ready for the next morning.

It was early evening of the full moon the day before Thanks Giving holiday, all six of the group met in the den, waiting for their time to enter the Realm. The full moon was the next day in the USA but somewhere in the world it started that night so the meeting was called. Seth was going through the meeting in his head of all the procedures needed just like the month before. Sue was going over what to expect with the girl's mothers when they get there and where they need to sit. The girls were reinforcing the moms and telling them not to worry but of course, the ladies were nervous.

The time came and the voice of the house told Seth to start his calling for the doorway. With a motion of his hand, he made an arch and the dark doorway appeared. Both the mothers made a small gasp but nodded to Seth that they were ready. Seth was the first to enter followed by the two girls, their mothers, and then Sue came in last. As before, when they reached the other side and they were in their room they were all robed. Kristle and Aprils mothers had on the same trim of light robin egg blue as their daughters. Seth this time was wearing the light-yellow stole with ravens on it from the moment he entered the room, unlike the last meeting where it came to him from another wizard.

On the walls were some new paintings which included the girl's mothers with their owls and Seth with his raven and Sue with her owl. There was a painting of the two girls together with their ravens, they looked more like sisters sitting together rather than being from different families. Then Sue noticed that on the collar of everyone's robe was embroidery of their animal friends. It was not fancy but it clearly showed the companions.

April and Kristle were pointing out through the doorway of the room telling their moms all about the seating and who should sit where. They could see all the people coming in and going directly to their seats but something caught April's eye. Seth's seat and their sublets seats had people in them again. She called Seth to the doorway and pointed to the seats saying that they had trouble.

Seth watched them for a moment and he noticed that they were acting very nervous. He said to the group that they were all going to enter the hall at the same time. When they got there, look at the people in the seats that are theirs and do not blink. At the same time, raise their right hand and point their index finger at them and he will do the rest. They all agreed and each picked a person so that no one was picked twice but Seth knew that would leave two of the sublet seats with people not chosen.

They gathered at the door and then with two steps they were in the hall. Seth pointed to the head table and his seat, which had the same person as last time trying to take his seat. The girls and moms did the same to theirs and then a spark came from their fingers and struck the people. It did not hurt them but did manage to scare them. The wizard at the head table that Seth zapped, clapped his hands and the complete group disappeared. Everyone else turned and peered at Seth and the group, however he knew they were watching and he ignored it and told the ladies to take their seats and get ready.

Seth walked past all the other wizards and sat in his seat ignoring all the eyes on him. He picked up the gavel and made two knocks with it and kept looking only at his group. As before, the Herald came to the front and called the meeting to order. Many were still stun by what just happened but they all sat in their seating area with their eyes fixed on Seth. Seth called for a motion to forgo the reading of the rules and go into general business. The motion passed, then he called for the reading of the last meeting minutes, after that was done he called for a vote on the minutes which passed with all hands.

Next was new business to be brought before the meeting. The wizard from England asked to be heard, then Seth let him have the floor and he stood at the pedestal. He had a look of being very serious almost as if he was both troubled and angry. He brought up the attacks that had happen to several of the Realms groups, just like the one that happen to Seth and his group on Halloween night.

"Many of us had visitors on the same night and they were testing the defenses' that we have in place. I believe that we need to start securing ourselves starting with this meeting place. I would like to have a vote to have this Realm locked so that no one can come uninvited. What just happen here today, is a good example of why we need to do this," the wizard said.

"Just what can we do?" Seth asked.

"We can modify the enchantment too only accept people that wait in the rooms before entering. If someone does come into the room that is not of one of the seven meeting trees then let the room send them back." The wizard from England expressed.

"Can we do that and not hurt the Realm," Seth asked.

"Yes," the wizard from the land of snow said.

"Then I would like to add that if the Realm cannot read the wizards thoughts clearly then the same thing happens," Seth added.

From the other end of the seven wizards came a comment, "That means that if you are a little under alcohol or on pain killers this could affect you coming to the meeting," that wizard from Africa said.

At that point, Seth and his party knew they had found the

right answer to the problem of people not following the rules. Seth then added, "If you cannot be of solid mind and thoughts then you should not be here, but let us put it to a vote, someone needs to make a motion to start the process."

The wizard from the east said, "I propose to have the Realm itself, look at each person that comes to meetings to see if they are of one of the seven meeting trees. Also, if it can read that person's thoughts through their ring, then allow them access."

"We have a motion on the floor. Is there a seconded motion to it," Seth asked?

The wizard from England seconded the motion and Seth asked for any questions. When none were given, he called for a vote and all but one wizard and his group voted for it. By the vote numbers, it passed, but that group that voted against it was not happy. Seth knew that this group was from Africa and they were the same group that wanted more sublet on the voting floor during the last meeting. He knew that this group was going to be a problem at times.

Seth called for the scribe and had him write down the incantation as it was passed. Then each of the wizards that passed it, signed under Seth's signature in the book. Just the one did not, and then the candles in the room flickered and it was done, the spell was enacted.

What happen next was not expected, all the African sublets and its wizard disappeared as well as several sublets from others different groups. Seth banged his gavel to return the group to order and said, "This is not a bad thing. When everyone gets home, you just need to check on these people to see what happen. With due respect to people out there older than me, there is a question to ask yourself, why do we need drugs and painkillers if we are healthy because of the rings. This means that drugs were used to get around the meeting trees ways to keep wizards pure of thoughts or that person has a drug problem. It is up to each meeting tree and it wizard to fix any problem within their group."

The next motion to come to the floor was to adjourn and was seconded very quickly. With a bang of the gavel, the meeting was ended. Seth stayed at his seat and groups that had someone disappear headed to their rooms and left the meeting room. A couple of groups stayed and came up to Seth along with the five from his group. They included the group from England with their wizard Philip Dooly, A thin man that looked to be in his fifties with a long gray beard. The group from Antarctica also came up; they are from an island off the southern tip of South America. Their wizard Sonia Pastel was a small framed lady that looked to be in her seventies with long gray hair and had a staff she used to help her walk, but it seemed more of a comfort item. Also joining them was the group from Australia with their wizard Radcliff Roth. Radcliff was a big man with very dark skin and gray hair and beard. He was very old and a few of his people helped him to stand.

He stood in front of Seth and this made Seth look up at this tall Aboriginal person. Seth stood taller than most kids his age but he only stood two-thirds Radcliff's height. Radcliff then spoke to him, "I believe that I am the oldest person here. I want to thank the youngest member that I have ever seen in the Realm and at the wizard's head table. You sir, have brought honor back to the Realm, thank you." He held his hand out for Seth to shake and as Seth did, his hand looked tiny in Radcliff's hand.

"We are the oldest of all the people on the wizards table," Philips informed him.

"Really, just how old are you," Seth asked.

Sonia spoke with a smile on her lips, "Mr. Roth is two hundred and eighty-one, and Mr. Dooley is two hundred and fifty-eight. I am a young two hundred and thirty-seven years and feeling good. Our rings have kept us from harm and aged us slowly. The other three wizards are less than sixty natural years of age. The man that is the wizard from Africa was one of the youngest until you arrived. He is also a strange individual as he is not of the people around the meeting tree. He and his sublets seem to be from northern Africa and they just showed up as a group. The original wizard, Berta Kibo disappeared; he and his group missed several meetings and no one could find out what had happened. The new wizard, Akmal Mustalph Kiral showed up with his new group and it was checked to see that he was of the bloodline and it was proven. No one knows what happen to the other eight people and their families. Even the meeting tree has no reading of the people, they were at a family event, and then there was nothing. You and your group may have found the reason why the meeting tree could not feel what happen to them. We already know that a blood exchange can make someone outside the family line become part of the bloodline and we knew that many decades ago."

"That means that a wizard does not need to come from the original family or bloodline," Seth said then added, "Maybe we need to research the group from Africa."

"It should be you Philip and not Seth and his group. He is new to this and we have friends around the world that can watch this group. Let him and his group, continue with the research they are doing," Roth said.

"You and your group have helped the Realm by bringing in a new study on the history of what we are part of. You need to keep doing what you are doing and we may be the better for it," Sonia told them.

"Maybe, maybe not, however I believe it is time we head back home, the lights are dimming and the room is telling us to leave. We will see you at the next meeting," Seth said and he motioned for everyone to head to their rooms. Once in their room, Seth looked back into the meeting room and it went dark just as before. They went through the doorway to their house and gathered in the den as the doorway faded from sight.

"Well ladies what did you think of the Realm," Sue asked.

"It was just as the training showed us it would be, also it was exciting," Aprils mom Janet said and Kristle's mom agreed. After some light talk among the group about what to do next, it was decided to call it a night and everyone went home.

Seth and Sue got things setup for the next morning then got ready for bed knowing that Sue had to get up early. She had to put the turkey in the oven early, so that they could eat around one or two in the afternoon. Each went to their room quietly to check their emails and social media pages then when they were done, they laid down and it was not long before they were both asleep.

The next morning Sue was the first to rise and straight to the kitchen she went. She warmed the oven, when it was ready, in the turkey went then she started her morning routine just as she did the many years before. After she had got everything being cooked or cooled off, she could sit for a minute and just rest. Her thoughts went to her husband, how so many times they spent this holiday together and with him deployed with the Army. She sat there with tears and her hands over her face wishing he were there. The memories are there and she can see Seth being so happy with the excitement of the day's events and the things they did as a family. The last time they were together as a family Seth was between twelve and thirteen. His events were now more geared toward a very young man that did not want to hang around his parents as much. That was the last time he had a holiday with his father because he was shipped out two weeks later. That meal was the last time they were together as a family and happy, even with Seth's teenage thoughts.

When Sue looked up she saw that she was alone sitting at

the table, but she knew the house was there, "You must think that I am a sorry person," she said to the house in her thoughts.

"No, we do not, because Jeb felt the same way about his wife and son when he lost them. We did not understand it at the time because we were new to being with a human, we only knew what the Realm had, and it did not let us feel the emotions. Nature has its own feelings but the human feels both sadness and anger at the same time and we are still learning it. We are sorry for your loss and we know that we can never fill or replace that void that you feel," the voice said to her.

Seth had just made his way into the kitchen and he looked as if he did not sleep well that night. His eyes were halfway shut and he looked tired. He looked at his mom and gave a half smile and a small wave with one hand as he got a drink from the refrigerator. With his cool bottle of water in hand, he sat at the table and asked, "What's up."

"You look like you have been up much of the night," she said.

"I could not sleep well, had dreams that made me wakeup," he told her.

With his answer, she knew that he was still tired and told him go back to his room and put some music on and get some more rest, she would wake him when breakfast was ready. The arms on the old clock showed that it was just 6:30 when Seth looked at it. With that, he drank some more water and put the bottle back in the refrigerator and shuffled up to his room. She has seen him like this before and she knew that he was half-asleep and needed more rest. She remembers the days after they got the news about his father, how he would walk around the house looking like a zombie, because he had not slept. When he put his music on and he would lay down, it would just be minutes before he was out and would wake later rested and ready to go.

Now it was time for her to pull herself together and finish

the prep and breakfast for the two of them. She got up from the table and dug in to make a nice meal for them both, all the time fighting to keep any bad thoughts out of her head.

After two hours, Seth came down after being awaken by his mom and sat at the table. Sue told him that he looked much better and to get the cereal and make a small bowl for himself to eat with the eggs and ham. She also said that if he wanted he could put the TV on and watch the New York parade. He did as she said and sat with his meal and watched the show while eating. Sue joined him and they talked about the different floats and bands as they came on the screen. As they sat and watched the show, Sue would get up and do what needed to be done to the cooking turkey and other items on the stove, then sit back down.

As it got closer to the turkey being done she became more of a cook then a show watcher. Even Seth had to join her to set the table for the two of them and keeping in mind that they will be having guest just a few hours after they eat. At the end of the set-up Seth handled the small food items and made sure they had a place on the table while Sue handled the turkey. They had everything ready for them to sit down and Seth stayed standing behind his chair, looking at the table. "Mom before we sit can we do one more thing, can we set a place for dad," Seth asked.

Sue's eyes began to tear up and she could see that Seth did not have tears. He had a determined look on his face and she said, "Yes we can and let us put him beside me across from you, just as we sat at home."

Seth took no time in setting a place for his dad and took care to make everything just right. When he was done he came back to his chair and as before stood behind it and looked at the table and said, "Now we are setup just as it should be, thank you mom."

Sue was fighting the tears back; however, she fully understood why he did it, even without the house linking their thoughts. It is still less than a year and she knew that he just as she, needs to have somethings remain the same. The councilor that they saw after their loss stated that small changes, a little at a time with help ease the pain of the loss. She knew it was not going to be easy for her but she worried about Seth because he may seem stronger at times, she knew better than anyone that he was just a young teenager.

They sat and Sue led them in a short prayer that wished all service personnel and families a good holiday, then they dug in to the meal. They tried a little of everything, talking about it in between items and before second helpings. They finished and both agreed that they would have to wait for desserts, that they were stuffed. They cleaned the table and got it ready for guest with covers on any food item they placed on the table. When they were finished both sat in front of the TV to watch a show and just like many other people this day across the land, they fell asleep.

It seemed like minutes that they had been sitting but it was nearly two hours when they heard the doorbell ring. Both were a little sluggish to get up but Seth made it to the door before Sue. When he opened the door, there was April and Kristle followed by their parents. Their parents had small trays of food that they wanted to add to the snack table and said it was a little of their home to help with the holiday. Sue brought the adults into the dining room and the girls went with Seth, both taking one of his arms and lead him into the den before letting him go.

"Well how do you like this holiday up here," April was the first to ask.

"Well it is not much different with how you do everything, but there are different foods," Seth replies.

"Are you ok with us asking you about things you do for this day," Kristle asked.

Seth looked hard at them and said, "we are friends and relatives, of course you can talk about things with me." After finishing that statement, he turned and sat in a chair. After the girls sat next to him they talked about what each family has done in the past on this holiday. There were some laughs and some joking around but they talked into the evening. The adults looked in on them throughout the time there and everyone had a turkey sandwich, the way each like it with plenty of other drinks and desserts. The kids even played a little with some of the tricks they could do with their given powers, including levitating things, changing colors of things like clothing, hair, and furniture. They were vigilant so that their fathers did not see any of it from where they were sitting. It was a good night to be with family, however in the back ground was the voice and the house listening, learning without saying a thing throughout the evening.

18

Two new girls join the house

It was now December and everyone was getting ready for the Christmas holiday, with the week off from school for the holiday. Seth and his mom had made sure that they had Christmas gifts early and they were rapped weeks before the big day, so that they had time for other things. The outside of the house was decorated with lights but each window was setup with a single white candle, with a bulb that looked like a flickering flame. For Sue and Seth this was for a tradition that they did when Seth's father was away from home, as did many other service families for many generations. They decided to carry on this tradition even though they had no-one in the service, it is for the men and women who were still serving away from home during the holidays. However, there was one special candle on the mantel of the fireplace for some-one special this year. It was a real flame candle, not like the battery-operated ones in the windows. This candle was in a special holder, which helped it burn slow and steady. It could also burn safely day and night for twenty-four hours a day, for many days before needing replacing. Above it was a picture of a man in uniform and his wife and young boy with the words in the frame that said, Michael Mason Hawthorne and his loving family. It was Seth's father in uniform with Seth and Sue with him, a military family portrait, with the candle being for Michael. Engraved in the top band of the metal case of the candle frame are the words "Michael, we will always love you and remember you until we are together again." Then on the bottom, it said, "You will always be our Hero, Love Sue, & Seth." Sue had this made special just for the holidays this year, to remind them of his love for them and in a way for him to be there with them. Michael always had candles on the table for dining; he told them that it was from his family's way of having a meal back in England. Then during the Christmas holiday, there was a candle lighted for as long as the tree was up and someone was home. Therefore, this was Sue's way of continuing what he started with them, only now the candle stays lit for him.

Many times, the girls, their mothers, along with Seth and Sue went out on Christmas shopping sprees and just Christmas light decoration viewings. Both Seth and his mom had never seen any of the holiday lighting in New England, even with the little snow on the ground, it looked a lot like the pictures used in Christmas cards.

One evening Janet receives a phone call from one of the girls that she gave blood to a few years ago. That girl, Elizabeth Miller also knew the second girl Sarah Simpson and told Janet they were great friends. After talking to her for some time on that first call, they set up a date to meet at the house too meet everyone. Everyone in the group was so happy, because if they agree, they will become the last to fill the seven sublet seats, also they would be added to the family in a way.

The meeting day finally came and when they pulled into the driveway, everyone was there to meet them. They all talked in the driveway for a short time then they all filed into the living room where the questions started.

"So, tell us about yourselves," Seth asked.

"Well, I am nineteen and I am going to school by using the computer to take classes online. Also, I am working part time until I finish classes," the girl named Elizabeth tells the group. Now she was average height and very light skinned with sandy long hair.

"I am sixteen and am a senior in high school and I have been working at the mall," the girl named Sarah tells them. She was almost the same height as Elizabeth with the same skin tone but just a little darker hair. Her age and grade did come to the groups thoughts but they figured there was a story behind it, and they felt it is best to talk about it some other time.

They were having some small talk about the house and learning about each person that met them, while having snacks and soft drinks. Then Seth decided to get straight to the point, and asked, "Do either of you like stories or games of wizards"?

"Yes, we both do and we play a role board game at a comic book store once a month," Elizabeth tells them.

"That is so neat, we have a game that we play here, would you be interested," April asked.

"Yes, that would be fun," Sarah said.

"Here, we start with these, just put them on and we will start," Kristle told them as she handed them two sublet rings.

The two girls looked over the rings and then place them on their hand. As they settled, they felt a little faint then the voice was heard.

"Please do not be scared, you are with friends here," the voice said.

The girls looked scared and looked around as they stood. Sarah followed with, "What is happening"?

"There is nothing wrong, please listen to the voice, all will be told to you," Sue said as the shade lowered and the doors shut.

"Sarah and Elizabeth please sit and we will tell you a story that you are a part of, because you became part of a family's bloodline, when you were given its blood. It started over a hundred years ago...." The voice went on to tell the complete story and the girls became very calm and interested. When it was all told and they were asked if they wanted to become part of the family bloodline, they became very excited and said yes without any hesitation.

As before with everyone else, they were told to sit and the ring would become part of them. They did what was asked and they fainted but this time they stayed passed out and the voice spoke to Sue and Seth only.

"There is a problem with these two. There is a section of their thoughts, which says they need to report what happens here to a man named Sayoie. It shows that they have been what you call hypnotized, what would you have us do with them Seth," the voice asked.

"Can they be returned to normal and protected after they are ok," Sue asked.

"Yes," the voice said.

"Do that and fast," Seth told the voice, fearing that in their state of consciousness they could be hurt.

The two girls were under just a minute longer after Seth's decision, then slowly they opened their eyes. "Sorry to the both of you. It seems that someone had you hypnotized and tried to gather information on what you do when you meet us. It seems that it was just a few days ago and the commands were removed that they hid in your mind, you are now safe," the voice, told them.

"We had a hypnotist at one of the group sessions that we go to, because of this blood condition we have. He said he could help us deal with it in our thoughts, so that it would be easy on us, we agreed only if it would help deal with that problem," Elizabeth told them.

"You no longer have cancer in your body and you will stay that way," the voice told them.

"You mean that we are healed? We are not sick anymore," Sarah asked.

"You are healed but for now you must go along with how the blood test will show your problem getting better and better over time. It is for your safety and protection, not to give away your new secret. You will learn more as you sleep but now Seth has one thing to do. He will make it so your rings are invisible to others not of the bloodline," the voice said.

Seth then had the girl raise their hands and he repeated the words "Cuddio neilltuo o'r golwg" while looking at each girl's ring. He then waved his hand and both rings disappeared and felt as if the rings were not there to the girls. They were in awe at what just happened and wanted to know more.

The meeting went on into the night with both serious talk and laughter. Both Elizabeth and Sarah had just got the best news of their lives, 'not sick anymore'. They also loved that they were taking part in something that they were fascinated with and dreamed about for as long as they could remember. They setup dates to meet and with the group now being able to be contacted by the meeting tree and the house, information exchange was now a snap. The night ended and everyone went home but both Elizabeth and Sarah drove home excited and in awe, they could not wait for their checkups to see if it is true. Just then they heard the voice in their head that said, "yes, it is true but we understand that you need to see the test, you both have been sick for so long."

"Are you mad that we need to see for ourselves," Sarah asked.

"No, we are not and we would like to see you happy," the voice said.

"Can we talk to you at anytime and anywhere," Elizabeth asked.

"Yes, and you will be able to talk to the others in the group after some training and whatever Seth sets up," said the voice.

Now the girls could not wait for their first night of sleep and training.

Over the next several days, the girls contacted the group and told them about their training. Several times, they all met for a meal and exchange of ideas and information at the house. The girls were fitting in with ease, as if they were born into the family and they felt that somehow, they also belonged in that house. Both Elizabeth and Sarah were excited to get a chance to go to the Realm and take part of something, that they only saw in video games or movies or play within board and card games.

Both the girls felt that this holiday season, they received the best Christmas gift that they could have received. They now joined the group during the holiday shopping trips and are planning to join the group in their holiday parties; they felt they needed to be there not as guest but as family.

Both the girls have families at home but their life differed there. Sarah was an only child and she had only her mother at home. Her father had abandoned them many years before, it happened just as she got sick. He has never been heard from over the many years and they both fear that with his bad habits he may be dead. Her mother works and goes out nights and sometimes does not come back until the next day, then sleeps all day. When she met Elizabeth at the hospital treatment center, she felt that she had met her older sister. There were many times that Elizabeth's mother would pick Sarah up and bring her to the treatment center. This was because Sarah's mom was unable to drive because of one of the many bad habits she had. It got so bad for Sarah with her mother not being there for her, that Elizabeth's mother got parental permission papers for her treatments. Then after a couple of bad times with Sarah's mother not being there for several days, Elizabeth's mother became her guardian with the help of the court.

Elizabeth's family was very stable and she was the youngest

child of three. There was seven years between her and her older sister and nine to her older brother. They both had married and moved away just after they graduated high school, which left Elizabeth home with her parents. When she got sick eight years ago there was just the three of them left in the house. When Sarah came into her life and with her problems at home, she also felt that she had gained a younger sister and always wanted to help her.

Both Elizabeth and Sarah now live together at Elizabeth's parents' house as a family, to the dislike of Sarah's mother. Elizabeth's parents filed papers with the court along with her doctors to remove Sarah from her mom for reasons of health and welfare. Her mother has full visiting rights under supervision but she must also provide for her health as part of the agreement, and she has fallen far from doing that. This had strained their mother daughter relationship, to the breaking point that she hardly ever sees her mother now. The last time Sarah saw her mother she was high on something and very violent. Now contact is by phone or with a guardian present are the only ways they see each other. This has been a strain on Sarah because she still loves her mother even with her many faults.

Elizabeth's parents have high hopes for the girls but they both know the reality of their health. If the girls do not beat their health problem, their life will be sadly different then they want. They are however, very confident that all will be well because the success rate now a days is greater than seventy-five percent. To them only time will tell, however, they are in for a surprise now with both Sarah and Elizabeth's new lives making their hope come true. Both the girls want to tell them but they know that if it just goes away overnight it arouses suspicion. They also must deal with the person that hypnotized them, when they see him without giving away their new secret. Just whom Sayoie is, is a mystery but he was part of the team to help them get better. They however will be ready for him on their next appointment, with the help of their new training and some use of cell phones to get a picture of him.

A couple of days later both Sarah and Elizabeth along with Elizabeth's mother went to the treatment center in the early morning. As they entered the office, paperwork was completed and blood was drawn as they maintained the routine just as they have done for many times before. They were now on the check and wait end of their last treatment so no medicines will be administered for some time. After a half hour passed by, the nurse came out and said that they wanted to draw more blood to run the test again. Both Sarah and Elizabeth looked at each other and they knew that this was a good thing. Then after another half an hour, both the girls were called into their doctor's office. The team that was helping them was there and everyone was around the desk looking at the test results acting with disbelief.

The two girls and their mom sat in the chairs and Elizabeth's mother was the first to speak up and ask, "Is there a problem?"

"There is no problem at all, we have some great news for the both of you. Your blood is nearly clear of any trace of the disease. It looks like the treatment has made you better and we had the test run a second time to be sure of the findings," their team doctor said to them.

Both the girls stood and gave each other a hug, then turned to Elizabeth's mother and hugged her. The room was full of handshakes and hugs and then at the end of it, pictures were taken with everyone. When the follow up appointments were set, and they got to leave the center, the three of them went out to have a celebration meal at a local restaurant. That is when Elizabeth's mother called her father about the news and they were ecstatic that both the girls had a new chance of a normal life. However, the girls knew that this was the confirmation of what had happen to them at the house.

Then as they ended their thoughts the voice from the house said, "we told you that you will be well again, are you happy"?

"Thank you," Sarah said in her head.

"That is the best news that could have ever been given to us, thank you," Elizabeth also expressed to the voice.

The three of them celebrated for a few hours and then returned home for the evening. Sarah gave her mother a call and told her the good news but Sarah could tell by the tone in her mom's voice that she was not clear headed. After she hung up the phone, she asked the voice if there was anything, that could be done for her. The voice told her that they could not interfere with free will but maybe she could ask the group if something could be done. She spent the rest of the night talking to Elizabeth, her mom and dad hoping that somehow, she could help her mom.

The next day the group met at the house, both Elizabeth and Sarah were glowing with happiness over their news from the doctors. They had pictures of the group that helped them and they were passing the phone around with the pictures. When it got to Sue, she looked close at the group and with a gasp, she noticed that one of the people, Sayoie was the banker, Kendell Solara that they had when getting the bank box. Seth joined her and the voice spoke and said this may be a problem. The mood of the group now changed from happiness to wonder about this person. Questions were now being asked, is this the person who made the attack happen on the house and the group that night.

"The problem may be closer to us than we thought, by

someone who may be working with one of the other groups that want to control the Realm," the voice said.

"What if this is someone that was with a group but was driven off, or if it is someone that knows of the Realm and was not allowed to become part of it," Seth asked.

"So, the question is, is there a way to tell if someone is part of another blood line without them knowing of our bloodline? Also, how to get around the mind control issue, if they use drugs or alcohol, if we need too," April asked.

The group all gathered in the den and sat in the seats around the room. The voice started the meeting with some questions to the new girls to see how their training was going. Next, was Seth going over the past meetings in the Realm they had gone to, and how they will meet in that room before the next meeting. Sue then reminded everyone that their training has given them the protocols that they will all need to follow. In addition, she let them know that no matter what happens Seth is the head of the group and we must follow him. After some talk about how the last meetings went, both Elizabeth and Sarah stated that, they could not wait to go and see everything that happens. They continued with how this whole thing has given them a new outlook on life and their future. The rest of the group went on congratulating them and welcoming them to the family.

The next thing to be brought up was by Sarah about what could be done for her mother's problems. The voice reminded the group that they cannot interfere with free will of people not in the group, and it is also the same for people in the group. However, people in the group can be stopped by the meeting tree if they go against the rules of the Realm.

"This may take some time to fine if we can do something, but what if we do something about the drugs or the alcohol, so that it is somehow bad for her to take it. This way she decides not to do it, does that interfere with free will?" Sue asked with a look of deep thought on her face.

"The rules say that you cannot use your power to force someone to change their mind or right to choose free will. If you do not use magic, it is not a problem. Changing how items taste with magic, that is unclear with the rules that we know of. How it makes them feel is again a free will choice, to feel that way or not to, that is the choice. This all needs to be checked," the voice informs them.

They ended the meeting on a happy thought by telling the new members how happy they felt for them. Everyone said their goodbyes and ended the night, however, something new was added to their thoughts, what to do to help Sarah's mother.

A couple of days later the group meets again, to talk about the Realm meeting that is in a few days, but first they sit around talking about how Elizabeth and Sarah were feeling and doing with their better health. It was more girl talk than anything else was, Seth felt out of place so he went and sat in the den. While in there he thought about how he was sick as a kid with all the typical thing kids get. He thought how he would see people on the TV that were asking for help for different conditions. He had never met anyone before that had a health condition like the one the girls had, only people with the common colds, flu's, and broken bones. This really was new to him and now he was the only boy there, with a group of females talking about things he did not understand.

The rest of the group came in the den after a period and sat as if nothing happened when Seth left earlier. They started talking about what the meeting should be about and what has happened in the last couple of meetings that they were involved in. The house filled them in on information that it had and reminded them of the rules. When everyone was happy and felt that they had covered everything, they moved on to other things.

The group talked about Sarah's mom and they now have the answer to the questions about changing the taste or reactions she has. The Realms answer to it is, that it is all free will and that any action that directly changes her ways is interference. However, indirect actions when she is not there such as, removing the alcohol from all the drinks in your house is not interference. The same as making all pills in the house a placebo, she still takes it when she wants but not the real drug. The fallout from this is that she will seek more or better things to make her feel good. The other thing is that you would have to be with her 24 hours a day, 7 days a week, then anticipate what she is going to do before she thinks about it. Because if you do it as she is thinking about it or taking it, you are interfering with free will action. See, once she sees it or has it in her hand, that is her free will to do what she wants with it. You cannot use your powers for any change of free will; however, you can use yourself as a human to help or force the change without the new powers.

"This is hard to have these powers to do good, but not to be able to help change someone who is in trouble. You can remove the trouble without them seeing or feeling it but they themselves with try again or do something else. Is this what they call human nature or the human weakness," Seth asks.

"Yes, this is the real hardship of being powerful where there are rules. We can see many time in the Realms history that this has been a problem and the answer is always the same, we have to stop you," the voice tells them.

As everyone leaves for the night at the end of the meeting they now fear that they have answers but are no closer to helping Sarah's mother. They also have feelings for her as if she was a blood relative even though she is not.

It has been a couple of days since the last meeting and both Sarah and Elizabeth came over to the house by invite of the voice. In fact, everyone was there as was their animal friends who sat around the yard in one of the many branches of the old trees around the house. No one had any idea why the meeting was called and what the house had planned. Everyone was sitting in the den talking about the up and coming holidays when the voice spoke.

"We now have all seven sublets for the meeting and of course you have both new family members, friends and of course a new outlook on life. There is one last thing that is missing from the group and that is animal friends and watches for Sarah and Elizabeth. The animal friends of all of you have found two that want to be with the girls if they want them," the voice said. The window in the room facing the front of the house opened and two very young ravens landed on the sill. They were purring as they jumped down to the floor and each walked to one of the girls and sat on the armchair. The voice then said, "These two are juveniles and were born just this year and have been friends since they came to be. Every one of your friends thought that these two represent Sarah and Elizabeth's friendship and have their faith to each other just as the two girls have toward each other."

While the voice was telling them about the birds they were looking at each of the girls, turning their head around and moving it back a forth. Both Sarah and Elizabeth were hesitant at first to touch the birds, but after a short minute they reached out to them and started running their hands along their back feathers. Each of the ravens closed their eyes and let the girls pat them as they made a very soft purr sound.

"How do you like them," Seth asked.

Elizabeth was the first to answer, "He is so nice, I feel so relaxed just petting him. If he wants me I will call him Calm," and as she said that he rubbed his neck and head along her arm as she pets him to show that he excepted her.

Sarah was still petting the raven with her and she was smiling and saying little things to it, "aren't you a cute thing, do you want to be with me and be my lookout and keep me safe? I like you, do you like me?" When she asked that question he made a loud long purr as if he was a jet airplane. That gave Sarah the idea for his name, "Jet, his name is jet," she said.

After a couple of minutes, the two ravens gave a loud purr then a low caw sound, then flew out the window to join the other birds to watch the house. The window closed and the voice was the next to speak, "That now completes the group. Girls, the birds will follow you around and will always be nearby if you need some friendship. If you have not seen it yet, you all have friends of a feather and that is what the tree picked so many years ago. The tree found that with all the hills, rivers, lakes, and mountains, winged creatures could spread the messages faster and see danger better from the top of the trees. Seth that is why your meeting clothing has the raven on it. Now that we have things in place, we need to keep a lookout for this Sayoie or Kendell Solara, whoever he is. If any of you run into him again your friends will follow him and report back to you whatever they see or hear. That is all we have and now we will retire so you can be with each other," the voice ended the meeting.

The group now moved into the living room where they started talking about the holidays, telling Sue of all the stores in the nearby towns. Seth stayed in the den and put on the TV to a Christmas show and he just sat there semi watching it, while listening to all the talk in the next room. However, in the back of his thoughts he was thinking about his father. He knew that they were taking a trip in a couple of days to go see him and he was not sure of just what will happen. He answered questions that were sent his way through the doorway while staying seated. He did not mind the girls gathering, because it gave him some time to think. As the time got late the group said good night and went home, ending a long day. When everyone headed homeward so did their friend, carefully watching, always on guard.

19

ARLINGTON TRIP

THIS WAS GOING TO BE A HARD CHRISTMAS for Seth and Sue. Even though Seth's father was not home last Christmas where he was deployed, there always was hope that he would be home the next one. However, not this time or anytime ever again, now that he is resting in the National Cemetery. Sue knew that Seth was not showing that he was hurting from the loss but it was there, just as it was for her. She has plans to take Seth down to Arlington for a day visit to place a wreath on his father's grave this year; still she was not sure how either of them would handle it. When the trip came up in conversation with April and Kristle, they also wanted to go, and showed both excitement and concern toward Seth. Sue gave some thought about the girls going, she wondered if this would be a distraction or a help, she concluded after some time that it would help Seth to have friends near him. The girls felt that they needed to be with Seth and they wanted to pay their respects to their relative. So, the trip was planned on very short notice, the four would fly down together in the early morning and fly back late the same day. This was going to be a fast trip with just one agenda, pay respect to Michael Mason Hawthorne.

The flight was not long and once at Dulles Airport, it was a rush to get to their rental car and get on the road. Sue had called ahead and set up a wreath that was waiting at the Cemetery with some honor guard personnel. As they parked their car, they were met by four men in full Army dress uniform that served in Michael's unit. Sue greeted them but Seth did not know them because as a child he was not interested in the adult world. They introduced themselves to Seth and the girls and then escorted them with a military formation to the row of headstones, where Seth's father was laid to rest. The Army personnel then made two lines, two on the right side and two on the left side so that Sue, Seth, and the girls could walk between them. Seth was holding the wreath, and as they started walking through the men, the men gave a hand salute until they passed. They dropped the salute and followed them to the site, keeping in a military formation march, with adjusted steps to not hurry the group.

Once at the headstone, the men stood on each side two by two and came to a stance, where their feet were slightly apart and their hands in front of them over each other. Their heads were tilted down, as if they were looking down into the earth and you could not see their face, only the top of their hats. They were motionless and silent; all you could hear was the sound of cars in the distance, and some birds in the trees.

The headstone was the same size as the thousands that could be seen all around and many had wreaths on them. The stone was curved on the top, with a cross at the top above Michael's name then his rank and the words, Army Special Forces. Next were the words Bronze Star, then the names Afghanistan and Iraq. Last on the stone near the bottom were dates of his birth and the last day of his life. On the very top of the stone, were some coins laid across the length of it, some pennies, nickels, dimes, and a few quarters. The girls never saw anything like this so they asked what did this mean.

Then one of the soldiers spoke, "Traditions have it that, leaving coins on a headstone of a military person has very specific meaning for military burials. Leaving a penny shows that you knew the deceased, a nickel meant you trained in boot camp with them, a dime shows that you served in the same company or unit, a quarter told the family that you were with them when they left this world." The girls thought about what they just heard quietly, so not to disturb Seth or his mother.

Seth laid the wreath at the base of the headstone, then each of the girls tied a small decoration with a tiny ribbon on it. The four of them held each other's hand, wished him Merry Christmas, then Seth and Sue followed with how much they miss him. Then each knelt, touched the stone, and stood back up in tears. They were just barely holding it together, when the four men in uniform all reached over and put a quarter on the top of the headstone. Then one said "Attention, hand salute," they snapped to a right-hand salute, held it for a minute then one of them said "two" and they slowly brought their saluting hand down together and remained at attention. That was it for Sue and the girls; they were in full crying mode. It was several minutes before everyone was back in composure; however, the men stood by at full attention until they were ready to leave. When the group started to walk away from the site one man reached out to Sue and held out his arm for her to give her support while walking away. One gestured to Seth to walk beside him, then the two others did the same for the two girls as the first one did for Sue.

The group made their way to the cars where the soldiers gave their regards and shared stories before leaving to head back to the base in North Carolina. It had been almost four hours since they arrived at the cemetery and they headed straight back to the airport. They could see many of the buildings of Washington DC but they were not in the mood to admire the sites, besides all of them had seen the sites before. They did not say it aloud but they knew that they all needed something to eat and to get their thoughts back to a happier time. The girls knew before they came that this trip may be hard but they were not prepared for what happen with the coins and service men. In many ways, they felt that they are really part of this family and Seth was like a brother to them.

Seth was running everything that happen through his head, also remembering past Christmas times both good and bad with his father being away. He remembers how he was brought up knowing that this was the way of the military family and until recently, he knew no other life. He still wishes that things were different but knows those thoughts clash with the new life they have now. He feels that he has two choices, live in the past and be sad, or live with the new adventure that they have become part of and see what happens.

Sue was thinking about the day and felt that it was needed, however, the soldiers helped and added to the healing. She feels that there is still a long road ahead but she was glad the girls were there for Seth. Although she knows the girls saw more than the average kids see in a life time. The graves and the reason for the coins, she knew they learned something about their family. She knew this was going to be the roughest holiday yet and knows that it is going to take time. She had to be both a hurt and support family member. It was time to head home and work with all these feelings for the holidays and beyond.

20

Christmas day and the Realm

THE DAY STARTED EARLY on this day of Christmas Eve at Seth's house. He awoke to the smell of his mother baking Christmas cookies as the sweet smell filled the house. The two of them made last minute adjustments to decorations and furniture for seating during the evening. This was the first Christmas away from the Army base, which was the only type of Christmas that Seth had ever known. Sue however remembers the years that she spent the holiday with her family and was now trying to bring it back into her life by sharing it with Seth. The country setting would make it easy to do that but she also knew that they had to keep some of the traditions they did as a family, while on the base with Seth's father. This was going to be hard for them both but now with the new family, this was going to be a challenge, not to lose what little traditions they had left. The decorations that they brought with them were set up in much the same way that it was done in their small base housing unit. They were mostly southern scenes with no snow, some even were service related having family there with one person in uniform. The new decorations had a New England and Canada theme to them, with much snow and very colorful cheerful displays. As each piece went up they would stand back to see how it looked, which led to some many moves until it was right. However, the old family decorations always remained where they were first setup. At one point, all boxes and bags were empty and the tables and rooms looked great to them, the decorating was now done, just in time for guest.

Christmas Eve dinner to Sue was about having both family and close friends, near and close to you for well wishes and support if needed. The event starts with people arriving and the household receiving them, however, new to her and Seth is when they arrive they have heavy coats because of the cold weather of New Hampshire. The coats went to a room upstairs, which was Seth's job, and any dishes of food they brought went to the serving table between the kitchen and dining room. There it was placed by its food groups; Snack, Main Dish, Dessert.

Now if they had a gift and everyone did bring something, it went under the tree. However, there were two types of gifts, one was a personal one, marked for a person by their name, the other was for a game where everyone got to choose a gift and they could swap it.

Everyone arrived, even a couple of Sue's relatives that were close by, April and Kristle and their families, Elizabeth, her mom, and dad with Sarah. Sarah told people that her mother said that she had made other plans with people that she worked with, she told her if she could, she would drop in. Sarah did not tell people this but she did not expect her to show.

The group sat down to the main table where there was an empty spot with a goblet with a red drink in it. Because of the vast amount of food dishes, the food was on a separate table and the main table was set up with the place setting and their drink only. A small wrapped gift only two inches cubed was on the center of each plate with a tiny bow on it. The gift matched the ones that were hanging on the decorations around the room and people looked at the item at their setting with wonder.

Sue stood, and then used her knife to lightly tap her drinking glass to get everyone's attention. The group became silent and faced her, Seth was beside her and standing as she spoke. "Thank you for coming, I will tell you about the gift in a minute but I want to turn this over to Seth for a toast," she then put a hand on Seth's shoulder.

Seth raised a glass and said, "Please stay seated but raise your glass of cheer and toast to those that are here, and those that could not make it here." He looked straight at Sarah after saying that, then followed with, "And those that we have lost, Merry Christmas." Then he touched his glass to his mothers, then his mother touched it to April's mother's glass, then it went around the table until it came back to him, then they all sipped the drink. This was an old way of toasting and Sue let them know how to do it before this night happened. With the lights out, and the candles on the tables and in the lamps providing the light, it was if the olden times were back. It was magical and Christmas at the same time. Then Seth spoke again, "A moment of silence please, to honor our faiths," everyone looked down or shut their eyes, then after ten seconds he said, "thank you."

Sue then spoke, "The gift in front of you is yours but do not open it. This is the season of giving and I ask that you all pass the gift you have to the right and with a handshake or kiss, wish the person Merry Christmas, then open the one you receive from your left." They all did as she asked; this caused a lot of merriment to go on around the table and when everyone opened the gift, there was a Christmas candy truffle in it. "From our house to yours, the first taste of the Christmas meal," she finished with. People then took a bite of the dark chocolate and wished Sue and Seth Merry Christmas.

April started the group up to get their food and people followed in a friendly line. There were all kinds of food from the small peas with a white sauce to the main dish of baked stuffed fish with a shrimp and bread stuffing. The meal went on for two hours with all the desserts finishing the meal. At the end, some of the people helped clean up and many of the leftovers were divided between guests to take home. With all the help and the laughter, the cleanup of the evening meal was done in no time. The main table was cleaned so that only the centerpiece and candles remained, and everyone was now in the room by the Christmas tree. The music of Christmas carols could be heard lightly in the back ground as people were having fun just talking between one another.

The time had now come for the event of the gift swap. Everyone was asking what game they were going to use because there are so many, however, Seth came up with this one. Everyone's name was put on a small piece of paper then it was put into a hat and shaken. The oldest person in the room, which was Elizabeth's father, then drew a name from the hat and that person went and picked a gift. The person picked first was April's mom Janet and she picked a small gift from under the tree. Seth then told her to open the gift and she did as he said to do. After removing the wrapping, she found two movie passes and free drinks with popcorn. He then had her draw a name from the hat which was Sues name, this brought her to the center of the group. He then told everyone if Sue likes Janet's gift she could take that gift and give a new gift to her to open. For the fun of it, Sue chooses a gift she brought to the fun and gave it to Janet. Janet now opens the new gift, which was a dinner for two to a nice restaurant and a show. Now Seth had his mom pick a name and this time it was Sarah. She now had the pick of the two opened gifts, she could give the unopened new gift to whomever present she chose. She could also keep the one she picked then open it, that was her option. This went this way all around the group and the twist to this game is, that what you give to the person whom present you took, may be better than the one you got from them. Of course, the first person to get a gift gets to go again, but there again is the twist, all the names are put back in the hat and she picks who she wants to trade with or she can keep her gift. She picks Seth out of the hat and he had nice a multi screwdriver set, she had bath soaps and candles and she kept her gift. People found it different and fun and there were a lot of laughs.

The Evening got late and the group started to thin out after the swap because it was almost ten pm. The private gifts were given to people by whom they were from and they were opened. People were having a great time and the only people left at the eleven o'clock hour, were the girls April, Kristle and their parents with Sue and Seth. They made plans for the next day because both the girls were going to be there Christmas morning to open gifts with Seth. The three mothers felt this was best for Seth because he had only his mother and the girls were both friends and family. So, the time was picked and the girls and families went home after a good night and Merry Christmas wish with a hug.

Now the hour was late, Sue put on the cable TV, and there was an old Christmas movie on, she curled up in the chair to watch it with Seth for a while. The time neared twelve and Seth put on his jacket, hat, shoes, and gloves then went out the front door. He sat in the chair on the porch and could feel the night's bitter cold air on his face and hear sounds of people up the street. He also could hear the light wind blowing through the trees and then he heard a hoot from Snowy his mother's owl. Shortly after that, he heard the purr that a raven makes to others to let them know he is nearby. Now it was silent but he still could barely hear some of the TV movie coming through the windows glass, he could hear the bells from the show, which were ringing for Christmas morning. He looked at his watch and he noticed that it was less than a minute into Christmas day, he thought it was funny how and if, the network set it up so it would happen that way.

Seth put his head back in the chair and looked up at the sky, with the snow and the colored lights, it was hard to see if any stars were out in the sky. He shut his eyes then inhaled a breath of fresh cold air, with that he relaxed and he felt a feeling that someone was beside him. It felt as if it was his father, just like when they would come outside and look for the Christmas Star on this very night together. When he opened his eyes, he found he was alone but something made him look up, to the west through the trees, to his amazement he could see one bright star, the only one. He watched the star until a cloud covered it, then he shut his eyes again and said "thank you dad, Merry Christmas."

Seth had not heard her, but Sue was just at the door after shutting off the movie and most of the lights but she had not opened it. Although, through the glass she could see the star. She heard Seth thank his father and that was it, she was in full tears of both sadness and joy. She managed to somewhat pull herself together and called to Seth, "it was time for bed." After she heard his acknowledgment and the door start to open, she went quickly up to her room so Seth could not see her tears. When she heard Seth come up the stairs she wished him good night and Merry Christmas. He stuck his head into her room and said the same. She met him at the door now that she got her composure back, then gave him a good night mother, son hug. Each made their way to their beds and began their way to dream land. Both however, laid in bed and thought about past holidays, while the house was not saying a thing because these were personal things, it knew that only they, could work these feelings out.

Christmas morning was here and the gifts had been around the tree since the day before. They were kept at the back of the tree, covered under a Christmas cloth during the party's gift swap. The girls would be over in an hour, so both Sue and Seth had a light breakfast from some of the leftovers from the night before. This was mainly cookies, breads, and eggnog; it was much the same as they had done in the past. There will be gift openings this morning and then later in the day the group is coming back to go to the Realm. This year the full moon fell on Christmas day and Seth was still learning the ropes of being the Chancellor, even after the meetings they had already gone to. He found with the help of the voice that meetings could be canceled because of events, holidays, or spread out over months. The only meeting that could not be moved is the big yearly meeting and every one of the head wizards had to be there. Seth has thought about meeting every other month like the Realm history says was the common practice. He needs to talk to the other wizards to see what they would like to do, then put it to a vote. He thinks that maybe it would be a good topic for the big meeting.

Before he realized it, the hour had gone by while thinking about the Realm, now the girls were at the door. They came with their families and had an arm full of gifts, which they put under the tree. Kristle put on the music and Christmas sounds filled the air as they moved gifts to the front of the tree. They all gathered in chairs around the tree and Sue then started passing out gifts with a Santa hat on her head. As people got a gift, everyone stopped and watched that person, open it and thanked who ever gave it to them. This went on until all the gifts were open and in a stack beside the chair they were sitting in, however, there was a large stack of ripped paper in the middle of the floor from the wrappings.

Seth got up and put all the paper in a trash bag while Sue pulled out of the tree two specially decorated envelopes with bright colors. "Ok, everyone here knows that Seth and I fell into a lot of funds thanks to the relatives of Seth and his father from many years ago. Well, Seth has a fund for school and now we have something for two special people," Sue said as she walks to April and Kristle and hands them the envelopes after wishing them Merry Christmas.

Both the girls' hands were shaking as they opened the envelopes given to them. In it they found a card with prints of Christmas bells and many colors with a Christmas wish. Then they found an account number and the information to Sue's relative the lawyer. There was also a check card with the amount of $400 written on it. They started jumping up and down while screaming very happily as Seth and Sue watched them. Then in front of everyone both the girls grabbed Seth and with one on each side of him they hugged and kissed him on the cheeks at the same time. He turned bright red and acted as if he was attacked but they were not letting him go. Both the mothers went to Sue and took her aside to ask her more about the account, when she whispered in their ear; they went white as if all blood was drained from their face. They then started acting as if they were as young as the kids. The ladies went to the husbands and whispered in their ear and just as they did, it looked as if all blood left them.

What the girls still did not see or know at that moment, is that they were setup with a school and trust fund, that could put them through college for many years, with some funds to spare. Not on the card but in the minds of Sue and Seth, were plans to use the money to take their new relatives on trips and many other things, they want to share. Since the day Seth's mother passed out in the lawyer's office after hearing how much money they had, Seth did not care about any of the money. He was so worried about losing his mom that nothing meant more to him then her. Since that day both Seth and Sue had talked about what to do with the money, since they found out how much was left to them. They both figured the girls needed it more than anyone and they did help to find it, so they should get some without anything attached to receiving it other than to use it for school. When Sue brought it up to her cousin he knew just what needed to be done and set it all in place. The girls are set just like Seth to have help for their future.

After a while everyone calmed down, the girls were told about schools and funds, both the girls still would not let go of Seth, each still had an arm. Seth had asked several times to be released but they were not hearing it and were clasped tight to him. After an hour, they finally released him and the group now divided into kid and adults with each being in different rooms. Each had things to talk about and eventually the girls and their parents went home so that the girls and their moms could make it back for the meeting that evening.

The Group all showed up within half and hour period, everyone got ready in the den for the doorway to appear to the Realm. This was Elizabeth and Sarah's first time to the Realm and you could see how scared and nervous they were. The group and the voice went over the rules and everything they needed to know, however to Elizabeth and Sarah this was a dream come true for them. They use to dream about this so their illness could go away and here they are, living it. Seth looked at the wall and shut his eyes then with his right hand made an arch motion and the doorway opened. The group just as before then walked into the waiting area of the large hall. Some of the groups were already in their seats and no one was standing. Seth led the way into the hall and all the girls went to their seating area and sat. Seth went to his seat along with the other five at the head table, it was obvious that the complete group from the African tree was not there. Seth called the meeting to order and a motion came just at the opening from Sonia the Wizard from the land of snow. She motions that the meeting be recorded for attendance, if there was nothing to come before the group then we adjourn for the holiday. Seth let all the formalities complete and called for a vote and it passed with all present and the meeting ended as fast as it started.

Just as Seth's gavel was banged, the lights around the hall changed to a red and green color. At that point people were wishing each other happy holidays with handshakes and hugs. Sue turned to Elizabeth and Sarah and said this is not the normal way the meeting goes but this was also their first time here for this holiday. The other five wizards filled Seth in that this has been what they have done in the past, when the meeting is near or on the holiday, to let people get on with their holidays. The groups stayed about a half hour then began to leave one by one as groups, until Seth and his group were the only ones left.

Seth had everyone gather in the waiting room so Elizabeth and Sarah could see how the hall shuts itself down. He was the last to return to the house and the doorway closed as he cleared it. The group talked for a couple of minutes, then went and sat near the Christmas Tree, where everyone had gifts for Elizabeth and Sarah, they in turn had some for everyone else. Talk continued about the Realm and then about Christmas into the evening, when April and Kristle's fathers showed up and joined the group. This was a family in so many ways but just a year ago, none knew that there were family members that were so close to them.

21

New Year's party with new family

THE WEEK SINCE CHRISTMAS DAY was filled with fun in the snow for Seth and the girls. This was a week of sliding, learning how to ice skate and have a good snowball fight, however the hot chocolate drink as a way of warming was very welcomed by Seth. There was no time that Seth was bored and at night, sleep came easy because the four girls wore him out.

It was the last day of December and officially the last day of a long year for Seth and his mother. They had to make some life changing moves, a few months after the start of the year and now their lives changed again. They have new family members that they never knew existed before they arrived in South Hampton. They have a substantial fortune in funds from Seth's bloodline and they live in a magical house with a magical world. Just six months ago, they were trying to rebuild their lives after the tragic loss of Seth's father, Sue's husband.

This night however, was going to be a party of parties. They had hired a party company to setup an evening of food and decorations unlike anything that was ever in the house before. Each room had plenty of seating and snack tables in it so that the whole family could sit. The television was in the den for movies and the countdown from New York. The fireplace was in the living room with a small fire for some relaxation and conversation. The kitchen had a drink station setup for both kid and adult drinks to last the night.

Sue and the mothers decided that it would be best for the group to meet there for the evening and night festivities. They could walk home from there where it was only a five-minute walk to the furthest house.

Now that April and Kristle have someone else from their family, not just the people on their father's side, they felt more like a larger family. Up to this year, they only knew members from their dad's side because their mother's side only had their mothers as the surviving member of the family. Their father's side kept a family tree in writing but they only knew that their great Grandmothers, on their mother's side had lost contact with the family in the fifties. There were no attempts to trace the family tree; life just went on.

Since they have been at school even their friends have changed. Not because of Seth, because with their new powers, they can see people as they really are. Friends were not real and people that they stayed away from were better people. This was all so new to them and with the new adventure with their cousin Seth; it was as if their favorite movies and stories are real. They were also growing up and seeing things that happen in the world that other kids their age just let pass by. Life for the both of them has got exciting in this small town in New Hampshire.

The party started with a family dinner at six pm with people to wait on everyone through the evening. They had the makings of a Thanksgiving and Christmas dinner combination. There were all kinds of fixing from cranberry sauce to a large turkey. Side dishes of potatoes, peas, carrots, butternut squash, fish, bread, stuffing, and Christmas colored drinks. The desserts were puddings, Christmas cookies, and the everyday favorite ice creams. There was something for everyone.

In Sue's family, they had a tradition of a little handheld

gift given to start the New Year. She had always given pencils, pens, and things to write things. This year Seth and Sue gave everyone, an old style-writing pen with an ink cartridge with many tips for different styles of writing. Each had their name on it so that it stood out for all to see. Others did not know that they were doing it and felt that they should have done something, but she told them that it is just something from her family's customs. This was done so that everyone could write their New Year's plan in writing so they can be reminded about it. When she told them this, they thought it was a great idea and started talking about things they could write during their meal.

After the meal was all cleaned up and portions were set aside for everyone to take home when they left, it was time to sit and relax for the adults. Sue and the parents of the two girls sat in front of the fireplace, which had a warming fire burning in it. They talked about family, friends, and things happening around town. The three kids retreated to the den where the video game was set up and they played a fighting game. They were waiting for the time when their music program started on the cable channel and all the parties across the country were shown.

The voice then asked, "We are trying to understand just how the game you are playing works. We see and feel the things that you do but how do the other things and people move? Can you tell us this"?

"We move our things with these controls and there are people on other computers somewhere in the world moving their items reacting to our moves. The computer makes it all happen together through the software. The internet links all the computers together," Seth said.

"This is what we do not know because we cannot feel the computer or see what it sees," the voice said.

"How can you see things that are on paper but not on anything else," April asked.

"As we understand it, paper was once part of a living tree or thing connected to the earth by crystals, water and soil. Animals have always been connected to us since the first day. People are the hard part, we can see things through them, feel what they feel but never control them. We can only fully communicate with people that we share blood with, and now we know that this can be interrupted with use of drugs or alcohols. We feel there is more to this but something is blocking it," said the voice.

"That is why we must keep looking for answers the best we can," Kristle added.

"Yes, but also keep it low key, so that we don't let anyone find out that we have made this our real quest. Let us get back to playing," Seth said and they went on with the game.

Minutes went on into hours and before they knew it, it was near midnight. Attention now turned to the TV and the last hour's countdown was started until the ball dropped in New York's Time Square, where everyone started toasting to the New Year. Someone over the state line into Amesbury Massachusetts was letting off fireworks, which lit up the sky. After five minutes, the sounds were gone, the still of the night was on them, even though, the smell of fireworks was in the air. Everyone in the house talked about what was coming in the New Year, however outside looking out of a hole in the barn was a watchful set of owl eyes.

It was a brisk cool night and the stars were out but the smoke from the fireworks was still in the air. The very slight breeze was moving the smoke to the east and it moved like a fog rolling along the ocean shoreline. Through the leafless trees, lights in other houses could be seen going out as people now retired for the night, a few cars were seen moving on the roads because of their headlights reflection off the snow. Some of the time if you listen closely you could hear the car's tires making noise on the asphalt of the road, as it moved from snow cover to bare road. The moon also gave some light that made the area light up with its light reflecting off the snow. In all, it was now peaceful out over the fields and in the woods around the area.

Snowy has been on watch the whole time this evening. She knew the area was protected but this was a warm nesting place, and all the animals knew that other attempts would someday be made on their friends. Each of the animals were in areas where they were protected from the cold air and out of site from anyone in the area. This made it so that they could watch their human partner and warn them of any danger. Their instincts told them that something was about to happen but just what it was, they did not know. They did what they can do best, watch over them all, making sure their path home was safe.

22

Αττack aτ τhe house

IT WAS A SNOWY JANUARY DAY; the girls and their parents were at the house for a good old meal of grill cheese sandwiches and tomato soup. There was not much snow on the frozen ground and the snow was not heavy that was falling; however, it was falling gently and steady with a small amount expected to build up that day. This was Seth's first year of being in snow and he found it much better than the wrenching cold weather, on the base when they get it. The snow was a new item for him if there was more than an inch on the ground, because at the base they never got more than that ever, that he could remember. Today however, they were sitting around the fireplace, which had a small fire in it and they had a large cup of warm soup and a plate of sandwiches. This is just the right combo meal on a cold, snowy New Hampshire day.

Conversation tones changed as different subjects were talked about but was always on the friendly side. Topics ranged from early family life to politics, but never to the Realm and the family power. Both the fathers were still unaware of the real thing that brought them all together, mainly because they were not a blood relative to Seth. To them this was just a family gathering with their wives long lost family members. A New England January day can come in many different conditions being snow, rain, windy, extreme cold and as a January thaw, the latter of which all snow lovers hated.

The afternoon went on joyfully, until the house started feeling a small rumble, then the people inside started feeling it. The house let Seth and the others know that the land around the farms protective barrier was moving. The voice also told them that it is protecting itself from an outside force, that seems to be coming from everywhere but only affecting this house. As the attack started both the fathers were frozen where they sat, by the house, so they could not see or feel what happens.

Seth made his way outside the house and could feel the ground shaking, he then placed his ring hand on the ground in a fist then said the words, "Atal y grym," in Welch. The rumbling got less and less until it was gone. Seth removed his hand, stood up and looked around to see if anyone was causing it nearby. No one could be seen and no one else from the homes close to theirs were even stirring, it was a normal day to them.

"It only took the words, stop the force. Just what caused it" Seth asked the voice?

"It seems that several other meeting trees around the world had the same thing happen to them, the Realm is letting us know," the voice tells Seth.

"Why, was this an attack or a test to see if we can protect ourselves, and if it is will it happen again? How can we stop it from happening again, if it does?" Seth asked the voice.

"We were in no danger because of our protection on the house and the tree; it seems that this was to get your attention. The Realm cannot tell were the source came from but three of the seven meeting trees did not feel this.

"This will need to be brought up at the next meeting, and we should be ready for anything to happen. The meeting is on January 23rd, so we have some time to get ready," Seth said. Then he remembered the girl's fathers, they were still frozen from the second the vibration started. "Everyone get to where you were when this happen, we have to let the fathers go" he informed them.

They all got to their spots then the house released them, they never knew any different. Seth, the girls, and the mothers all looked at each other and they knew that they will need some day to let the fathers know about this new life. They had talked about it but could not come up with a way that would not scare them or put them in harm's way from outside forces. However, after today's events that day needs to happen and they all know it.

Later that day after the fathers went home, they gathered in the house's hidden room. Seth asked the first question, "This is twice that something happen to us, can we make it so nothing from another person with powers can affect our homes or even us."

"The voice answers with, "we can expand the area from the meeting tree to whatever you wish, however there will be many other homes inside this sphere. Those homes have other families not of the bloodline, how do we act around them if something happens that includes them?"

Seth thought about it and so did the others, and then Sue came up with the answer. "What if you made it so no one outside our bloodline could use their powers while inside the sphere."

"That will put them inside and able to reach the house or the tree, we now make it so that they cannot come near the house and tree" the voice said.

"Then let us have a sphere in a sphere, can you do that? Let's make something that they call safety zones in the real world, a new sphere with the area say 5000 feet covering the tree. This will include the other two houses of our relatives and all the land around this house. No one from another bloodline can enter the tree or house spheres as it is now. Then no one other than our bloodline can use his or her power inside the larger area which include all the other homes. In addition, wherever we go we must protect ourselves with our own little tight sphere, like the ones on Aprils and Kristle's dads." Sue said, as the group pictured it in their heads and all agreed.

The voice then said, "that will work, however, let us put a sphere around the two other houses along with the house of Elizabeth and Sarah. These house spheres will work the same as the one on this house. As we spoke to you, we put the large sphere in place along with the house spheres." They all felt that this was the best until they could find a better solution.

They also talked about the meeting of the Realm and made plans to have several meetings to prepare for any event that may arise. They all agreed that not knowing what could happen scared them some but prepping was best.

With all that was happening, the three of the kids were able to get out and play in the snow. From sledding down the hills to ice skating and riding on snowmobiles, with Elizabeth and Sarah joining in, it was a fun time to be young. After a day of outside frolic, they would go to one of the three houses, to sit and enjoy a warm cup of hot chocolate and laugh about the day's events. Sometimes it was not just playing around, it was all the schoolwork they had, they worked together to get it completed, the group learned to help each other to finish work. Sue kept an eye on the three of them so that no powers were used to finish any school work, she found that she did not have to worry about Elizabeth and Sarah. Elizabeth and Sarah would help Seth, April and Kristle but being older they knew to only help and not do the work for them. The three, Seth, April and Kristle were young but Seth seemed well ahead of his age group because of his father's events and the gangs at his school. His life has not been that of a normal country youth, he has something call street smarts, which come from the careful ways to avoid the gangs at his old school. In addition, the large amount of kids in the classrooms gave a sense of watching out for ones-self. When people first meet him, they place him well into high school as April and Kristle did when he first said hi. Sue still worries about him but she now knows that he is in great company with the girls.

It is the full moon and time for the Realm meeting. As they have before they line up and Seth opens the doorway, they walk into their waiting room. From there they watch through the doorways mist where they could see other groups being seated. This time everyone is standing by their assigned seats except the group from the African meeting tree, they have not arrived. Noticing this, Seth and his group come out of the waiting room and take their seats, receiving greetings from the people already in the room as they passed by them.

As they were getting ready to start the meeting, people began coming out of the waiting room for the African meeting tree. They filled their seven seats and more started to line the back of the hall until all standing room there was gone. Then a man walked out of the mist of the meeting room, like all that came before him he was not of the native people that live at the mountain area where the meeting tree is.

With a loud voice he said, "Those who have checked on us to see if we are real, here is my bloodline. You have asked question about us and to prove we are real, we used the Realm to show that if we were not real, it would not have let us in. We are real and there are many more of us."

The wizard for Europe spoke, "But you are not Berta Kibo from the village at the base of Mount Kilimanjaro of the Chagga people of Africa, where is he and his people? This is a change of people from this meeting tree, just what is going on with the Chagga people."

I am Akmal Mustalph Kiral, which stands for 'the perfect selected supreme leader,' and these people with me are of my people. We are the people of the bloodline and this should prove, that I could not have opened the doorway to come here if I did not have the will of the meeting tree." After making his announcement, he walked down to the head table and sat in his chair at the end of the table. All the people including Seth watched him as he sat and acted as if he was the king of the room and everyone should bow to his commands. After a little time, the six remaining on the head table looked at each other and with only eye movements they showed disbelief. They then all made a motion that said let's move on, they became ready for the meeting.

Seth called the meeting to order and called for the reading of the last meeting, then after they were read, he called for a vote. That is when the wizard from Australia called for a stop to the meeting. Seth asked him to explain, and he stated that per the bylaws, only the seats may vote and that the African group had several times more people than allowed. He then called for a vote on the removal of the group except for their assigned seats. The wizard from the group refused, and stated that they need to enlarge the number of sublets allowed. Now the group was in a rage and people were yelling. Seth was pounding his gavel and only a few at the head table responded, the ones that were working with Seth. There was one last thing he could do, he learned it while sleeping and it was needed now. He has the power to start the meeting and he has the power to stop it.

With a hard bang of the gavel and the thought to stop the madness, the lights went out and everyone was frozen in the spot where they sat or stood. The lights then came on but the people could not move. Only Seth could move and speak but he just looked out over the group, shook his head, and then spoke. "Many of you said I was too young and not experienced to hold this rank of office," then with a move of his hand he freed up his group and the head table. When a couple from the head table started yelling, he moved his hand again and they could not speak again. Then he said, "Look who are acting like little kids, gangs, and bullies, not me, the young one, but you the so called wise ones? I have it in my powers to do this and do the following, each group will only be allowed seven sublets, one wizard and a guest by permission of the group, which must be given before the guest is to show." He waved his hand and all the people could move but not speak except the wizards from England, Paititi, Antarctica, Shambhala, and Australia, they could both move and speak. Seth held his hand up to them to tell them not to speak and followed with. "This meeting is over until the yearly meeting next month. You all need to read and study the rules for that meeting because I will not let it get out of hand." With a bang of the gavel, everyone was gone from their seats in the blink of an eye, except his group and the five other wizards he told not to talk.

As they looked at the rooms coming into the main meeting area, they could now see each group through the mist in the doorway which normally you are not able to do. He had sent them to their rooms and they could not come back through the doorway. The group from the African meeting tree was packed tight in their room. Through the doorway, their leader could be heard making threats against Seth and the rest of the group. "Wow, he is mad, and that is why we think he is behind the attacks. His meeting tree has let other trees know that it is not happy with its group but it cannot deny that they are of the bloodline," wizard Radcliff Roth from the Aboriginal people said.

"How did you do that," Woo the wizard from Shambhala asked.

"There are many things that I can do while in the meeting as long as it has no personal gain, and they needed a time out. I know that I did not make any friends today but they need to follow the rules of the meeting. Next month will be no different, I will act as needed," Seth said.

Seth's mother was looking at Seth in wonder, thinking about this young little boy that she was worried about. However, now she sees both her and his father in him and she feels that maybe he will be all right.

The group talked about the others for a while and made plans that if they hear anything good or bad they will send messages through the trees. Seth started shaking his head and laughing and everyone was asking him what was wrong. He looked up and said with a smile "tell a tree, tell a phone" and the group started laughing. Sue looked at Seth and said to herself, "there is my boy."

"This meeting showed us that none of the original Chagga people of the African meeting tree, are part of the group, this is a mystery. However, what we must do is have our trees find out what is happening and only they can fix it. Let us leave this place and go home to ponder the events of today," wizard Juande_Eguiluz from Paititi said.

The group made their way to their rooms and the people of the other five wizards were waiting in the room, since Seth put them there. Each wizard explained what happened and all the groups, including Seth, returned to their homes. Seth's group all chose a chair and they sat and talked about the meeting, also what could be done about it. However, Seth also had the voice telling him all that was known about the people that showed from Africa. It seems that they are not from there but are from the northern shores of the continent. It also tells him that the wizard Berta Kibo from the Chagga people in Africa is alive, but is very ill, and is not at the tree. Beyond that, information is scarce and hidden just like when his mother drank the wine.

Seth now suspected that maybe drugs and blood transfusions might be behind a takeover of one of the trees. Something that helped Elizabeth and Sarah health could be used as an evil takeover of a people's way of life. This looks like a takeover for power he thought, but he also hoped that it could not be that easy. Also, he wondered if it is, can something be done to fix it to prevent it from happening again.

Over the next few weeks, this was talked about with the group in the house, and looked for on computers to see if anything like this was ever heard of before. To their surprise, it was found on some video games out of the Mideast area of the world. The group made sure that they left no trail of what they were looking for. They used computers at gaming centers, and other public venues, with fake ID's for on line gaming. They also took notes, however it seemed that the worlds of gaming, magic and drugs were all working hand and hand. It was not long before Seth began thinking that he had no idea about any of this while growing up down south. However now he could see why some of the kids in the groups acted the way they did.

23

The Big Realm Meeting

It is February and the snow has stopped falling for the most part, but small snow storms come every other day it seems to Seth. There was a lot of work shoveling the walkway and driveway and Seth has found something that he hates, the snowplow working the street. Several times, he had finished the driveway when it came by and pushed the snow from the street and the snowbank into his nice cleared driveway. The girls had fun teasing him about it and told him he should make it so that something happens to the truck, before it gets near the driveway. The voice and Sue quickly reminded the three of them, that it was personal gain and someone could get hurt. They said that they could dream can't they.

The whole group went out for Valentine's Day to Boston for a day of fun and food, paid for by Seth and Sue. With their new funds the family is again one of the wealthiest families in the area. Still the two of them would trade it all for one thing, Seth's father's life. No matter how wealthy anyone is, loss of a family member changes people and so it has for Seth. To have the three of them together is the riches thing he wanted.

Sue had rented a van with a driver to take everyone: her, Seth, April and Kristle's family, Elizabeth, and Sarah so they could fully enjoy themselves without putting up with the traffic. They started with a breakfast in Boston, then a tour around the city, which ended up with ice skating in the park during a light snowfall. They then went to a show and a diner at a medieval restaurant in which they all were made to be part of the act. At the end of the day, they were falling asleep on the ride home. That night none of them needed the help of the sandman to fall asleep.

They have found that they live in a world of many different worlds. There is the world of happy people going from holiday to holiday making life happy for themselves and other around them. Then the real world where it is dog eat dog to get somewhere in life and people meet each day with the feeling you must fight to get ahead. There is the world of drugs and lost people who have given up on the everyday status quo. You could become one of the people keeping this world going. Doing what needs to be done, and go home at the end of your day to be with family, friends or the internet and TV. This last of the known worlds could be part of the gaming world, which covers everything from board games, computers, and/or live play. Then there is the world that Seth and his group have become part of, magic and power.

Seth, Sue, and Seth's father never really got into the gaming world very heavy, only as an item to pass time when needed. Seth had done more of it because the kids in his last school were always talking about it and playing it on their phones. Even in school, some of the kids were doing more gaming then learning from the needed class work, Seth always felt.

Now Seth and the girls had their only little gaming world. On slow or snowy days, the three or five of them when Sarah and Elizabeth are there, have fun using their powers. They create games out of thin air and play them. They are careful not to break the rule about personal gain by making sure that at the end of the game no one keeps anything. These games

are anything from a floating checkers or chess board with figures that are life like, to driving games where they have set
up a course in the study and they race around it using their
thought. They set a rule among themselves that none of their
games would hurt any character that they made up. If they
set up two armies to battle the one that was the looser, would
just disappear with no cries or blood. They all in many ways
despise the death and gore scene of games, and Seth has seen
firsthand what war can do to a family or friends.

It was now the full moon and the meeting was gathering
in the Realm. Seth and his group were at the archway in their
house getting some updates from the house on known past
meetings. Seth was thinking that from the sound of the past,
none of the meetings have been routine and he feels that this
was going to be the same. Seth led the way and they gathered in their chamber, and they saw that they were the last
to arrive. Seth and Sue watched the group to see if anything
looked odd or as a fuse to an event that has not been foreseen
by anyone. Most everyone was seated just the group from
Africa was standing and looking out over the group, pointing,
and talking among themselves. Even their leader was not at
the head table but was standing with the group. Seth pointed
it out to everyone in his group and told them to keep an eye
on them as they entered.

Seth started the group through the mist in the doorway,
then stood so that everyone could make it through the doorway
into the Realm meeting room. After a very short time standing
there, they made their way to the seats for their group, after a
glance around the room they sat. Only Seth was now standing
out of his group as he made his way to the head table. Each of
the wizards greeted him as he walked by and in turn, he also
greeted them, however the wizard from Africa was still standing with his group. On the head table was an hour glass, about
eighteen inches in height and eight inched across, with red

sand in it that was just about to run out signaling the start of the meeting. This has always been there in the past meetings but the sand was always white, which represented the light of the moon. This is the first time that Seth is seeing that it is red; however, he knows from the training while he sleeps that red means all wizards must be there. It works so that at the right time, everyone would meet. All trees knew the time, and they make sure that the wizards would be there before it ran out and reset itself. Once the meeting starts, it flips itself and the sands starts running for the next meeting time. A clear dome protects it, so that no hands can touch it, and will adjust to the meeting schedule set by the Realm and the Chancellor.

Seth watches the sand of the hour glass and it ends its fall, he then bangs his gavel twice to call the meeting to order. The Herald stands and walked to the front of the head table, with the staff bangs the end on the floor while calling the meeting to order. The African group however remains standing, again the Herald bangs the staff on the floor and calls for order. Now all the eyes including the Herald are looking at the group and for a third time the staff is banged on the floor. The group then acts as if they were saying "Ok, ok were doing it," and they moved to their seats then sat.

Once everyone was seated the Herald returned to sit after turning and nodding to Seth. Seth banged his gave once and said, "The meeting is now open can we have the reading of the rules for a reminder of our laws."

The Reader stood and made his way to the pedestal with the large book on it. He stood on the step to make it so he could reach to the top of the book page and he began to read all three hundred and forty-five rules.

After nearly one hour of reading all the rules, people were a little restless but Seth followed the finish of the rules with, "thank you for the reading of the rules. Because this is just the reading there will be no motion to the rules," and he banged his gavel once. "now can we have the readings of the minutes of all the meetings including the main meeting one solar year ago."

Without hesitation, the scribe moved to the minutes log and read all notes for every meeting during the year. This was a much shorter time and at the end with a nod from the scribe, Seth asked, "are there any questions or missing information from the minutes." He looks out over the meeting room and no one raised a hand, then he asked, do we have a motion to accept the minutes as read." A motion came from the head table and a seconding motion came from the sublets. Seth then said, "The motion to except has been raised and has been seconded, are there any questions." Seth waited and then said, "All in favor raise your hand," as they did the scribe counted them. With a nod from the scribe he then said, "all those opposed please raise your hand" and none did.

The scribe said, "All voted to except minutes, none apposed," and he wrote it all in the book.

Seth banged his gavel once and said, "Vote is excepted and logged"

"Next is business to be brought to the general assembly, with the head table's permission I would like to bring something to the table. I would like to submit that we change our meeting to the following: That we meet with a meeting once every other month and if there are two moons the month that we meet, then it is always on the 2nd moon. The skip will start next month."

A motion came from the sublets from the Shambhala group, with a seconding from the Paititi group from South America. Because Seth brought the item to the floor, Radcliff Roth ran the meeting now, he asked, "are there any questions," and none came. All those in favor raise your hand," and just as before the scribe counted, when he was done he nodded to him, then he asked, all apposed and the African group all raise their hand. At the same time as the vote, that group's leader started making statements about how bad of an idea it was.

"The time to bring up questions and comment has passed, you are out of line," Radcliff told him, however he kept making statements then Radcliff stood. "I now run this meeting as per the laws that were just read. Do you need to be removed as you were before, I will do it"?

With that statement, he became very quiet and sat. When the eight hands were counted the scribe made the announcement of the count and Radcliff banged the gavel once and stated, "The motion passed." When that happen the size of the hourglass changed and there was now more sand in it and the sand changed to white.

Seth now was given the gavel by Radcliff where he regained control of the meeting. "Is there anything else to be brought to the business at hand he called."

As he finished his words, the head Wizard from the African group jumped up and asked to speak. Following the rules Seth recognized him and let him speak, "we are now at the required meeting and as groups have done before, we want to propose the expansion of the sublets to equal the size of the population. We are in a different time then when this was set up, so this needs to change." As he was saying that, there was a mass of grumbling from the rest of the sublets seated in the room.

"Ok, everyone let him speak," Seth said as he banged the gavel several times, then Radcliff asked to be recognized and Seth asked, "Is it about his proposal?"

"Yes, it is, and I am asking that it just be tabled for a moment as we bring information that has direct input to this proposal," Radcliff stated.

"Per the Realm's rules, all information on items brought before the gathering must be allowed to be heard, so the request is valid," Seth informed everyone. Then Akmal Mustalph Kiral, head wizard from the African group started ranting. Seth banged the gavel several times again and stated, "It has not been dropped, but the rules allow for every item brought before this group to have comments or debates for and against it, to be discuss on the open floor of the meeting. This will be followed and everyone in this room will follow those rules, or they will leave this meeting," Seth directed the statement to Almal but meant it for everyone.

Now Radcliff had the floor, being a large man when he stood he towered over the people at the head table. He made his way to the front of the head table, standing at a podium just off to the side. He used it to keep his balance as he addressed the room. "We have been checking the claim of the wizard for the African tree, we started after the meeting a few months ago when there was a change of leaders there. What we, a few of the older members of the head table found, was that many of the new sublets here last meeting claiming to be with that group, were also in the group that claimed to hold the seventh tree which was found to be false. They could not come back after the rule was put in place that blocked them from the Realm. This was because it could not read the thoughts of any of them entering the meeting, however here they are in the seats for that group. After checking farther into the group, we found that the leader is not from the land of the meeting tree and none of the sublets are of that land. So, we looked for the former wizard," Radcliff stated with a deep voice that felt like it was holding you in the chair you were sitting in.

Seth hearing this went into action and raised his gavel and said, "Freeze the group and looked at the African group," then he banged the gavel once and they could not move.

Seth looked back at Radcliff then Radcliff spoke, "Thank you Seth. I am sorry that we did not let you know about this, but we felt it was best for us to do this because we know many of the people, and you are new to the Realm. We found that it was true what you found out about drugs and mind control, which seems to have been used for many decades. We also found Berta Kibo who was drugged and hidden from the tree as well as several of his blood relatives," Radcliff raised his hand and Berta appeared out of the ready room of Radcliff's people. You could see that he was dressed in the clothing of the Chagga people as he walked to where Radcliff was standing.

He stopped at the side of Radcliff and stood holding the staff in his right hand which looked as if it was helping to hold him up. Radcliff started with, "this man was drugged and locked away under guard along with many of his people. There was a takeover of the tree using blood injections, drugs and death while being on drugs. This has taken years to set in place and it is a threat to our Realm and we need to put safe guards in place. However, there is something that needs to be done first. Chancellor, may Berta Kibo address Akmal Mustalph Kiral and see if the tree returns him to his position."

Seth answers with, "Is this still part of the item brought before the assembly?"

"Yes sir, it brings in the answer if the person who made the motion could really ask for the motion," Radcliff stated.

Seth banged the gavel once and said, "So be it."

Berta walked behind the head table and made his way to the far end, because Akmal was in the farthest end of the head table. None of the group could move including Akmal, and as Berta reached him, he put his hand on his shoulder, the gown, regalia, and the ring disappeared off Akmal and appeared on Berta. Berta then waved his hand and said in his own language, "Remove all these people to my waiting room and keep them motion less." Just as he finished, everyone in the seats for his group disappeared and he sat in his seat, turned to Seth and said, "Thank You to all of you. As I sit here now the tree is removing all the stones from the people that were not part of my group. I have a few people at the camp that are setting things in place to protect the tree and our village, we never had to worry about this in the land but now evil has come to our land. We will deal with the people that hurt us and I promise that it will be what the rules let us do to them. There memories and people they know will be removed."

Radcliff had made his way back to his seat and raised his hand for Seth to see. Seth called on him and Radcliff stated, "Chancellor, with the outcome of this item brought up by me, I motion that the item brought to the floor by Akmal be canceled since it was not his place to address the Realm."

It was seconded by many people in the sublet seats and Seth asked for questions. When none came to the floor he banged his gavel once and the hall was filled with hands clapping and everyone stood for Berta. Berta just raised his right hand to a thank you wave, then with both his hands made a motion with his hands in front of him for the group to stop and sit down.

Seth banged his gavel several times and waited for the people to sit. When it was quiet the wizard Sonia Pastel from the land of snow asked to be allowed to speak and Seth allowed it. She stated, "We now have a problem, our blood can be used to make people who can come to the Realm. This is the same process that a mother has happen to her if she is not of a bloodline and has a baby. If we fix it the wrong way we could make it so that she could not be able to join the Realm. How do we fix this and make it so that evil people do not use it and can we remove people that have this done?"

Just then Seth remembers the two girls in his group that had the blood exchange. He thought for a second than asked, "we have two in our group that had a blood exchange and it was done in the line of medical treatment. It also allowed them to join us and the tree could save their lives. How can it be done to save the really good people of our groups?"

Then the wizard Juande Eguiluz from Paititi spoke up and said, "This is very easy, the tree must test each person and it should be able to see the history in the memory of that person.

We must recheck all our sublets, tighten our checking, and maintain our group. The tree is the test but the wizard has the responsibility to question the trees findings. This is not a disrespect toward the tree, it is our job, we can put up guards to protect our trees, and areas and we need to do it before anything else happens."

Wizard Philip Dooly from England then stood and said, "With all this information Chancellor we should end this meeting for a couple of reasons. First because Mr. Berta does not have any sublets and to be fair in any voting he should have whom he wants here. Second, we should go home to check our groups and tree to make sure that things are safe there. Berta, you should make sure that you are safe and if you need help please contact Radcliff or myself."

Seth called the meeting to an end and after the motion was made and the gavel was banged, many sublets left, however, the seven at the head table remained seated and talked. Much of it was making sure that Berta was going to be safe and he assured them that the tree has already told them that everything was locked up and people were safe. With that assurance, the seven of them said goodnight and returned to their rooms. When the last person entered their room, the lighting in the main room lowered and the misty doorway between the main hall of the Realm and the ready room became solid. This was the first time that Seth noticed this, the voice of his tree told him that the Realm locked all its doors so no one could enter the hall, only on a meeting day or a special meeting called by the Chancellor. This time it locked quickly because it sensed the problem that was the main event this night.

The group sat in the den and each had a confused look on their face. Seth sat and looked at the floor slowly shaking his head from side to side. Sarah and Elizabeth had a look of sadness in their eyes but also a look of guilt. The others in the group saw this and asked what was bothering them. After being asked a couple of time they said that what saved them made the life of that man horrible. They all knew just what they meant and told them that they did not instigate the problem so do not feel bad. It took the group several times to convince them it was ok but they still had feelings for the poor man.

Seth was still shaking his head and for the first time was thinking that he wished that they did not get involved. They talked for a little while and then Seth asked, "House, can you train us to defend against other people like us with power, and to use our power if needed to fight."

"Yes, we can, you all have the power, however Seth because you are the head of this group, you can limit or give unlimited control of use of power to each person. Also, training can begin at any time and you can use your hidden room," the voice told them.

"Great, we start in a couple of days," Seth told them.

Sue was dumbfounded by what she had just seen and heard with Seth. She was thinking that he just took command of a situation, fixed it with help from other leaders and was thinking like an adult. Who was this son of mine she asked herself? He was the only male in this group and it has crossed her mind that maybe he needed a male role model, but she questions that thought now.

After some nods and a couple of "Oh wells," the group decided that they should call it a night and everyone headed home, this time a little somber. When the last person left Sue turned to Seth and asked if he was ok. He looked up at her and said, "Yah, people are the same everywhere in the world and some are just plain stupid. I am glad dad showed me how to be strong." He gave her a hug, said good night, and went up the stairs. Sue just stood there and watched him go up the stairs and disappear through the door to his room. For the second time tonight, she had been surprised by what he said and at that point she now realized, that her son has grown up from the lost boy she remembers coming home from the school on the base. She thought about how proud she was of him as the tears started to flow down her cheeks.

24

Attacked

THE GROUP WAS NOW SETTLED after the last Realm meeting, and has had several meetings with discussions with each other along with the house's voice. They sometimes would practice defensive moves and shields of many type, in the house's hidden room where the book, stone and group pictures were hung. As always, the room seems bigger each time but the voice tells them, that it can be any size they want with any amount of light they need. With each training session came a night of sleep training and the next day of feeling great. This was one of the side effects of sleep training, it gave you a well-rested night.

They came up with many fighting or attack situations, of course many were from games, shows and movies. Seth came up with an idea and the group went back and forth with it for many hours, then they tried it out. The spell was for a bubble to surround you and act as a shield so no matter which direction someone tried to hurt you from, you were covered. However, they found there were several problems with this, what would happen if the wind was strong or they used a spell of wind or force to move you, and it started rolling you around. When they tried this, they had fun rolling each other around the room. They decided to put an anchoring spell on it to keep you in one spot on the ground and make it so the bubble does not collapse or dent. Next was the problem of air, they found an easy fix for that, only pure air can penetrate it as well as, anyone of their bloodline, in case that person needs protection.

Then came a question from Sarah, "we are anchored to the ground but what if we are on water or if the attacker makes the ground move or disappear"? This raised a lot of questions of being in planes, cars, boats and if there is non-bloodline people nearby.

After some thinking about it, they talked about some of the movies and shows of half science and Hollywood special effects, they came up with some ideas. The first if on water you stay at the same spot and will move as you need, you have control of the bubble, it will always float. The more challenging was if the ground disappeared from under you and as with many other things they had fun with testing this. Seth came up with the idea of a bubble, neither weighted nor weightless; it was just there at that very spot. It could not turn, lift, or fall without the person inside the bubble wanting it to move and only they could move it, not an outside force. This took care of wind, force, or gravity. With all the thinking and trial and error, this was as science would call it, a force field barrier. Each of the group practiced it, learned to move with it and how to just walk with it in a group or crowd. They had to learn how to still have it around you without it pushing other people around. This training went on until each person mastered the protection spell.

Along with this was offense training, which each person found hard to create something to fight back with, that could hurt the other person. The house and voice kept reminding everyone that this is why they are good people, it was because they cared even about who was fighting them. They developed skills that could make all kinds of balls; stone, ice, water, metal, and fire, they could also be any size. The main weapon was a bolt from the hand and it could be fire or ice, but the most efficient was lightening. However, there were other tricks that they could use, one was of course making the ground or water disappear then reappear. Moving objects was very simple, but to make your opponent relocate was difficult because they could also have a protective barrier. It was also realized by the group that this could be a battle of who had the better tricks and strength to stay and fight. They all found that they believe one thing, that no matter what happens it is their duty to protect and stand your ground until everyone is safe.

It was a nice clear day for an end of march day, with some snow still on the ground and because of the little warmer temperature you could see some of the melting. Elizabeth and Sarah had gone to lunch at the mall and Seth, April, Kristle and their moms joined them. They ate at one of the sit-down restaurants and enjoined a relaxing meal and great conversation about almost everything under the sun. Seth being the only boy there sometimes did not feel like it was a place for him in many of the conversations. He managed to turn his attention to a feeling he felt since coming to the mall and was trying to track down just what it was. The voice even was helping him with it and he did not let anyone else know about it so they could have fun if it was nothing. He looked around and could not see anything that looked out of place, however he saw that there were a lot of people here and that he felt that maybe the problem. He still had problems in areas where there are large amounts of people since his days at school on the base.

The meal was finished and everyone was walking out into the main mall area when something sounded and felt odd. Almost at the same time everyone in the group noticed that there was no sound, then they noticed that the other people in the mall were not moving. Seth, without hesitation but up a bubble shield around the group and just as he did a lightning bolt hit them. It came from the second level and the eight of them turned to where it came from, and there stood a man pointing he arms at them. He was the person that was in the hospital staff for Elizabeth and Sarah, who was also Kendell Solara the banker that was at the town bank, when Sue and Seth got the old safety deposit box. He held out his hand again then a bolt came from it and hit the bubble, Seth immediately followed with the same. His bolt seemed not to touch him but Seth also made the floor under him disappear and he fell to the 1st floor. He did not land on his feet and he looked very shocked at what just happened. He managed to get back on his feet after throwing a couple of fire balls, but Sarah made the next move. She made all the chairs and tables pile around the man, then Elizabeth hit him with a force that threw the pile at the wall behind him. To everyone's amazement he stayed standing and un hurt, however the group started heading for the doorway to go outside.

As the group made it into the parking lot, there was a lot of movement out here because the man seemed to only have affected the inside mall. He had made his way outside also and kept throwing fire balls which everyone around could see, which now made them run for cover. Seth told everyone in his group to hit him and they threw water balls at him. What he did not see was that Seth had waited until the water covered his view and he made the ground open under him and close-up over him. He was now gone, but people were still running madly around.

Seth then said "yn dychwelyd i normal fel o'r blaen yr ymosodiad" (return to normal as before the attack) which put everything back to normal in the mall where people had just started unfreezing. The outside was a different story and Seth had to think quick of a way to hide what had happen. He spotted a fire hydrant just to the side of the entrance and without thinking said, "dechrau d r yn llifo fel ffynnon" (start flowing water like a fountain). This now had everyone's attention in the area and the group made their way to their cars where they met earlier in the parking lot. Without hesitation, they got in them and made their way back to the house, while leaving Seth thought about the cameras all around and with one thought he erased any recordings for the last twenty minutes. This way it covered any chance of the event leading to them in any way. Once at the house they felt safer but the question was still on their mind, 'what was that and why.'

The tension was now high among the group, everyone was talking at once when the voice told everyone to sit down. When they were all there, the next thing they recall is waking up feeling very relaxed and a little confused. "Sorry, we did that to calm everyone down, you were out only five of your minutes so that your bodies could catch up with your head. What happen was an attack on the group and your training worked well for you. We must let you know that man does not show anywhere in the Realm yet he had power equal to yours without your tricks that you included, the voice said.

"I felt that there was something happening before it did, when we were in the restaurant, and I thought it was just the size of the crowd," Seth told the group. Each of them told how they felt a little uneasy also but put it to just not feeling well. They then swapped what they felt with each other, asking if it was about the same time.

The group then decided to call the husbands and Elizabeth's parents and they were all fine.

Then the question came up by April, "do you think that he will be back or is he gone?"

The voice was first to answer, "We do not know, we did not know that he had power. It is clear that he is a threat but now that we know that, we can watch for him. I know that this is a hard time for the group of you but we need to know, do any of you want to leave?"

With the last question, the group looked at each other as if looking for the first person to say yes. But after a few awkward seconds everyone answered "no."

"Good, we have some work to do," the voice said

It is the last day of the month and Elizabeth and Sarah are having dinner with Elizabeth's parents at their Newburyport home, when they receive a knock on their front door. Elizabeth's father excused himself as he went to see who was there, then in a short time he walked back to the table. "Sorry everyone but we must go sit in the living room, there are some people here that need to talk to us," he stated. The three ladies being curious asked each other who could it be but quickly made their way to the room.

In the room were two police officers sharply dressed and standing tall and proud, with their hat under their left upper arm. Elizabeth's father had already made it to the room and was standing beside an arm chair, he motioned where the ladies should sit. He had Elizabeth sit with Sarah on the couch and had his wife sit at the chair he was standing at. He put his hand on his wife's shoulder and she looked up into his eyes and he had tears starting. She managed to get four words out before she her self teared up, "what is it dear?"

Elizabeth and Sarah were watching them closely when the older of the two officers spoke, "we are so sorry to interrupt your meal but we have some bad news," he said. The fathers hand tightens on his wife's shoulder but she was not looking at him, she felt that she had to watch the girls. The officer then said, "Sarah, are you Sarah Simpson?"

Sarah then replied with a, "Yes I am" and she grabbed Elizabeth's hand and held it tight.

The officer then continued, "we are so sorry to have to deliver you this news, your mother was found at home after a neighbor called for a wellness check. She has appeared to have died in her sleep. We do not know all the details but I have the information of the people that you need to contact." Sarah grabbed Elizabeth and both were holding each other tight. The parents without hesitation also joined them to comfort Sarah the best they could. Both officers were holding their feelings in, then after a couple of minutes walked over to the group and said, "we are so sorry for your loss," then handed the father the paperwork. He stood and thanked them and escorted them to the door, then with a hand shake they were gone.

While this was happening where Sarah was at, Seth, Sue, April and Kristle along with their mothers were also in tears at their own homes. Sarah and Elizabeth both open their thoughts to the group and everyone could feel the loss of Sarah's mother. Sue asked Sarah if she wanted the group to come over, but Sarah told them that not tonight, the next day would be better, she will need all her new family there.

That day and all night off in a nearby tree you could hear the cry of a single male blue jay. Some say there is a lore that their cry was a cry of death, and this night was a proof of that. However, with the cry of the blue jay, there sat two black figures just out of sight where Sarah was, watching and listening carefully were two ravens both with a tear in their eye.

25

New way to view the world

It has been a couple of weeks since Sarah lost her mother, and they had her laid to rest on a small rise in the towns cemetery. There were few people to see her off but there were people there for Sarah to support her in her time of need. When the reason for her mother's death was released, it was no surprise to Sarah or anyone that knew her mother. She had passed away due to an overdose of drugs and alcohol, and had been gone for two days, before the police found her. Sarah had a hard few days and everyone did what they could to help her get through it. At the service Sarah read a letter to the people there, those that knew her knew it was going to be meaningful. At the end of the letter were the last words she said, "Mom you had a hard life and I know you were hurting, you now can rest without the pain and have a peaceful sleep, I love you mom." There was not a dry eye at the service from that point on.

The group has got together and had a couple of informational, brainstorming meetings, but they have not been as intense as before. The group knows that everyone needs some time when bad things happen, and Sarah needs to know that they all are there for her. Seth has had a little different outtake on this, he knows that the girls are better helping Sarah then he is as a guy. Even Sarah came to him and said the she understands what he is thinking and agrees with him. However, Sarah and Seth do talk often just between the two of them, not like brother and sister or boy and girl friend, but as confidants. The two of them share one thing that none of the youth in the group can feel, and that is the loss of a parent while young.

One morning after a night of learning, Seth was sitting at the breakfast table still a little sad about the recent event. He was looking at pictures on his phone of the group, when he had a thought, what if he could see places without physically going there but view it as an image. He had no real idea why this popped into his head, but it sounded like a good idea to him. So, he spoke up and asked the house, "Can we see an area on the wall as a moving picture"?

"We can show you an image that you request in the mist of your doorway," the voice said.

"Can you show us what Stonehenge looks like at this very moment," Seth asked.

"Go to the den, open your door to your room, and let us try to bring up the image," the voice tells him.

Seth made his way around the corner to the den, then made an arch with his hand and the doorway to his room appeared. As it appeared, it was full of a mist just like the doorway to the Realm. Within seconds, a dull image started to appear and people could be seen walking around the large monolith stones of the old site. The weather was a little gray with a light mist but it was as if he was standing there.

"Is this what it looks like at the site at this very moment?" Seth asked as he was watching the people walk around the site.

His mom walked over to him and was very impressed at the site and the way they were seeing it. She reached into the image and it distorted in the area around her hand for as long as her hand was there.

"Can you show us any area in the world," she asked.

"We can try many and see what we can do. We have never done this before and do not know much about this except the little that is in the Realm's knowledge. It says that it can be used to see areas that are not hidden from site by a meeting tree. The tree will block the area around and including the wizard's area and the trees location," the voice clarified.

"So, we cannot see any of the other meeting trees or the people," Seth asked.

"No, we cannot, although we can see many old ruins and places," the voice told them.

"To call a place to see, what do I need to ask," Seth asked.

"We can show from your thoughts or an area that you choose from a likeness of the world as we know it. We are not as experienced as many other trees because we have not interacted with humans as long as the other meeting tree's. However, we must tell the both of you that your knowledge that you have in your memories that we can see, seems to be sizable with all that you have learned from what you call the computer. There is one thing that we find very different though, we see images of what you call movies and shows, that portray land, time, and events that we know as legends. We see them as real things in your memories," the voice informed them.

Sue then added, "I think I know what you mean. These are all the movies and things that we watch that were made by other people, and recorded to play back as entertainment, or to help in our learning. It is not all real, but there are some things that are recorded of real events, that we have watched which now have become part of our memories. It's no different than the same way you remember things along with the Realm memories."

"Seth, you have a memory of a cave where Merlin went to rest, to regain some of the power he lost as he got tired. Sue, you have a memory of him being trapped there by his fellow wizard in a crystal forever. Those are not the only memories, there are many more with them, always having a cave, crystals, and Merlin. In addition, the both of you seem to have many images of a lost world call Atlantis, that also has the same, caves, crystals, and people with power. It is hard for us to see which is real and which is make believe. Is this how the people of your time see everything, as what you call a movie or show? Do they not go and find things on their own and feel what is like to hold it or see it happen in front of them? Does everything have to be done by the TV or the computer?" The voice asked them.

"This has been the question that many people have feared and been asking since these items have been invented. Learning has now come to a point that you do not have to hold it in your hand or see it in your presence, it is what someone tells you, or you see on a screen. Even books are becoming a thing of the past, being replaced by the computer. Simple learning has been replaced with complicated machines and even physical things such as walking and work is now done by machines. Life also has become very fast now, with people doing many things fast and not enjoying or learning from the hard work of getting there. Many books, papers and even shows have been made about this but it still goes on," Sue informs the voice.

"Tell me if I am wrong, but you do the same with your information stored in the Realm. You show it to us just as if it was a computer," Seth asked.

"You bring up a good point but we rely on someone to see, hear, or feel the information. If it is not real, we store it as yarns, made up stories and keep them in an area that is just regarded as falsehoods. We are the youngest of all the meeting trees by means of being with humans, however, we are the same age as all the lifelines of the known meeting trees. We have missed so many years of learning from humans compared to the rest of the trees, but we do have memories from the other trees, which show the humans growing in knowledge. It also shows us how they masked information from the Realm as they learned the power of the crystals and nature. We can show you all that is in the Realms history from the wizard's point of view, and we can show you everything seen or done by a living thing. We can also show you everything that you have for knowledge, however, you must remember that if you do not block it from the Realm, they will have it as memory also once we show it," the voice tells them.

"We have blocked things before from all of us, so from now until we tell you differently, block all from this group's memories and feelings from entering on to the Realm's knowledge," Sue said.

"Seth being the head wizard do you want this?" The voice asks him.

"Yes, please do as my mom asks" He said as he was in deep thought about how much this seems like many of the games he has played on the computer. Then he got an idea and asked, "Can you show us all the caves that have crystals in them?"

"Yes, we can," the voice says.

Then slowly an image of the earth shows in the mist and then many areas show red. "Are the red areas where there are caves," Seth asked.

"Yes, these are all the known caves to us," the voice informed them.

"Can you show us caves nearby," Seth asked.

"Yes," the voice said and the image changed to a close-up of the northeastern United States. What became very visible were several areas but an area to the west of where they are living now was showing brightly.

"Why is that area so bright," Sue asked.

"We do not know, however that site shows as bright as several areas in what you call Great Britain. The Realm does not have any information on any of these sites however there seems to be an area in the Realms history that is blank as if it was removed before the first meeting. Also, the first meeting shows that there were nine wizards on the head table but no other information about that meeting is given," the voice informed them.

"So, can this mean there were nine land masses in the beginning, and can we count the number of meetings up until now so we can see the age of the Realm?" Seth asked with hope in his voice.

"There are meetings but they have no date or time given, as if the records were not clearly kept. However, the time line only adds up to fifteen hundred years which would put the date as you know it as 580 AD. We do know that the meeting trees go back much farther than that, at least 2500 years beyond 580 AD.", the voice said.

"Then that means the trees family is 4000 plus years old. Can you show us caves and sites 1400 to 4000 years old", Sue asked?

The mist changed and then the sites came up. There were sites in Great Britain, and one on each of the continents with six showing up in New England. Seth pointed them out and two were in New Hampshire, two in Vermont and the last was in Connecticut.

"Do you know anything about these six sites here in this area of the country," Seth asked.

"No, we do not, they are just there as are the sites in Great Britain but the others around the world are in the same area as other meeting trees. It may be safe to say that the sites just to the west are part of this meeting tree, however that is unknown. Now you can call all that you see on this view at any time and add more to it as you wish," says the voice.

At the next meeting plans were to study the sites, then they felt that maybe they needed to visit some of these sites, to get a firsthand look at them. Everyone agreed that it would be best if it was done closer to the summer months. They then changed the subject to the meeting at the Realm and what they were going to talk about at the meeting, mainly about the attack that happened last month. Discussions were aimed at everyone knowing what to say and when, this time notes were taken so no item or action was lost from memory.

The time has come as the full moon has become visible in the sky, and the call has come to start the meeting. Seth and the group have made their way into their waiting room, where they watched the other people come in and take their places. They could see that the six other head wizards are in a heated discussion at the head table, but it was not an argument just lots of talking. Seth lead his group into the hall and the girls took their seats as he made his way to the center seat, without talking to anyone he sat and readied himself.

"Did you not have any problems," Sonia asked.

"Yes, but we need to bring it up during the meeting, so please let us get started and bring it to the floor," Seth told her and he called the meeting to order. The formalities were followed and people followed the rules of the meeting.

The next thing to come to the floor was a motion to open the floor to open discussion about what has happen to groups over the last two months. The motion was seconded and it was open with the rule that the head Wizard must do all the talking. One after another, the people at the head table told a story about some type of attack on one or many people in their group. When it came to Seth's turn whom was last, the description of the attack was much the same as the others, however they were the only group where all eight of them were attacked at once. This bothered several of the head wizards and they asked the girls in Seth's group directly how they were, and if it was as Seth described. This was allowable and it is what they practiced for. Once Seth had control of the meeting again, a motion was made to stop the discussion and with a motion of the closure and a vote, it was back to a controlled meeting.

Philip Dooly then made a motion that all trees, houses, and groups close their area and make safe all that are part of their group. He also added that any person that attacks anyone have their image be given to all trees, so that they can use it to protect their land. With motions and votes it was passed. Then a motion was made to have anyone that attacks anyone of a meeting tree group to be sent to the containment zone, it was brought to the floor and there was a gasp from many in the other six groups. Seth and his group were looking for information on this and Philip could see that they did not understand, so he asked for a clarification for new people. With that Roth told the group that it is a containment zone, where a person is alive but no powers can be use by anyone who is placed there. They float and only the Realm can remove a person in the zone, however only with one hundred percent vote of all present at a Realm meeting can it be done. That person is aware but cannot eat, drink or sleep, a limbo hell is a close description of it, darkness with not even a hint of light and no sounds.

"Thank you, I believe we now understand and our tree can fill us in when we get home, but why have we not heard of this before" Seth exclaimed.

"This is for the containment of the enemy of the Realm, if we are in a war against someone, this lets us hold them and figure things out as a group. Your tree was never at a meeting before you came to it, so there are somethings that it did not know. As of tonight, your tree has full access to the Realms records and even more than any of us have because of your position that you hold. There is one thing that needs to happen when someone is sent to the zone, the Realm will contact all heads of meeting trees and justify the placement of this attacker into the zone. There should be a meeting called to see if there is a better way that is humane to deal with this attacker, just as we did with the person that took control of the African group. Now if we may finish the vote on this motion," Philip asked. The motion was acknowledged and voted on and there were many hands that went up slowly but there was a one hundred percent vote. It passed and everyone received a message from their tree that training will take place for the power to use this. There was then a motion to end the meeting and passed as if it was lightning and the meeting was closed.

Now the noise level in the hall became very loud as everyone started talking. The head table was abuzz with how to adjust to the use of the containment zone and Seth felt that it was best that he gets together with his meeting tree and learn about this. He spent his time listening to people and waited for groups to leave the meeting hall. When the last groups were off the main floor and in their waiting room, he watched the main hall shutdown and lock itself. When all was closed they made their way to their house and sat in the den, while Sue brought everyone a juice drink.

The group talked about the meeting the rest of the night, the voice told them that they will be given information during their sleep. They will learn about this and then during their meetings be shown how to use it. When everyone was calmed down they headed home and reflected on the meeting in their homes.

26

Spring is here

THE MORNING CAME and Seth decided that he was going to spend the day fishing the Powwow River, which is the name of the river that runs under the bridges near his home. He had dug some worms the day before and had them in a plastic butter container and with his rod and tackle box, he went to the bridge. He jumped the guardrail and sat on a rock just off the water. He baited his hook, set the red and white bobber then casted the line into the open water. He sat back and listens to the water run past the rocks and bridge walls. The water is higher than when he first came down there to meet the girls at the end of last summer, and it was moving much faster because of the snowmelt. This year though, the snow was light and even as high the river is, it is lower than he was told that it has been in the past.

Seth also was thinking about the sounds he was hearing that had nothing to do with the river. There is a slight breeze and the new leaves were making some noise, as were the autos that could be heard coming down the hill, just over the Massachusetts / New Hampshire state line. There were many apartments along that road and the autos would come and leave to make the hill. Every so often, an auto would come to the stop sign, or go over the bridge as he watched it. He thought about the base he was at, just a year ago and how it was never this peaceful, and how he liked this so much better.

Just then, he heard two familiar voices, it was the girls and they had their fishing gear also and joined him. They each put their lines in the water but in a way so that they were in different areas then each other. They asked him what he was thinking and without hesitation, he told them, knowing that he could trust them. They sat there talking about his thoughts and many more that came up between them. Every now and then, they got a bite on the line, even catching a few yellow perch, and quickly releasing them back into the water.

Before they knew it, it was late afternoon and time to head back to their homes. Before they left they confirmed that they all were going to the historic site the next day then said their goodbyes. That night the three of them were on the phone in a conference call talking like three teenagers. The house voice stepped in and talked to all three at the same time. It asked, "the three of you do not need that device to talk to each other, why do you not use the powers to talk?"

"I guess it just the thing to do, all the kids do it and we are kids," April stated.

"I don't care either way," Seth stated.

"Just like a boy," Kristle said with a laugh, then the three of them laughed.

"We will never fully understand the humans and the items you use," the voice said to the three of them and stayed silent. The three of them finished their goodnights and hung up.

Seth then addressed the house, "I am sorry about that, but there are somethings that we need to do to just be kids. We still also want our privacy so we can just be ourselves and have our space. I guess it is a human thing."

"Someday maybe we will understand everything but until then we will also learn as time goes on," the voice tells him. Seth tells the voice goodnight and heads to his room for an appointment with the sandman.

The morning was here and the day is a perfect morning with

the weather. Seth and Sue got set for the arrival of April and Kristle with their moms, for a trip to American Stonehenge in Salem New Hampshire. They arrived just after eleven and then they all piled into the minivan. The ride took them through a couple of small towns to the west on back roads. While in the van they talked about many of the other Stonehenge's that they saw on the computers and in shows.

The group arrived in the parking lot, looking around, they were overcome by the beauty of the tall trees that surrounded them. They met up with Elizabeth and Sarah then they made their way to the visitor center, paid the entry fee, and made their way out the door to the site. They had to walk up a short hill trail and began to see rock formations just off the path. These structures were made from stone slabs and carved stones arranged to make cave like buildings and walls. Following the marked pathway brought you farther up the hill and to more structures. There were deeper cave type tunnels and table stone slabs. An area that looks like an alter with a speaking tube can be seen, when the girls were at the table slab, Seth made a low howling sound and gave them a small fright. This had the group laughing. There is a fence around some of the sight to keep people from damaging it by walking on it, and from falling over some of the stones.

The site is all built on a side of the hill, when they got to the top, there was a gazebo platform where you could see all the cleared areas. This allowed you to see the stones set out several hundred feet all around the site that made up the solar calendar to see the solstice. To the group this was a wonderful place. It is very different then the sites like Stonehenge on the Salisbury Plains in England but it is just as magical. Sue being the history teacher she is and Seth's curiosity set them to thinking, are there more sites like this, maybe near their home. They spent some time talking to people that run the site, where they were given leads on other sights nearby.

Later that day after they got back home, Sue and Seth started researching the web for sites in the New England area. They followed up on some information given to them at the American Stonehenge site, that hinted that there were many more sites in just New England alone. One was just between the site they were just at and their home, in a town called Danville, it is called the Beehive Hut. When Sue looked this site up, she did not find much information on it, she found that it does match other sites all over the world that were made facing the sun. It is not known how old the site is, legend has it older then the natives that lived in the area though.

Seth came across a site on the computer listed in South Woodstock Vermont, over two hours travel by road from their home, with a mysterious underground chamber. There are also the four stone chambers of Putney Vermont, with standing stones and large open areas. The computer showed all the sites have one thing in common, stones.

The next site was found by Sue and it is called Gungywamp in Groton Connecticut. The name in Gaelic means "church of the people," however there are some people that believed it is also an ancient Native American name and this feeling is also common on many sites. There are chambers, beehive type hut sites and stone circles as well as large stone slabs, pillars and stones that form astronomical lines to make the site. The function of this site is as much a mystery as the many others sites.

Seth also found a megalithic site located at what has been call, Druid Hill and LeBlanc Park in Lowell, Massachusetts. This is a site of weathered megalithic stones, on an earth mound which looked as if it was the same that were spread across Great Britain and Europe. It measures 112 feet long by 56 feet wide, the stones seem to provide astronomical alignments. Although the site is believed to have been moved due do a 1900's construction it has many mystery's surrounding it.

Both Sue and Seth found many sites on the web, that men-

THE MEETING TREE THE HOUSE & THEIR WIZARDS

tion how many inscribed flagstones have been found through-out the New England states. They were used for stonewalls to mark boundaries of farms and foundations. It is even believed that many ancient sites could have been removed without the farmers knowing what they had done. They talked about how maybe the stone that led Jeb in his quest over a hundred years ago, may have been part of a site that was destroyed, by people moving stones for foundations and walls. They agreed that there is no real way to find this out, though they feel that so much history has been lost by people destroying sites not knowing what they were at the time.

Before they knew it, it was two in the morning the next day. Because it was Sunday morning they knew that they would be sleeping the morning away so they retired to their rooms. It was not long before they were off in dream land, but both of their last thoughts were of how many sites of prehistoric man have been destroyed throughout the world.

Seth and Sue have managed to map and logged all the known sites, that had an age range greater than one thousand years on to Seth's wall map into his hidden room. With some help from the house, he could have a wall in his room that showed all the sites, he could see the site live like a television set.

There is a holiday that all veterans hate to see come and that is Memorial Day. This holiday means that to honor it you pay respect to fallen veterans of the past that have lost their life because of time or have fallen in battle. No matter which way it is a somber holiday to them. Sue and Seth have planned to go to Arlington National Cemetery to do just that, honor someone they had lost. Seth's father had visited the site many time to honor lost comrades over the years during this holiday, however it was his turn to be honored. Both Seth and Sue were not looking forward to this but they would not miss it. This was Seth's fathers first time to be honored as a lost hero and that day was here. This time the girls did not go because they wanted to have things ready for Seth and his mom when they come back home. Sue and Seth met some friends there that had lost loved ones. They also walked the fields of stones, each marking the spot of a resting place of a Soldier, Marine, Sailor or Airmen. Peaceful as it was, it really was not. There were families there walking to sites, loved ones on a blanket at a grave crying, prayers being said and the reminders of the hell of war. Heartbreaking, best described the place with people with lives that were changed forever with no chance of reversing it.

They arrived for the ceremonies and Sue made sure that her husband's flag was flying straight and tall for him. As you looked out over the stones each had a small American flag by its side, waving as the breeze flowed pass them. Both Seth and Sue remained strong through the ceremonies and at the end spent time at the grave to talk to him in their thoughts. This was not a happy day and it was not a day that they want anyone else to have, but it was Michael Mason Hawthorne day, and all the people like him that gave their life to serve.

Seth and Sue did not stay in the Washington DC area overnight; they made a late-night flight and came home for the cookout at Kristle's house the next day. The girls had made plans to make sure that Seth or Sue did not have to do anything that day. They wanted to let them relax and try to have a fun time. Both Kristle and April remember the time they went down to visit Seth's dad and how moved they were with the site. They cannot forget the graves of service personnel, and how Seth and his mom reacted with such sorrow. However, the servicemen that knew his dad told them the story of the coins, then when they all put a quarter on the stone remains still a strong memory to them. This affected them to the point that they will never forget it, ever, even as they think about it many months later it still brings tears to their eyes.

When Seth and Sue arrived, the cooking on the grill was well underway and close family and local neighbors were already there helping. The girls made sure Seth was ok as did the parents with Sue. The party went into full cook out mode and fun was the order of the day, Seth just joined in on any game or conversation and Sue rested with the adults. In the trees around the house just out of sight were six companions, three ravens and three owls, watching and on guard.

27

Graduation

THE MONTH OF JUNE comes with warm and sunny days,
having just the right amount of rain to help anyone that was
planting gardens. Early crops were planted a month ago but
many people are planting flower gardens with their favorite
plants. Trees are full of leaves with the lawns bright green with
new grass showing. Many people are on bikes and the nights
have a slight coolness to them, that was warm enough not to
have a jacket on. Seth was sitting on the porch thinking about
all that he sees within his sight, and he is comparing it to what
would be happening back down south. There the days are very
much warmer and have been for some time, what he is seeing
here is what he would have seen a month earlier there.

They have been at this new home for just about ten months,
he still has not got use to the seasons in this area, however
being in snow during the winter was fun he thought. Just as
he finished the thought, Mason his raven landed on the railing
and began to purr very softly. He hopped down to the ground
and grabbed a small stick, then flew up and dropped it in Seth's
lap before landing back on the railing. Mason kept turning his
head from side to side, and flapping his wings very tightly near
his body. "Do you want to play fetch?" Seth asked and Mason
gave a loud caw sound. Seth raised an eyebrow and then threw
the stick to the far side of the front lawn. Mason jumped off
the rail and glided over to where the stick landed, picked it up

in his beak, and returned it to Seth's lap on a fly over before landing back on the rail. "Well this is different; most people play fetch with a dog; I'm doing it with a raven." When he finished saying this Mason let out a series of caws as if he was laughing. Seth threw the stick back out and Mason did the same fetch and return. The both of them did this for some time before Sue came out of the house and sat in the chair on the opposite side of the porch. Seth said hello and he and Mason kept playing with the stick.

Sue sat and watched the two of them playing and her thoughts returned to one year ago back on the base. They had just lost Seth's father and had received the news that they would have to move off the base. She had come up here one year ago this week to look at the house and interview for her job. It was not an easy time and she does not miss the feelings that she had at the time, of both being lost at what to do and the grief of the loss of her husband. Life is not what she thought it would be one year ago but at least it is a life. Now here she is watching Seth play fetch but with a raven, she thought to herself how funny the sight of this looked.

The week went by, and the time in school for the girls and Seth was both dragging and moving very fast. In a few days after all the test are done and books and gear have been turned into the school, they would be graduating heading for high school. It was a time for excitement and sorrow with a scary feeling of starting a new school. Seth however was not as moved by the moment as everyone else; this was because he is still new to the area and had his big move with the overdrive of feelings almost a year ago. For him it is just another move but he was enjoying how the girls were acting. He felt anything was better than the last school he was in, and he did not miss that school at all.

Seth's and the girl's graduation were held in the gym of the school and all the families watched as each student received their certificate and awards. It was small because there is only sixty plus students in all eight grades of the school with less than a dozen in his class. People were friendly and the main talk between the parents was where their son or daughter was going to high school. A few were going to other schools around the area other than Amesbury High, but the girls were headed there along with Seth. Some of the other parents of kids also heading to Amesbury made it a point to talk to Sue, because she was a teacher there and they want to know what to expect. Questions were many for her but the kids broke into groups for the last time in the school, they were in tears and happy at the same time. Even though the school was small this was no different than any other school that does this, however being so small it was more of a group being a family.

Later that day the families got together at Aprils house for a graduation party for the three new high school freshmen. All three families a year ago had no idea that in just a couple of months they would find out, that they are all family, be it distant but they are family. In many ways, this has made it easy for Seth to know that his father did have family, not what they had been told. Even though Seth would not show it, he was glad he was not alone.

The parents were gathered together around the grill and food tables, while the kids including the relatives were out playing and walking around. There were only a few other kids because none of the families wanted to have large families. Some had no kids at all being in their early twenties and starting careers. It was a beautiful day with blue skies with warm temperatures, and because the fields of grass were still a little short they were running around in the fields. Sue every now and then watched Seth, and felt great that he was being a kid and letting out some energy. The parents were talking about their latest trophies from sports or games and wealth gains from the markets showing much pride in bragging about it.

None of the people outside the family knew about the wealth of Seth and his mother or the wealth that was given to the two girls. Everyone involved feels it best and safer for the kids.

Also showing up for the party a little later in the day was Sarah and Elizabeth; Sarah had graduated the week before from her high school. She was now moving on to college courses at home just as Elizabeth has been doing since leaving her school. Sarah however was still young being only seventeen, and she will become eighteen after the start of the new year. She had skipped the fifth grade because she tested out, she scored high enough to jump into sixth grade. She still to this day feels that she should have not done that because she had left all her friends in the lower grade. When she got ill the next year she did not have the support group that she would have had if she was with her friends. However, she met Elizabeth that year just as her family fell apart, and she and Elizabeth hit it off as if they had known each other forever. Now here she was with her new extended family, and friends with a great outlook for life and an adventure that people just dream of. She now felt life was good and had a new friend with Seth, who had felt some of what has happen to her. She felt that beside Elizabeth, she could talk to him about things even though he was a boy.

After the food was served and people ate, there was a short time for yard games, then it turned into a pool party. The above ground pool had a deck that made its way half way around the pool and had chairs and umbrellas that swing out to provide shade from the sun. The day stayed very warm to the point of hot and the pool was a welcome cooling to the day.

Some people left during the afternoon to beat the weekend traffic home, however just as many showed up after going to other kid's parties. The cookout went well into the night and Seth, April Kristle, Sarah and Elizabeth found themselves floating while sitting on a raft together in the pool. They were watching the adults and sometimes picking on something they were doing, however they kept it between themselves. Then Kristle says, "You know, we are another year closer to being them."

"I don't think that we are ever going to be like them with what happen to us this year," exclaimed Seth.

"I think our life along with our parents is never going to be like the other people up there, or even their kids. Our lives will never be the same as it was before," April said as the group floated until it was the end of the night.

The day was here and the moon is full, the call has been given, it is the meeting day in the Realm. This is the second meeting since the dates were changed to every other full moon, plus it was the first time after the zone was put in place, for people that attack Realm people. Since it was enacted there have been no reported attacks, and the person that attacked Seth and the group, has not been seen since that day. Two things could have happened that day; first he did not survive the hole and the refill that Seth did to stop him, or second, he is waiting for the right time to do it again. There was no way to know which if either fate he had met.

Seth opened the doorway and the group stepped into their Realm's waiting room. People were coming into the main meeting hall from their waiting rooms and going to their seats with greetings along the way. Seth as he does each time lead his group in and they went directly to their seats without hesitation. It had taken a minute but the room got all settled and Seth called the meeting to order. Without interruption, the rules reading was skipped and the minutes of the last meeting were read and acknowledged, then they were at the start of the new and old business part. The Wizard Woo from Shambhala, made a motion that all wizards and sublets that come to the Realm be trained in the full use of power that will protect them. The question came to the floor for him to explain what he is talking about. Then he explained, "There is information in the Realm of training and knowledge of the old ways, with incantations that will protect us from evil and give us the power to fight back. However only a head of the Realm and meeting tree can assign or allow sublets to have such knowledge, but this knowledge has been forbidden to use. The Realm does not allow us to see all the information, and will not unless all the wizards agree to the use of the knowledge. There is also a warning that this power can change people, it has in the past been a problem but there is no information of how."

Seth then asked, "Can we table this motion and then motion the Realm to explain the knowledge?"

Then Radcliff answered, "Yes, we can with each item, however we at the head table must petition the Realm for the information. The Realm will then let us know what must be done and who can see the information. This has not been done since the last world war and that was terrifying."

Sonia then made a motion, "Realm, show us the forbidden knowledge of incantations and ways to protect us from evil."

The motion was passed and as Seth finished the banging of the gavel, the chamber lights went out, then a light blue haze appeared over the seats of the sublets. Seth could see that all the sublets were not moving as if frozen in time, a figure was now becoming visible in the blue haze. It was becoming clearer with each passing second until a hooded figure was standing in the air above the sublets. It then spoke, "you all seek the knowledge of the old ways but are you ready for the responsibility of such power? The last time this power was used it nearly destroyed the world, which is why it was sealed and labeled forbidden. This power will expand your way of thinking; however, it will also expand your good and bad characters also, that is why it was removed from everyone and sealed."

Then Radcliff replied, "We seek the power to be able to protect the Realm and ourselves against people that have attacked us already."

"Then you seek it as defense, however it can be used as an aggressor force also, to do evil by people that do not follow the Realms rules, how will you stop that? Power to control and to destroy has always corrupted man, and this has been the down fall of so many. The question that is before you is, how will you control it in others, such as the sublets? This is the warning that was put in place when the power was removed from everyone the last time." The figure finished speaking and remained still.

"That is what we put in place the last time we used this, then the Realm wiped our memories of the event. They nearly removed all the memory of its existence," Radcliff said as he wiped is face with his hands. He then asked, "Can we set it up so that the power cannot be used by people that cannot come into the Realm, just as we did for not being able to read their minds. Also make the person sick somehow if they were trying to using it for evil."

"Let's ask it," Seth said and he repeated Radcliff's question to the figure.

"The figure started moving again and said, "yes that can be done and remember that the zone can also be used for people that miss use this power. The responsibility of the power is in the hands of the meeting tree and the head wizard of the tree. Set yourselves in such a way that you see all that your sublets do and the seven of you at the head table must watch each other," the figures final words were a warning before it disappeared. The room cleared and the sublets started moving again.

Seth banged his gavel and said, "Ok everyone, please remain calm. We got our answer from the Realm and it was only meant for the heads of each meeting tree."

Wizard Woo was the first to make a motion that we use the power that was shown to them, then Sonia Pastel seconded the motion and when put to vote, all voted yes and none no. Seth acknowledged the vote and it was logged. Just as all was finished the lights dimmed and a voice told everyone, that this will be done by your meeting trees and the head of your group. Then the lights came to normal power.

There were no other items brought to the meeting, it was closed, but no one left quickly. They broke into groups and talked just as all the head wizards did. Conversation was mainly about the new power to come to them, and questions were asked of the people that were there through the world wars. However, they could not remember anything about that time or having power as the figure said. They stayed for an hour and then everyone started heading back home. As every meeting before, Seth and his group were the last to leave as they watched the room shutdown before going home.

Now the group had many questions at the house, mainly about what happen when they were frozen. Seth told them about it with the voice filling in the missing parts, it also told them that after Seth receives his training, each of them will also be trained. Then the voice told them the same warning that Seth heard about the miss use and how the zone was used for that.

The end of the day came and everyone went home, Seth and Sue were alone in the house when the voice said, "I did not want any of the others to see your expressions when we told you this. We are going to train the both of you first, then you will decide if this training is ok or should it be modified for the group. We have never used this before, because of our late coming into the Realm, so we need what you call feedback of all this training. Is this good for the two of you?

They both agreed and the voice told them that the training

would take a few days, then there will be a test and it will take place in Seth's hidden room out of site. With that statement, it was off to rest to start a new day in the morning. They said their goodnights, then went off to their bedrooms, but rest was not on Seth and Sues mind, wondering about what power could be so powerful to make someone become evil.

28

Summer day's cookouts and Mysteries

JULY HAS COME and the first big party of the summer is the fourth of July, where there is a cookout at April's family house. Burgers, hotdogs, chicken and potato salad, were the chosen meal of the day along with the dip in the pool. Everyone was there including Elizabeth, Sarah, and their family. The day was sunny and had no wind but water splashing was the event of the day. Later that evening a fire in the fire pit was warming and the marshmallows on the stick were toasting over the fire.

Next were the fireworks and April, Kristle and Seth were waiting for this. They have been planning to have some fun with the girl's fathers using their new skills to make things interesting. They started with firecracker's and the girls made them fire off slow so it seemed to be in slow motion. They would let some go regular then play with them as the two fathers set them off. It had the fathers all confused.

When the fathers were done with the first items, they moved on to bottle rockets and Seth was waiting. He let the first one fly as they normally work, then he made them fly very high and then sideways. The fathers were just scratching their heads, as the group was trying to keep from laughing. Then they set two off and Seth made them fly around sideways to complete several circles. Then he had them fly straight up and make a sound ten times louder than how they should have sounded. The fathers were so confused that they turned to face the families and threw their hands up into the air. Sue finally told the three of them by a voice in their heads, "please give them a break before they run and hide." The three of them responded the same way and agreed to leave them alone and let them have their fun.

The night continued without any more unexplained firework tricks from the fathers, which made them happy and relieved. The group remained around the fire and laughed, had snacks and drinks until everyone left after midnight. The three families of April, Kristle and Seth would get together like this over the next several weeks, less the fireworks for some relaxing times. During the day, the kids would do different things such as bike riding, hiking, and fishing, also spending time at the beach with one of the parents. Sometimes Sarah and Elizabeth would join the group as one big happy family. However, they were always on guard for something or someone that may try to hurt them. They did not like the feel of that but it was now a way of life for them. While they are at home during free time they logged onto the computer and followed up on any leads or ideas that would help them find more about the Realm. Seth uses his window of mist to visit and find places or events, then writes it all down so that it could be revisited later. He feels that they are finding useful things all the time, only time will tell if that is true.

After a short time, Seth and Sue had completed the new training and found some of the dreams that it caused very shocking. The power goes way past the do no harm clause that they had in the very early training, however this new training is more like the training a person in the military would receive for war. That was just the defense part, the offense part was based on destroying, both Sue and Seth had problems with that.

In Seth's room, they were tested with attacks against them and how to fight back. There was a fun part of it which was more like target practice where they would have both moving and stationary items. They would have to hit them with varies things like water, ice, flames, lightning and even move objects around them to hit it with. The most fantastic thing was how to slow things down, so to you it seemed like time was slow, when in reality, you were speeded up in thought and movement. The bad part about the speed trick is that you use twice the energy to do it, so your strength fades fast. Both Seth and Sue saw this as near unlimited power and both can see how this would be easy to become evil.

At the end of training the test was now in play and both Seth and Sue were doing well, for the finish there was the test to see if they could do evil with it. They were both given an innocent rabbit to use harsh spells on and when both tried, they got ill and wanted to stop. It worked for them but the question was, will it work for everyone? It was decided that the group would go through the training just as the two of them did, however ethics training will be done to everyone. It is based on simple teachings taken from many books such as the bible and laws of nations. They felt that a good foundation will help with control of the powers. However, how the meeting tree watches them will be the real factor of keeping everyone under control. They knew that they still had much to learn and practice, even though the main training is complete.

One clear comfortable day, Seth, April, and Kristle, were sitting on the river bank beside the bridge just wondering about the rest of the summer. Much of the conversation had to do with the new school, filled with new classmates, boys, girls, and teachers. They were talking about the classes that they signed up for, and could not wait to see if they were in the same class rooms together. They even were kidding each other about finding boy and girl friends, also about keeping each other safe as close friends.

Seth threw a rock into the river and it made a larger splash then it should have, which got the attention of all three of them. As they were watching the area where the rock hit the water, a figure started coming up out of the river. At that point, the three of them went into defense mode and put a dome of protection around the group.

As the figure came fully out of the water and now was fully formed, it was around six feet tall and covered in a dark gray hooded robe. There was a sound coming from it and it got louder and repeated. It was in Welch and said, "ydych yn agos at y gwir, peidiwch â rhoi'r gorau iddi, ar eich cyfer yw'r rhai dewis i ddod o hyd i mi."

They understood immediately that it meant, "you are close to the truth, do not give up, for you are the ones picked to find me." The figure then sank into the water and the three of them looked at each other in bewilderment. They were asking in their head, what did we just see. All three of the ravens were squawking in warning calls.

Sue and the rest of the group saw what the kids saw in their heads, and they all were asking what it was. Everyone was excited and terrified at the same time, but the kids were not thinking about running, just what was it. Then the voice from the house said just one word, "Master!"

THE STORY CONTINUES,

PART TWO,

The Journey

Time moves on and so do the lives of all young people, however where the lives of this group of eight heads could turn two ways. First is to the side of good and second is to the side of evil, just which way will things turn. What have they planned for the days ahead in a new school with new kids as peers?

Who was the figure that rose from the water of the river? Could they be making their way to solving one of the biggest mysteries of all time or did the evil person that attacked them survive? Could that person be setting them up in a grand scheme to claim the power of the meeting tree and house? The future has so many questions.

DISCLAIMERS

Note that the following names and sites are in no way claimed or copyright by this author. They are used as common points on a map or historical records used in the book to give the reader a name to research, follow online or by reading books to learn about the real story known to the public.

Druid Hill and LeBlanc Park in Lowell, Massachusetts

American Stonehenge in Salem New Hampshire

Beehive Hut located in the town woods in Danville NH

Stonehenge in England

Gungywamp in Groton Connecticut

Arlington National Cemetery

Merlin a Welsh legend or lore

Atlantis a mythical Island or lore from ancient tales which has been associated with Plato

Plato a Greek philosopher that lived in both Greece and Egypt

Shambhala" the Sanskrit name for a mystical land believed to be in East Asia

Paititi a legendary city believed to be east of the Andes in the amazon of South America.

The Author

STEPHEN FRANCIS JORDAN presently lives in Exeter, NH with his wife Cheryle. They have three kids between them from prior marriages and have four Grand Daughters from his oldest son. He has degrees in Applied Science's and many certificates in electronic, alarm systems and coaching. He also has been a scout leader and has run camps for scouts and young kids to get out, play, and learn. He currently is a level 4 archery coach, and also competes in tournaments, as well as brings people from a local archery shop, Big Al's Archer's Paradise, to events as a team. He is teaching kids and adults to enjoy and/or compete in the sport of archery.

As a scout leader, he always had a pocket full of stories and lore's to entertain young scouts and adults at a campout. From Native American stories and lore's, to real history and mysteries of the areas he has lived in. While in school during his youth he disliked history, however, when he started traveling while in the US Navy, he found much that he was taught about history was wrong or missing parts. He spent time learning all that he could to be used later. Now from much of his notes he is able to put together stories and put them into books for people to read. His thirst for knowledge had led him to many sites and areas to discover a world that many people have never heard of or just ignored. He has walked beside dinosaur tracks, crawled through ruins, walked along volcano rims, repelled inside the cone of an active volcano and many dormant or extinct ones. Also, while in the US Navy on a shore leave from his ship, he skied on Mount Etna, a highly active volcano in Sicily. While he was in the Navy he made the best of his time while serving his country. During this time, he has flown and landed in a jet on an aircraft carrier as well as traveled to bases in areas with vast amounts of history.

He has become a person with many stories and adventures to tell people and can spin a yarn with the best of them. However, he has also learned that many people will not believe a story even if very factual and true unless they see it on the television or movie screen. Here is where he finds the problem; people no longer reach out for adventure in the real world. The real world is now on the computer or a screen to most people.

CHARACTERS

- Horton Crocker- 1st settled in house in South Hampton New Hampshire

- Catherin Crocker- Horton's wife

- Jeb Crocker- Horton's son

- Rebeca Mills- Jeb's wife, Bonny's mother

- Mathew Crocker- Jeb's 1st son with Rebeca

- Bonny Crocker- Jeb's only daughter

- Bonney Lee- Bonny's daughter

- Sherry Hawthorne- Jeb's lady in England, mother of Garry Hawthorne

- Trisha French- married Garry Hawthorne

- Seth Hawthorne- Michael and Sue son born 2002

- Sue Hawthorne- Michael wife and Seth's mother

- Michael Mason Hawthorne- Seth's father

- April Morse- dark haired girl lives that lives in 5th house on street

- Janet & Mike Morse- married 1998, April mother and father

- Kristle Blake- blonde haired girl that lives in 3rd house on street

- June & Jim Blake- married 1998 Kristle mother and father

- Elizabeth Miller- young girl that is friends with Sarah Simpson

- Sarah Simpson- young girl that Elizabeth's family took in to help her

- Nicolas Faith- Sue cousin the lawyer

- Mike Chris- bully in kid's grade

- Kendell Solara- Bank president of Amesbury bank

- Sayoie- hypnotized Elizabeth and Sarah and is Kendell Solara the banker

ANIMAL FRIENDS

- Sue's White Snow female owl named Snowy.
- Seth's companion is a male Raven named 'Mason' after Seth's dad.
- April's companion is a Raven with a small white patch under it throat named Star.
- Kristle's companion is a Raven with white on tip of bill named Tipper.
- April's mom Janet is a Barred owl named Hoot.
- Kristle's mothers June companion is an Eastern Screech Owl named Bright Eyes.
- Elizabeth Miller companion is a young Raven named Calm.
- Sarah Simpson companion is a named young Raven named Jet.

WIZARDS OF THE REALMS

- <u>Seth Hawthorne</u> from Markland (North America)

- <u>Sonia Pastel</u> from the land of snow, (Antarctica)

- <u>Philip Dooly</u> from Salisbury area near Stonehenge in England

- <u>Berta Kibo</u> from the base of Mount Kilimanjaro from the Chagga people Africa

- <u>Akmal Mustalph Kiral</u> new leader of Africa

- <u>Radcliff Roth</u> from the Aboriginal people of Australia

- <u>Woo</u> from Shambhala the Sanskrit name for a mystical land, (East Asia)

- <u>Juande Eguiluz</u> from Paititi the legendary city east of the Andes in the amazon (South America).

CPSIA information can be obtained
at www.ICGtesting.com
Printed in the USA
FFHW011248050519
52236435-57619FF